Praise for *Your Perfect Life*

"*Your Perfect Life* has all of the ingredients that I love in a book—relatable characters who made me laugh out loud, a delicious, page-turning premise, and sweet and surprising insights about how the perfect life may be the one you've already got."

—Jen Lancaster, *New York Times* bestselling author

"I loved this from the very first line (which will go down in history as the funniest, bravest first line ever). Hilarious, honest, and truly touching, Liz Fenton and Lisa Steinke are two important new voices in women's fiction who write about life in such a real, relatable way."

—Sarah Jio, *New York Times* bestselling author

"For every woman who's ever wondered about the path not taken, Fenton and Steinke mine—with tremendous humor and insight—the mixed blessing of unexpected second chances."

—Emma McLaughlin and Nicola Kraus,
New York Times bestselling authors

"Liz and Lisa's voices are warm and comforting, like a relaxed chat with great friends while wearing cozy PJs and sipping wine. I highly recommend *Your Perfect Life!*"

—Beth Harbison, *New York Times* bestselling author

"Liz Fenton and Lisa Steinke blend their voices seamlessly and hilariously and remind us that even though the grass often looks greener under our friends' lives, nobody gets *happily ever after* unless they go *after* it. *Your Perfect Life* is clever, quirky, fresh, and ultimately, empowering!"

—Claire Cook, bestselling author of *Must Love Dogs* and *Time Flies*

"*Your Perfect Life* puts a fresh twist on a 'Freaky Friday' scenario: What if you switched bodies with your best friend, and got the life you'd always secretly coveted? I adore Liz Fenton and Lisa Steinke's witty, winning style and gobbled up their debut novel."

—Sarah Pekkanen, author of *Things You Won't Say*

"Sassy, heartfelt, and smart, *Your Perfect Life* is a clever take on switched identities that will make you think hard about the choices you've made in your life and what matters most to us all in the end."

—Amy Hatvany, author of *Safe with Me*

ALSO BY LIZ FENTON AND LISA STEINKE

Your Perfect Life

the status
of all things

a novel

liz fenton
and
lisa steinke

WASHINGTON SQUARE PRESS

new york london toronto sydney new delhi

Washington Square Press
An Imprint of Simon & Schuster, Inc.
1230 Avenue of the Americas
New York, NY 10020

First Washington Square Press trade paperback edition June 2015

WASHINGTON SQUARE PRESS and colophon are registered
trademarks of Simon & Schuster, Inc.

For information about special discounts for bulk purchases, please
contact Simon & Schuster Special Sales at 1-866-506-1949 or
business@simonandschuster.com.

The Simon & Schuster Speakers Bureau can bring authors to your
live event. For more information or to book an event, contact the
Simon & Schuster Speakers Bureau at 1-866-248-3049 or visit our
website at www.simonspeakers.com.

Manufactured in the United States of America

10 9 8 7 6 5 4 3

Library of Congress Cataloging-in-Publication Data

Fenton, Liz.
   The status of all things : a novel / Liz Fenton and Lisa Steinke. —First
Washington Square Press trade paperback edition.
      pages ; cm
   1. Time travel—Fiction. 2. Social media—Fiction. 3. Female
friendship—Fiction. 4. Chick lit. I. Steinke, Lisa. II. Title.
   PS3606.E5844S73 2015
   813'.6—dc23   2014039814

ISBN 978-1-4767-6341-5
ISBN 978-1-4767-6343-9 (ebook)

To Cristine, for being so much more than my mom

To Matt, for making this dream possible

the status
of all things

CHAPTER ONE

....

In less than 24 hours, I'll be walking down the aisle.

Something borrowed, something blue? Check.

Something old, something new? Check.

The love of my life? Double check! #whatcouldgowrong

I upload my status to Facebook, tuck my cell phone away, and try to savor the only minute alone I've had all day. Sitting on the veranda of the bridal suite, I stare hard at the waves crashing against the Wailea coastline. I tug on the unforgiving fabric of my black peplum dress, having just fought my way into it moments ago. Stella, my wedding planner, with a permanent flush to her round cheeks and steely look in her eyes had unabashedly yelled, *suck it in!* as she yanked the zipper until it stubbornly found its way to the nape of my neck.

Embarrassed, I had immediately sent her away with a checklist, to place the gerbera daisies in the vases—two orange and one white in each—and to confirm that the ginger-glazed shrimp skewers and crispy spicy tuna rolls would be passed at 7 p.m. sharp. I also reminded her to make sure my mother and father, divorced for almost two decades, would be sitting not just at different tables, but across the room from each other, my mom's quiet anger over my dad leaving her still easily triggered like a scab that gets scratched and starts bleeding.

"And please don't forget to deliver Max his groom's gift!" I had craned my neck out the doorway as she'd jogged down the hall, giving me a thumbs-up without ever turning around, no doubt trying to put as much distance between herself and the memory of forcing the folds of my lily-white skin into a size 8 dress.

I had spent months scouring Pinterest boards for the perfect gift for Max—finally settling on a vintage Tag Heuer watch, lightly engraving *You're still the one* on the inside of the band, a nod to the Shania Twain song we'd danced to at the wedding where we'd been introduced by my best friend, Jules, three years ago. I couldn't wait to tell Max the story of how I'd found the antique timepiece on eBay, then engaged in an intense bidding war with Shaggy202, my eyes burning and my hands sweating, all while Max slept soundly next to me. I waited patiently for the final seconds before the auction closed, then punched in a final bid, a number that far exceeded my budget, sending Shaggy202 retreating into cyberspace as I silently pumped my fists in the air and mouthed the words *take that, bitch!*

But if Max received the watch, he hadn't told me. I'd texted him several times coyly referring to a *special delivery* he should've received—and it wasn't like him not to respond. I push the thought aside as I watch two little girls giggling as the turquoise ocean water splashes up around their knees. I close my eyes, knowing I should take a cue from them and inhale the warm Maui air and *just be*. That my mind shouldn't be swirling like the tide as I second-guess practically everything—including my decision to get Max the watch instead of the cuff links. But when you devote a year to planning one day, you want everything to be perfect.

"Knock-knock," Jules says as she pushes the door of my suite open and I spot the familiar yellow label on the bottle of champagne she's holding before I see her. I smile as she giddily holds up my favorite bubbly. From the moment we'd met over fifteen years ago on the first day of freshman orientation at UCLA, bonding over a shared disdain for our smarmy tour guide and his repeated use of the word *homeboy*, she'd had an uncanny ability to anticipate exactly what I needed. That day, as we'd paused in front of the student union, listening to our guide ramble on about the *off the chain* clubs we could join, at the precise moment I didn't think I could take one more minute of his *legit raps*, she'd stage-whispered, "I don't know about you, but I say we ask those guys to give us the rest of the tour," pointing to a group of frat boys tossing a football in the quad. Jules looped her arm through mine, and as we muffled our giggles and inched away from the group, I knew I'd made a best friend.

"Hey." She pulls me into a deep hug then steps back. "You look absolutely gorgeous," she says, knowing exactly what I need to hear.

"Are you sure?" I prod, smoothing the material of my dress that's buckling slightly at my waist and trying not to think about the way the shapewear underneath it is cutting off my circulation or the offending red indentation mark it will leave around my middle.

"Will you stop?" Jules pleads and grabs my arm, guiding me in front of the mirrored closet door. "Do you know how much I would kill for *this* hair?" She touches one of my strawberry-tinged loose curls. "And *this* face?" She smiles as she runs a finger across my lightly freckled nose and over my cheekbone, my powder-blue eyes peering back at me, wanting so badly to see what she does. I don't understand the fuss she's making. Staring back at me is an average-looking girl who easily blends into the crowd—with limp locks, a button nose that's too small next to her round cheeks, and a few extra pounds she hasn't been able to lose since college. I can't help but envy Jules, whose naturally lean figure towers over me, whose body has never needed the assistance of spandex underwear, whose nonexistent love handles have never been shoved into anything.

I tug at a straight strand of my hair that has lost its curl. "I'm not sure I should wear this up tomorrow."

"No updo?" Jules frowns.

"Maybe not . . ."

"But you were so happy with it when we did the trial run last week. It looks great with the dress and jewelry. Very elegant."

"I'm just rethinking the pictures." I pause and gather my hair on top of my head. "I'm not sure I want to be *that* bride. Maybe I should go for a more casual look?"

Jules waits a beat before answering me, the slight frown that flashes across her face giving away her frustration with my indecisiveness. "What do you mean by *that* bride? Did something happen? What's making you second-guess your hair in the eleventh hour?"

"Are you friends with Anne Freeborn?"

"On Facebook?" Jules squints at me as if she's trying to conjure her face.

I nod.

"Yeah, but I think I hid her from my feed after the last election—her political rants were making me crazy. Why?"

"She's getting married next month and she posted two pictures this morning asking people to vote on which hairstyle she should go with. Up or down? Tight bun or beachy waves?"

"Okay . . ." Jules continues to look at me skeptically.

"And way more people said down—something like 112 of her friends were against wearing it up—they commented that she'd look more carefree if she wore it loose."

"Okay . . ." Jules says again.

"So it just made me think—maybe I should wear mine down too? I don't want to look uptight. Like I'm not having a good time."

"Because you won't actually be having a good time?" she asks gently.

"No, but it's something to think about. The hair," I say slowly, suddenly feeling self-conscious as I stare at Jules' face, still registering confusion and doubt. "What?" I challenge. "I can't make a last-minute change?"

"Of course you can, but—"

"But what?"

"Never mind. You're right. It's your day. Down it is!" She claps her hands together, the sound echoing loudly on the balcony.

"Tell me what you were going to say."

"It's just . . . you should do what you want and not worry about what others think of it. It's going to be the biggest day of *your* life—not theirs."

I know she's right—that it's my day—but I also can't ignore the words on the tip of my tongue, even if I wish they weren't perched there, like divers about to sail off the board. The truth is, I care. *I care a lot.*

"I can't really explain it, okay? It's just how I feel. And anyway, maybe I should take this as a sign? Maybe I was supposed to wear my hair down, no matter what the reason."

"Maybe that's it." Jules smiles, and I can tell by the flickering in her eyes that there is a lot more she wants to say, but she lets it drop and I'm relieved.

"Sorry. I'm just kind of a mess. I want to get it right." I consider asking Jules for her opinion about why I haven't heard from Max, but worry I'll sound too neurotic after my hair up/hair down diatribe. My cell phone buzzes and I pull it out of the pocket of my dress and shake it at Jules. "And it's not helping that my mom refuses to stop texting me about Dad and *the wife*—"

"I cannot believe she *still* won't use her name," Jules says, cutting me off.

"Well, you know, it's only been *eighteen years*." I shake my head. "Apparently *the wife* has already offended her, and I quote, '*multiple times*,' today." I think of the last message from my mom demanding that I ban my stepmom, Leslie, from the family picture and feel my stomach tighten into yet another knot.

"I'm sorry you're even dealing with this! I told Stella she was supposed to keep your mom's neurosis from you—she's under strict orders to pass all of her complaints *my way*." She places her hands on her slim hips and narrows her green eyes.

"Cut Stella a break. She's had to operate way beyond her job description in other ways today." I pat my stomach and laugh as Jules gives me a questioning look. "She deserves hazard pay for helping me squeeze into this."

Jules rolls her eyes as she pops the cork and pours the champagne into two flutes and holds one out to me as the bubbles race to the surface. "I'd like to propose a toast. To your marriage tomorrow. Welcome to the club!"

I press the glass to my lips. "I know! Me? A married woman . . . *finally*."

"Thanks to my supreme matchmaking skills!" Jules pats herself on the back.

I clink my glass against Jules'. "How will I ever properly thank you?"

"You can start by naming your first child after me!" she teases.

"Maybe." I run my finger around the rim of my flute, thinking of the night Max proposed, his voice breathless after I'd said yes, like he'd just sprinted at the end of one of his long runs.

I can't wait to be a family, he'd whispered.

His olive-green eyes had brightened and then squinted as if he was picturing us with our arms wrapped around a baby. I knew Max would be a good dad—he had an instinct with children that didn't come as naturally to me. I loved kids and wanted to be a mom, but I was always afraid of something happening to any child in my charge. Even Jules' kids, Ellie and Evan, whom I considered my niece and nephew because Jules was like the sister I never had, would roll their eyes at me if I suggested taking them to the pool or for a bike ride. It was as if they could smell my apprehension. But they'd been calling Max Uncle M practically since the moment they'd met him, when he'd scooped them up, under each arm, and swung them in the air as if he'd done it a hundred times before. As they'd squealed in delight, Jules raised her eyebrows and pressed her lips together, her look saying, *this could really be the guy for you.*

I watch Jules smoothing a strand of her white-blond hair that has fallen from its effortless-looking sleek ponytail and I think about how it mimics the way she has always seemed to glide through life. She'd married her college sweetheart, Ben, almost ten years ago and had quickly produced Evan, then two years later, Ellie, both blond-haired, emerald-eyed replicas of her. And although she had no formal training, she'd always been able to whip up the richest masterpieces from the most basic of ingredients, quickly working her way up to her current position as the pastry chef for The Midnight Snack, one of West Hollywood's hottest restaurants. She seemed to juggle motherhood, marriage, and a career with the precision of an air-traffic controller, not to mention the confidence of one. It was probably the reason why people had always been drawn to her the way a bee is pulled to a budding flower.

As Jules and I nearly drain our glasses, a familiar deep voice cuts through the air. "Is everyone decent in here?"

Jules giggles. "No, we're hanging out in our lingerie even though the rehearsal dinner starts in fifteen minutes!"

Liam peaks his head out, his hazel eyes lighting up when he sees my arm wrapped around Jules' waist. "Well you two may not be half naked, but this still looks like some fun I'd like to get in on." He smiles and raises his eyebrows. As he ambles across the room, I notice his new charcoal-gray suit drapes perfectly over his tall, lanky body, smiling as I remember his moans after yet another jacket he'd tried on was too short for his arms, warning me that we'd better find something, *anything* soon because if he missed the Dodgers game there'd be hell to pay. He wraps a strong arm over each of our shoulders, the white pocket square the salesman talked him into grazing my cheek, me reaching up and touching his tousled light brown hair.

"Did you even bring a brush on this trip?" I tease.

"Haven't you heard? The messy look is in," he says with a laugh.

The three of us had been linked from the moment we'd traded deep sighs over our college professor for Economics 101, the insufferable Dr. Kinsey, whose jowled face, crusty demeanor, and steep grading curve gave us many sleepless nights that semester. Liam had nudged me at the end of the first day of class, flashing a crooked smile, his eyes narrowing from behind his dark-rimmed eyeglasses as he made a joke about how our curmudgeonly teacher needed to just get laid already. He wondered if possibly I was up to the task so I could save us all from our inevitable fate—dying of boredom before we were even twenty-one.

When I'd fake gagged and hit him with my notebook, he'd relented. "Fine. If not you, maybe your friend?" he'd said, pointing to Jules as she walked toward us. When she'd given him the finger after hearing his pitch, he'd deadpanned, "What? Didn't you guys see the size of his hands when he was writing our assignment on the dry-erase board? You know what that means, right?" As if on cue, Jules and I had cried, "That is so foul," and broke into a fit of laughter, silently sealing a promise of a lifetime of friendship.

"Okay, people. Time to head up to the restaurant," Jules says authoritatively, resting her empty glass on the wood table sitting between two deck chairs. "As your matron of honor, I feel it is my duty to get you there on time," she adds, elbowing Liam jokingly.

Liam clears his throat dramatically and tugs at the collar of his crisp white shirt. "Well, as her *best man*, I feel strongly that she should have another drink first—in fact, I brought something stronger." He grins as he pulls a tarnished silver flask from his back pocket—one I gave him when we were in college, instantly evoking memories of ski trips to Tahoe, late nights lounging on the deck of his fraternity house, and Fourth of Julys spent sunbathing on the bow of a speedboat in Havasu. I'd had it engraved. *Think of me every time you take a sip.* He swore that he did.

"Well, this isn't the Met Gala and Kate's not exactly Anna Wintour . . . no offense—" she says, turning toward me.

"None taken." I laugh.

". . . so being fashionably late isn't going to cut it," Jules continues, grabbing the flask and putting it up to her nose, releasing a small cough as she inhales. "Whoa—what the hell is in here?" She shoves it back into Liam's hand.

"Whiskey," he says with a shrug, and takes a drink, releasing an exaggerated sigh when he's finished. "And not just *any* whiskey—it's Pappy Van Winkle! Do you know what I had to do to get my hands on this? It's harder to find than my man card after I let you talk me into wearing those skinny jeans you bought me last Christmas!" He shakes his head at the memory.

"Pappy Van what, what?" Jules laughs. "It sounds like one of those shows my daughter watches on the Disney Channel, not a brand of whiskey!"

"Oh, Jules, you have so much to learn," Liam says before taking another swig.

"Well, I don't care if it's laced with gold—Kate's not drinking that. Her friends, family, *and fiancé* are expecting her to be there when the party starts! Not to stumble in late." Jules turns toward me. "Right?"

"I'm not getting involved." I wave my hands in front of me like an umpire calling a baseball player safe. "But I will say this is exactly why I asked *both* of you to be in my wedding—so you can fight over what's best for me. I love it!" I grab my iPhone and study the screen, my face falling for a moment when I realize my earlier text to Max has still gone unanswered.

"What is it?" Jules, who never misses a beat, catches my strained expression.

"Nothing," I lie.

"You sure?" Jules presses.

"Positive," I say.

Liam arches an eyebrow and I look away quickly. "Kate probably just has a little case of prewedding jitters, Jules. I know I'd be shitting bricks if it were me!" Liam laughs as he leans back in a lounge chair, his long legs dangling off the end. "Exactly why she needs some of this." He waves the whiskey in front of me and I happily take it. As I'm sipping the liquor, he scoots his chair close to mine, his eyes suddenly filled with an intensity that makes me pull the flask away from my lips. "But hey, Kate, you don't have to go through with this if you don't want to. Everyone will understand if you decide you aren't ready to settle down."

I stare at him, blinking hard, the backs of my eyes watering from the whiskey stinging my throat, unsure of how to respond.

"Will you relax." He slaps my knee. "I'm kidding!" he says, laughing. "But you should have seen your face. You turned white as a ghost. Priceless." He leans back in his chair again and I release the breath I'd been holding.

"God, you are terrible! I should fire you! And I blame this!" Jules reaches for the flask, but I hold it just out of reach as I take another sip, the whiskey going down much easier this time.

As Jules and Liam banter, I decide I'm just obsessing. Of course Max received the watch. And of course he loves it. How could he not? I saw him eyeing a similar one in *Esquire*, and that's what had sparked the idea in the first place. He'll show up tonight wearing it and wrap my hand inside of his protectively, the way he has so many times before.

"Okay, let's get a pic for our little Facebook whore." Jules elbows me playfully, bringing the dialogue in my head to an abrupt halt. "You know you want one!" She giggles as Liam holds my phone high above our heads, all of us jockeying for position as I give Liam instructions on how to angle the phone for the best shot, finally accepting that his forehead won't make the cut.

After I settle on a photo, Liam sighs. "I will never understand the effort that goes into taking a picture of women that's Facebook-worthy. I'm quite confident NASA spent less time helping the Apollo 13 astronauts get back home!"

I roll my eyes at him and pull up my page, filter the photo, tag him and Jules and then Max as well, knowing our picture will make him smile.

Feeling thankful! Lanai selfie with my besties.

• • •

My mother is the first person I spot as I enter the restaurant on the top floor of the hotel, Liam and Jules waving good-bye as Jules makes a beeline for Ben and Liam for his date, Angie, a leggy raven-haired beauty I just met yesterday.

"Kate!" my mom says, her sleek golden blond bob bouncing as she hugs me. "You're here. I was beginning to wonder if you were going to show up." She laughs, but the not-so-subtle disapproval drips from her voice like a leaky faucet.

"Well, I'm here now," I say, straightening my back as I scan the room for Max. "Speaking of being here—"

"Did you get my texts?" my mom interrupts, awkwardly tugging at the hem of her knee-length dress despite the fact that it fits her slim figure perfectly. Her body is more toned than that of many women my age—*including my own*.

"Have you seen Max?" I ask, ignoring her question as I follow her wistful gaze to my dad and stepmom, huddled closely in the corner like they are the ones exchanging vows tomorrow. When my dad announced he was marrying Leslie, who is only twelve years older than I am, my mother had scoffed, promising he and *the baby* wouldn't make it six months. But nearly twenty years later, they are still mad about each other, and I am still unable to admit to my mom that I have also come to genuinely love Leslie. She has kind blue eyes that still light up whenever she talks about my dad, and she always welcomes me with a warm embrace I can feel long after we've parted. It's as if her sunny personality radiates through her skin and transfers onto mine.

My mother grabs a mai tai from a passing waiter and takes a long drink, her ruby-red lipstick staining the straw. "I haven't seen him . . . I assumed you two were together." She motions her cocktail glass toward the crowded room without taking her eyes off my dad, and I fight the urge to grab her by the shoulders and shake the bitterness out of her like a coin you try to retrieve from a piggy bank.

I scan the area again, noticing most of the guests have already arrived, wearing colorful leis around their necks, sipping cocktails with umbrellas, a warm bronzed tone to their skin from their first day in the sun—or in the case of my uncle Louie, a shade closer to lobster red—but there's still no sign of my fiancé.

I frown. Max is *never* late. I think back to the morning we flew to Maui. At 6 a.m., he was already off on his daily six-mile run, his single black Tumi suitcase and garment bag sitting by the front door hours before we were scheduled to leave, his items thoughtfully and precisely packed the day before. Meanwhile, I was in our bedroom heaving my severely undercaffeinated body on top of my third piece of luggage, desperate to squeeze in one last sarong and pair of espadrilles *just in case*.

Where is he?

"Well, I'm sure he'll be here any moment," my mom says, as if she's just read my mind. "It's Max we're talking about here, not your father," she adds, an edge to her voice.

"Mom, *please*. Not tonight."

"So about my texts. Do you believe the nerve of that woman?" She presses on anyway. "It's a *family* picture!"

I bite my tongue, holding back the thoughts scrolling through my mind like the ticker at the bottom of a news program—that my mom's palpable anger was *not* an invited guest to my wedding weekend, that her lipstick is three shades too dark for her ivory skin, that I'm truly sorry my dad fell in love with someone else and even sorrier that she refuses to let go of the anger that's been eating her alive ever since. I shoot Jules a look across the room, letting her know I need her help.

"It's not a completely unreasonable request—they've been married a long time," I finally say gently, not wanting to hurt her feelings, no matter how foolish she is acting.

My mom starts to respond, but Jules intercepts her, swiftly grabbing her hand and guiding her toward the bar, mentioning something about the freshly shaved coconut in the piña coladas.

I turn on my heel to search for Max. I'm relieved when I finally locate him on the veranda, in deep conversation with Courtney, my friend and the other vice president at the advertising agency where I work.

"There you are." My gaze is immediately pulled to Max's empty wrist like a magnet. "Didn't you get a special delivery from me today? Stella swore it was delivered—"

Max glances sideways at Courtney, then back at me. "Stella didn't forget. I got the watch." He runs his hand through his wavy dark brown hair and across his stubble-lined jaw.

"Then where is it?" I chew on my lower lip as I wait for his answer.

"It's down in my room."

"Really? Why?" I say, my mind spinning. "You didn't like it." My cheeks redden with embarrassment as I catch Courtney's sympathetic stare. She looks away quickly. "I'm sorry, I thought—"

"No, I did like it—loved it actually," he says slowly.

"Oh, thank God. So you just forgot to put it on. No big deal. I'll see if Stella can go get it." I slide my phone out of my pocket. "I know you're probably dying for a scotch but I just want to take a picture with you first." I glance around for the best light. "Over there?" I say, pointing next to the railing, the sun casting a red and orange glow across the sky as it begins to set. I grab Max's hand and start to walk toward the edge of the lanai, then glance back. "Courtney? Will you take it?"

Courtney obediently follows us and snaps several pictures.

"Can you take one more?" I ask apologetically, noticing Max looks like he's posing for a passport photo in all of them. I turn to him, his jaw tight and his body rigid, whispering in his ear, "Will you please smile?"

But the corners of Max's lips still don't curve upward. "We need to talk," he says quietly.

"After this," I say through my grin, my hand perfectly poised on Max's chest as I tuck a wisp of my hair behind my ear and tilt my chin downward. "Trust me. You'll thank me when we're showing this photo to our kids."

"No, I need to talk to you right now," Max replies forcefully, and I step back, his voice sounding foreign to me—almost guttural. I glance over to see if Courtney heard his reprimand, but she's disappeared into the party like a ghost, the only sign she's ever been there is my phone, resting on the edge of a teak chair.

"What is it?" I ask slowly, our eyes locked. Something is wrong. *Very wrong.*

It's the moment I can feel him begin to slip through my fingers.

CHAPTER TWO

....

"I'm sorry, Kate," Max says, his eyes avoiding mine.

"For what? What's going on?" I ask, feeling off balance, as if I'm on the teacup ride at Disneyland, spinning around and around while everyone else stands still. "If this is about the watch, it's no big deal if you don't like it," I say, trying desperately to find a reason why Max has that terrible look on his face that I've never seen before.

"God, I thought I could do this. I'm sorry . . ." he repeats, his face pale, a small bead of sweat forming on his brow. As he reaches up to wipe it away, the reality of the situation hits me. I instinctively put my right hand over my left and cover my engagement ring. *This can't be happening.*

"Kate?" Max's eyes are watery. "Do you understand what I'm saying? I can't do this. I convinced myself I would feel better about things when I saw you tonight. That my doubts would disappear. But they haven't. I'm sorry."

Doubts?

"Hey, you two lovebirds," Stella interrupts—her singsongy voice slicing through the air like a knife. "As your wedding plan-

ner, I think I speak for everyone when I say you have your whole
lives to be alone together. It's time to join the party and mingle!"
She hands us each a glass of champagne and motions for us to
step closer to her. "So"—she lowers her voice before continuing,
"Aunt Kris is asking for a gin and tonic but we only have vodka—
can we make an exception or should I tell her no?"

"Make an exception," I answer just as Max says, "Tell her no."

Stella frowns as she studies our faces, her wide eyes finally
registering the tension. "I'll figure it out," she mumbles before
heading toward the bar.

I will myself to look directly into Max's eyes as "Brass Monkey," the first song on our iPod playlist, booms from the speakers.
Behind him, I glimpse Jules and her children dancing in a circle,
occupying the otherwise empty dance floor.

I force a smile when I catch her eye, fighting the desire to
wave her over, to make her tell me everything will be okay, that
my life isn't falling apart—not just in front of me, but in front of
the people I love most. To have her shake Max by the shoulders
and whisper just the right combination of words in his ear that
will make him change his mind. And then, if that doesn't work,
pull back her fist and pop him in the mouth. *Hard*.

Jules takes in my tight smile and gives me a curious look. "You
okay?" she mouths from across the room. I nod and blow her a
quick kiss to prove my point before turning back to Max.

"God. Katie. I don't know what to say."

"Do *not* call me that," I say through gritted teeth, the sound
of his nickname for me making me feel light-headed.

"I didn't mean to let it get this far."

"It's our rehearsal dinner, Max. What the fuck? You've had
over three hundred days to tell me you didn't want to do this.
And you choose now?"

Max rubs his neck. "I know—I kept thinking maybe I was just nervous, like I was having—"

Anger swells inside my chest as I remember Liam's statement from earlier—that he thought *I* was the one who was nervous.

"—wedding jitters? Cold feet?" I offer, my voice tight, scaring away an approaching waiter with a tray of shrimp, signaling it's now seven o'clock. In just seventeen hours I am supposed to waltz down the aisle to meet Max in the ivory strapless gown with a gray bow at the waist that Jules and I had found at the very first boutique on my list. I feel sick when I think of how we'd shaken our heads when we noticed the All Sales Final sign posted next to the cash register. "Who brings back a wedding dress?" I had mocked, and the saleswoman had remained silent but gave me a knowing look. Maybe I had jinxed myself.

Max stares at his shiny black loafers. "You have every right to be furious—to hate me, even. I want you to know this wasn't an easy decision. I've been sick about it—"

"So your mind is made up, then? That's it?" I ask, cutting him off, feeling as if I'm watching a Lifetime movie of the week. Because this doesn't happen in real life, does it? "I don't even get a say in this?"

His eyes well up with tears again. "I'm—" He doesn't finish his sentence and takes a large drink of his champagne. "I'm sure," he finally responds.

Tears prick the backs of my eyes and I press my thumbs against them, hoping the pressure will stop the drops from escaping. "Why?" I finally choke after I've regained my composure.

"It's hard to explain. I mean, there's a part of me that is freaking out right now, that can't believe I'm doing this." He loosens his pale pink tie.

"Then don't. Don't do it, Max. Please," I plead, hating the

desperate tone in my voice. "We can fix whatever's broken here." I grab his hand in mine, feeling the knuckle of his bare ring finger. "We've invested so much." I swallow hard, pushing away the image I've imagined for a year—the one where our eyes lock as I walk down the aisle, Max holding my gaze as I approach him, the goose bumps on my arm increasing with each step.

"I'm sorry. As much as I hate that I'm doing this to you, hate that I'm doing it here, it's still something that needs to be done." He gives my hand one last squeeze before letting it fall and stepping back slightly, as if he's already beginning to distance himself. "I know it doesn't feel like it, but I'm doing this for both of us. We shouldn't be married."

His words hang in the air like a deflating balloon, the finality of his statement cutting through my heart. Max was never one to make rash decisions, and as much I want to grab the lapel of his jacket, to pull him close and beg him not to go, that we could stay up all night talking it through, I knew there was no changing his mind tonight. Begging would get me nowhere.

"How do we tell everyone?" I ask simply as my dad and Leslie wave from across the room, holding up their tropical drinks to toast us.

Max furrows his brow, as if he doesn't understand what I'm asking.

"Well, you're choosing to call off our wedding at our rehearsal dinner, so I'm assuming you've thought this through? You have a plan?" I don't recognize the sound of my own voice, feeling like a doll with a pull cord uttering the lines programmed into me at the factory.

Max shoves his hands into the pockets of his black slacks and shakes his head.

"Why are you doing this?" I ask again, still desperate to understand what I did that was so awful that he would end things this way. But at the same time, not wanting to know. Not here. Not like this. I struggled when my boss rejected one of my pitches or my mom questioned my wardrobe choices, so I'm pretty sure finding out the reason why my fiancé was so determined to leave me *right at this moment* would break me into a thousand pieces, like a finished jigsaw puzzle that's been hurled onto the floor.

"It's not because I don't love you, because I do—so much," he continues, searching my face for a reaction. I stare at him blankly as I force my hands to stay frozen by my sides, not to reach out and pull him toward me like I so badly want to.

"You Give Love a Bad Name" starts playing and Liam is now dancing behind Jules, with his hands on her hips. She throws her head back into his chest and laughs, having no clue that my whole life is about to change.

I notice a clock shaped like a Tiki god hanging over the buffet table. In a few minutes, Max and I are scheduled to give our toast, thanking friends and family for coming. I shake my head as I remember the post I'd written on Facebook just that morning. That tomorrow was going to be the first day of the rest of my life—that I couldn't wait to start living it with Max. To think that I had been planning the rest of our life together while Max was trying to drum up the confidence to dump me spikes an anger that begins to spread through me like wildfire.

"Talk to me. Tell me what you're thinking?" Max asks.

"Honestly, how humiliating this will be to explain to everyone," I say.

"That's what you're worried about?" Max lets out an audible sigh.

"What's that supposed to mean?" I demand, feeling the muscles in my neck stiffen.

"Never mind," he says, forcing a smile when his cousin shouts an "attaboy" and slaps him on the back as he passes by. He reaches for my hand one last time and says gently, "I know this is going to be terrible. But I think it's time to tell everyone. We can't pretend any longer."

• • •

The day my wedding should have taken place is beautiful, the sun blazing in the cloudless sky and the wind calm, just as Stella had promised it would be. I pry my eyes open, the tears that finally fell last night bonding them together like glue as I slept. Jules is sitting in the chair by the bed, her own eyes also swollen from crying. "Oh, honey—" Jules gets up and comes over to me.

I struggle to form a thought, my mind foggy. After Max's announcement to the guests, Jules, Liam, and my mom had formed a protective barrier as they led me away, the shocked crowd spreading like the Red Sea as we passed. My mom had dug through her purse until she found two small white pills. "Take these, now," she'd demanded as we sped toward the elevator. I complied, desperately wanting the searing pain that filled my chest to subside. Liam pulled me into his arms as I sobbed into him. He whispered, "I'm so sorry," over and over, as if he had been the one to let me down. Then he guided me as if I were a small child to my room and stood over me protectively as I fell into bed. I pressed my face tightly into the pillow until darkness overcame me.

"Is Max gone?" I ask Jules.

She nods and wipes a tear from her eye. "Are you okay? Sorry, don't answer that. It was such a stupid question." She shakes her head. "You know I suck at this. Saying the right thing."

"Where's Ben?"

"What? With the kids, why?"

"I don't know. I guess I want someone to be with their husband." I choke on the word. "You know, since I don't have one."

"Well, I want to be here—with you."

I notice my wedding dress hanging on the back of the closet door, the satin heels sitting neatly beneath it. The outfit I've dreamed about wearing for a year that will now be sold on some website for brides-to-be looking for a deal.

"What now?" I ask, and Jules squeezes my hand, pressing my diamond into my palm. "Where do I even begin?" I ask as I twist the ring around.

Do I take it off? Send it back to him? Hock it?

"We need to get you home."

"I don't even know where that is. Is he moving out? Am I?"

"Let's just take this one step at a time," she says, and the look on her face matches the pity in the eyes of my family and friends as Max delivered the news that there would be no wedding. He had grasped my hand tightly the entire time, me feeling like one of those wives of a senator who's been caught sexting with his assistant—standing behind him but not supporting him. As he spoke, I concentrated on a black mark I had spotted on the ceiling, while my guests searched my face for answers. *Don't look at me*, I had thought. *I don't have them either.*

The digital clock on the nightstand reads 7:30 a.m. Shortly they would start setting up the white garden chairs on the ocean-front lawn. "Did Stella call and cancel—"

"She took care of everything," Jules answers before I can finish my sentence.

Could she take care of my broken heart too? Was that in her job description?

"Does everyone—"

"Yes. Everyone knows."

I lie back against my pillow and stare at a picture of a palm tree hanging on the wall until the image blurs into a streak of green, reminding me of the finger painting Jules' daughter made for me that's tacked to my corkboard at work.

My phone vibrates against the glass top of the nightstand and I grab it out of habit and click onto my Facebook page. Dozens of congratulatory messages flood my wall. My heart aches as I think about my dad *not* walking me down the aisle, Jules' daughter *not* carrying the flowers, Liam *not* giving a hilarious toast at the reception, where he finally makes good on his threat to tell an incredibly embarrassing story about me.

"Stop!" Jules reaches over and tries to grab my phone from my hand, but I hold it against my chest and protect it like a bird with a broken wing. "Just give me your cell and nobody gets hurt," Jules says, a smile in her eyes.

"I think it's too late for that," I deadpan.

"I warn you, I will use force if I have to." She crawls onto the bed and tries to pry my arms apart. "Remember the time I caught you drunk dialing that guy in college—what was his name? Started with a B—"

"Bobby. Bobby Jenkins. You know he just posted that he sold his software company—he's so successful he goes by Robert now."

"Makes sense—I don't think I could invest in a Bobby," Jules says.

"Whatever—the point is, maybe if you hadn't yanked the phone out of my hand that night, I would've married him and this"—I point at my wedding dress as if blaming it for last night's events—"would've never happened."

Jules rolls her eyes and snatches the phone just as I relax

my arms. "It's not a good idea to read this stuff right now. I'm saving you from yourself. As your matron of—" Jules freezes as she catches herself.

"Matron of *dis*honor now!" I force a laugh.

"I'm sorry—I wasn't thinking. I just don't want you reading that. No good can come from it."

"What am I supposed to tell everyone? What's my status report? *Feeling sad. Got jilted?*"

"Come on, Kate. That's the last thing you should worry about right now. Everyone will understand."

"People are going to feel sorry for me."

"No they won't! They'll feel *sad* for you. There's a difference."

"Well, either way, I'm going radio silence. At least for now."

"That alone should tell them something awful happened!" Jules jokes. Admittedly, I was sometimes guilty of oversharing on social media—checking in at my Pilates class, uploading pictures of the models from a photo shoot at work, even posting links on Jules' wall about the latest episode of *Girls*. I had never denied that I loved interacting with everyone online, that I enjoyed sharing all the best parts of my life there. But in my defense, I had always drawn the line at taking pictures of my food.

"I like keeping in touch with everyone," I argue weakly. "At least I'm not as bad as some people. You know who I keep thinking about?"

"Max?" Jules offers.

I cringe at the mention of his name. "Well, yes, but no. I mean Callie."

"Callie Trenton? From college?"

I nod my head. "Her wedding pictures keep flashing through my mind. She just posted them in honor of still being 'deliriously happy' after ten years. Did you see the one of her and her husband jumping in the air on the beach? It was the perfect day. The perfect shot. The perfect *everything*," I say, thinking back to the way my stomach tightened as I scrolled through her album, hoping I'd be able to capture the same sentiment at my own nuptials.

"It was her wedding day. She's not going to share the picture of her brother spilling red wine down the back of her dress or post how irate she probably was when her husband *actually* smashed the cake in her face. She's going to make sure she looks picture-perfect."

"I guess I just wanted to have that too. Now I never will."

Jules puts her arm around me. "You will. Just not today."

"Will I? Or do I just not deserve it?" I shake my head. "Because I look at people like Callie. And it's not just her wedding photos—it's everything. Her model-like kids, her exotic vacations—did you see the safari she went on? She kissed a giraffe! And I guess I want to know why some people have lives like that, while others"—I tap myself on the chest—"are sitting in their bridal suite with a gown they'll never wear on a wedding day they'll never have."

Jules considers this for a moment before responding. "I don't think anyone knows why things work out the way they do, Kate. But one thing I do know for sure is that people's lives are not always as perfect as the filtered photos or edited statuses they post on Facebook."

"True," I concede, pulling the sheets tight around my body and curling up into the fetal position. "But wouldn't it be nice if they were?"

CHAPTER THREE

....

Who says you can't drink seven mai tais on a five-hour flight?
#passedoutatthirtythousandfeet

I turn the key and push my front door open, watching it swing
wide and settle against the wall. The entryway looks just like it
did when we left—Max's navy-blue windbreaker is hanging on
a hook, right next to my black hoodie. We'd worn them to walk
down to the wine store the night before we'd flown to Maui,
deciding to splurge on a good bottle of red to celebrate. Why
couldn't he have voiced his doubts then, as we sat facing each
other on the couch while we sipped the Pinot Noir we'd pur-
chased, speculating about which family member would make
the biggest ass of himself at the reception?

As I step through the doorway, my heart folds inside my
chest. This homecoming couldn't be more opposite of the one
I'd envisioned. I'd pictured Max dramatically scooping me up
and carrying me over the threshold, me giggling as he nuzzled his
face in my neck, kissing me just below the ear, sending electric
charges through my abdomen. But as I drop my suitcase now,
the thud from the luggage hitting the hardwood floor echoes

through the vacant house, underscoring the emptiness inside of me.

I draw my breath hard into my lungs and release it slowly, remembering Jules' advice on our flight home: *just take everything one moment at a time*. I turn at the sound of her footsteps behind me. She's gripping a suitcase in each hand and has a tote slung over each shoulder, looking like a Sherpa as she walks up. After I'd dissolved into tears as my luggage descended the conveyor belt at LAX, she'd demanded that she carry *all* of my bags, only letting me be in charge of one small carry-on.

"I didn't get very far," I say as I reach out to grab the straw purse that's sliding down her arm—the one I'd planned to stuff with magazines and books and take to the private poolside cabana Max and I had rented for the first day of our honeymoon on the island of Lanai.

"You're inside. That's something." She presses her lips together forming a slight smile, releasing the rest of my bags around her feet.

I nod, my eyes resting on one of the pink luggage tags that reads Bride.

"So"—she laces her fingers through mine—"let's take a few more steps. If we're diligent, we might get to the staircase by nightfall." Her eyes are sympathetic as she nudges me with her elbow.

I turn to face her, my hand still tightly gripping hers. "Thank you."

"It goes without saying."

"Well, I'd still be in a heap on the floor of the bridal suite if it weren't for you," I say. Jules had called the airline and changed my flight; she'd neatly folded and packed all of my bikinis, maxi dresses, and even my lingerie into my suitcase; and she'd put my wedding dress into the garment bag—the sound of the zipper sealing it inside making me feel nauseous.

"You're going to get through this," she says, interrupting my thoughts. Then when she catches my skeptical expression, adds, "I promise."

"I'm going to have to trust you on this one, considering I'm not even sure how I'm going to lift my arms to brush my teeth tonight."

"I'll help you. I'm staying over."

"Jules, you can't. The kids. Ben—"

"It's already done. Ben loves you as much as I do and wanted me here with you. . . ." She pauses, amusement in her eyes. "Plus, better him than me dealing with the kids adjusting to the time difference!"

We laugh. It feels foreign, almost like a betrayal of my pain, making me wonder how long it will be before the laughter rolls comfortably off my tongue like it used to.

"Well, please thank him for me."

"Will you stop? It's an unwritten rule that best friends take care of each other and best friends' husbands understand. You'd do the same for me."

"Well, if Ben ever leaves you, I will kill him," I say matter-of-factly. "I need you to know that."

Jules smiles wryly at my declaration and then regards me for a few moments, no doubt taking in my disheveled appearance— my oily face and the dark circles around my eyes exposing the stress of the last two days. My unwashed hair is pulled back into a messy ponytail and I'm wearing the same pair of sweats I'd woken up in yesterday.

Finally, Jules says simply, "Well, you definitely *look* the part of someone who can wield a weapon." She points to my puffy eyes and my sweatpants hanging low on my hips. Jules grabs my hand again. "Now, follow me. One foot in front of the other."

I walk in step with Jules down the hallway that spills out into the living room. The remote control rests on the glass coffee table where I left it after we'd watched an old episode of *Project Runway* the night before we left for Hawaii. Feeling tipsy from the wine, I'd told Max he should start wearing sweater vests and he'd pretended he hadn't heard me. As Jules and I walk into the kitchen, the granite countertops gleaming—not so much as an errant water glass in sight—I have another flashback to the morning Max and I were leaving for the airport. I was gripping our freshly printed boarding passes tightly as I rushed around the corner, nearly tripping over the open dishwasher door. I'd wanted to be two hours early to LAX—*at least*—and Max had been hunched over the sink, his sleeves rolled up, running a round brush inside my cereal bowl that I'd forgotten to wash. He'd looked up unapologetically. "Can't come home to dirty dishes." *Or apparently he hadn't been planning on coming home at all.*

In the past twenty-four hours, I've thought about a dozen instances like the one that morning, wondering which marked the exact moment when he decided he couldn't marry me. While I knew it wasn't logical that he left me because I refused to rinse every glass and pan thoroughly before placing it in the dishwasher, I still wondered deep in my heart if it was part of what had factored into his decision. Had he finally grown tired of certain nuances about my personality that he'd once found endearing? Like my need to dissect the tribal alliances on *Survivor* every week? Or my inability to take out the trash before it was overflowing and too heavy for me to carry to the Dumpster? Or was it something bigger—maybe he wasn't attracted to me anymore? I glance at my reflection in the microwave and cringe. From the way I look right now, I can't say I blame him.

He'd texted me several times since the rehearsal dinner, saying we needed to get together to figure things out—my hope rising each time his name appeared on the screen, only to fall again when I realized all he wanted was to settle things and move on. While sitting on the tarmac as I waited for the flight back to LA to take off, I absorbed the plush West Maui mountain range, the same one that Max and I had planned to take a helicopter ride over before departing for Lanai, and had finally written back and asked him what "things" he was referring to, my heart sitting in the base of my throat as I waited for his response, hopeful that he meant *us*, but knowing better. He'd texted me a list that had nearly made me double over in pain: *the condo, the checking account, the credit cards.*

As I'd watched the wing of our plane start to move down the runway, my sobs rippling in the back of my throat like a hot spring, images of the honeymoon plans that would now never become real force themselves upon me: snorkeling on Molokini, hiking to Sweetheart Rock in Puu Pehe, and getting the couples' massage Max had insisted on booking for us. I'd made a bad *Bachelor* joke when he'd suggested it, but as we ascended into the blue, cloudless sky and the island of Maui became nothing more than a speck of green in the vast Pacific Ocean beneath us, I would've done anything to be side by side with him on those massage tables.

I'd thrust my phone at Jules to show her the text from Max and she'd unbuckled her seat belt and wrapped her arms around me tightly, despite the warning look from the flight attendant. "How could he be so businesslike about this?" I'd sobbed into her neck.

Jules shook her head. "I don't know. I don't understand him at all right now. I thought I knew him better than this."

"So did I—"

We'd sat in silence, both of us taking inventory of our memories of Max. I wondered what had become of the man I could always count on—the guy who once drove an hour round-trip to get me the only chicken noodle soup that sounded good when I had the flu, never questioning me when I told him it was something about the texture of the noodles and the taste of the broth. And doing it again a few months later, this time without even asking, when I'd been sick again. Where had the man gone that would always reach across and grab my hand while we lay in bed, folding it back over his chest and kissing each finger as I drifted off to sleep? And where was the guy who'd made my mom laugh so hard she'd cried the first time she'd met him, when he'd told her the story of how, after spending two months abroad in college, he'd excitedly hugged the wrong girl from behind at the airport, thinking it was his girlfriend. "Let's just say my jokes about them both having a very nice ass didn't go well." As my mom dabbed at her eyes, he'd smiled and squeezed my hand, knowing how much her approval meant to me.

"Do you want me to handle things with him when we get back—tell him you need some space and aren't ready to talk yet?" Jules said, breaking the silence. She looked down for a moment and I followed her gaze, noticing an airsickness bag that had fallen from the seat-back pocket. My stomach lurched as we hit a patch of turbulence and I contemplated picking it up. Finally she looked at me again. "I just feel so bad about this, like somehow I'm responsible."

"Because you introduced us?" I frowned.

Jules nodded.

"Just because you pushed us together on the dance floor at Deb and Eddie's wedding after you'd had one too many sangrias does *not* mean this is your fault," I'd sputtered through my tears, suddenly back to that night, seeing Jules' eyes brighten when she spotted Max—whom she'd befriended after he'd hosted his mom's surprise fiftieth birthday party at the restaurant where she worked as a pastry chef—and realized we were both at the wedding without a date.

"If anyone's to blame, it's me—how did I not see this coming? Clearly I missed some major warning signs. Because what kind of person just up and leaves his fiancée the night before he's supposed to marry her?"

"A stupid one!" she said, pulling me in for another hug, and I'd squeezed her tightly, despite the armrest pressing into my side.

"Really stupid," I said as I buried my head deeper into her shoulder, the smell of her lavender-scented shampoo comforting me. "And when you talk to him will you please remind him the condo is *mine*," I'd said calmly, but deep down, I could feel the anger bubbling inside me like a pot of boiling water about to force the lid off.

"Do you want a glass of wine?" Jules asks me now, but her hand is already on the corkscrew. She pours a bottle of Wild Horse chardonnay into two goblets and I follow her outside into the garden just off the kitchen—the selling point for me when I bought the condominium.

I'd been saving for my first home for years, deciding to buy a place before Max and I were engaged, wanting to be a home-owner no matter what happened between us. As I'd tailed the real estate agent through the interior, taking in the delicate crown molding, the built-in bookcases, and the newly finished dark wood floors, I had a feeling it was special. But it wasn't until I walked outside and saw the Spanish tile on the patio and the beautiful landscaping on the small but perfectly sized yard, completely hidden from others' view by two large orange trees, that I'd given Max *the look* that said, *I want this*. He was the in-house counsel for a small medical device company and told me he'd do the negotiating. And when he'd caught the seller's real estate agent watching us, he'd shot me a look in return—one that said, *if you want it, you need to put your poker face on—now*.

Max and I had later shared a laugh about how transparent I'd been, how I'd been unable to hide my wide eyes while a perfectly composed Max interrogated the agent about the asking price. You would never have known he liked anything about the condo, when in truth he was just as in love with it as I was. When the seller agreed to my offer, several thousand dollars less than it was listed for, Max and me high-fiving over the *take it or leave it* stance he'd held firm on, it had never occurred to me that his uncanny ability to hide his real feelings would ever come into play in our relationship. That it would prevent me from seeing that I was losing him.

I remember scrawling my signature across the bottom of the deed, a confident grin spreading across my face as I imagined it would eventually become *our place*. The thought that one day I'd simply be thankful I still had a roof over my head after he tossed me into the trash as easily as he would a carton of spoiled milk would never have crossed my mind.

• • •

My phone rings and Jules wrinkles her nose at the sound. "Sorry, I know, I need to change the ringtone," I say, and she gives me a knowing look, remembering that Max had chosen the last one—

ironically it had been "Wrecking Ball." It had become our thing, to steal the other's cell and select a song to play when there was a new notification.

I hesitate before checking the alert. Is it another email from a wedding guest who felt as blindsided as I had by Max's announcement—wanting me to explain *why*? Or was it yet another clueless Facebook friend wondering why I hadn't posted so much as a picture of my veil on my special day? So far, the friends and family who'd been at the rehearsal dinner had been rather tight-lipped about what happened, but I knew it was only a matter of time before word got out. Even the mailman, Henry, was wondering why I was back early. I'd overheard a hushed conversation between him and Jules as she was coming inside earlier—something about how *he'd thought* I'd deferred delivery of my packages for another week. I imagined his sun-weathered face contort in disbelief as she quickly explained what had happened.

Pity from the postman—that's all I needed.

It was hard enough seeing the sympathetic faces of my family and close friends in Maui as they heard the news. But now that I was home, I realized I was going to have to go through it all over again. And not just with the people in my everyday life, but also with the friends I interacted with every day online. I was quick to like their pictures and check-ins, and even though I hadn't had a live conversation with most of them in years, I still felt strangely invested in their lives—and was terrified to let them see that I wasn't the carefree girl who loved to shop at Target and play Candy Crush.

As long as Jules was here I could put off dealing with reality and continue to ignore the questions from curious people wondering why I hadn't gotten married. But eventually she'd have to go back to her life—to cheering on the sidelines of Evan's soccer games and posting pictures of her latest professional chocolate masterpieces on foodgawker. And then where would that leave me?

The alert turns out to be a text from my mom checking in to see if I made it home safely and asking if I want to join her for a power walk to clear my mind.

I look up from my phone. "It's my mom."

"Let me guess—she thinks a hefty workout will cheer you up?"

"Yep," I answer, pausing to write her and say thanks for the offer, but I'm too tired to go hiking with ankle weights and I'll call her tomorrow instead. "Her answer to everything—burning calories!" I take a long sip of my wine, deciding that for the rest of the night, I'm going to try my best not to think about why I'm sitting on an Adirondack chair in my backyard instead of lounging on a beach chair in the tropical sun.

• • •

There's that split second first thing in the morning when your eyes slowly open and your mind is still empty and your heart is still light. It's that moment when you are blissfully unaware of the pain that is inside of you—the dreams that danced in your head the night before still seeming possible. And then you see your best friend passed out on the floor, her mouth hanging open slightly, and it unleashes the memory. And instantly, like a wave of nausea, reality hits.

I force my legs out from under me and pull a sweatshirt and baseball cap from the hall closet, too emotionally drained to care about what I look like—to worry if my bad breath and raccoon eyes will scare off anyone I might run into while out in public. I grab a book from my packed floor-to-ceiling bookshelf and leave Jules a note that I'm going to Starbucks, and after I close the door behind me, I rest my back against it and squeeze the tears away.

Last night, I'd told Jules I wasn't ready to walk into the master bedroom, let alone sleep in the bed, so she'd swiftly grabbed a fitted sheet and tucked it around the cushions of the couch and covered me with a blanket as my eyelids became heavy from the wine. "You're a good mom," I'd said just before I drifted off to sleep.

Walking the two blocks to the coffee shop, I resist the memories flying to the surface of Max and me, walking hand in hand down the same street just last weekend. I'd been venting about the florist informing me that due to an inexplicable ordering snafu, it wouldn't be possible to get the exact color and type of exotic orchid I'd wanted to surprise my mother, my stepmom, and Max's mom with on the morning of the ceremony. As I'd clamored on about finding another person to handle the flowers, Max hadn't said a word, which, at the time, hadn't seemed that unusual since he'd been leaving most of the wedding decisions up to me. But now I wonder if his silence meant he hadn't been listening, or hadn't cared, because he knew he wouldn't be there anyway. I shake my head slightly—neither of those scenarios fit the man I'd loved for the past three years.

After I order my coffee, I sink into an oversized chair in the corner and open the novel I brought with me, the words blurring on the page. I shut it quickly and pull my phone out of my pocket delicately, like it's a loaded gun. I rub the sleep still wedged in the corners of my eyes and stare at the screen, instinctively looking around as if Jules might walk in at any second and scold me. And she'd be right. I shouldn't go on Facebook. Or Instagram. Or even Google Plus. Because there's no chance I'm ready to make an appearance on social media—to officially change my status back to single, and then explain why.

But like a bad habit, I still crave my news feed, and soon find my eyes locked on a picture of Max and me posing with beers in the pool at the Four Seasons the day before our guests were scheduled to begin arriving. Ignoring the flood of messages filling up my timeline and in-box, I click to update my status and stare at the empty space, wishing I could find the words to make my life seem right again. But for the first time since I joined Facebook years ago, I'm speechless. "I wish there was a status update that could fix this mess," I mumble before slipping my phone back into my pocket.

I head back up to the counter to order a mocha for Jules before going home. I pay quickly and lean against the counter as the barista, a striking woman with caramel-colored hair and chocolate eyes, wields the espresso machine expertly. I let out a loud sigh as I wait, and she looks up and smiles.

"In a hurry?" she asks.

"Not really," I admit, embarrassed she caught my annoyance.

She eyes me sympathetically. "Don't worry, your life will get better."

I tilt my head and take a closer look at her face. Had I met her before? I didn't think so, but something about the way she said that my life would get better—it was almost as if she knew me and knew what happened. But how?

She slides the mocha across the counter and I meet her eyes again, now certain I have never seen her before. *God, I have already lost my fiancé, am I losing my mind too?*

"You're going to be okay," she says as I grab the hot cup and slide a sleeve over it.

"Thanks, but I'm fine," I finally say more sharply than I intend, wanting to believe my own words, to escape this woman who seems to be able to see right through me. I swivel and walk away quickly, not looking back, even when I swear I hear her laugh and say, "Whatever you say, Kate."

CHAPTER FOUR

....

Feeling blindsided and stupid. How could I have missed the warning signs?

I mentally compose the status update I wish I could post as I climb the stairs to my front door, painted fire-engine red based on the recommendation of the feng shui consultant I hired after Max moved in with me. She had floated through the house like a fall breeze, shaking her head slightly every few minutes and making notes in her gold notebook. Several hundred dollars and paint colors later, she had finally given her chi blessing and convinced me that my happily-ever-after with Max was just around the corner despite the fact he'd been tight-lipped about his plan to propose.

As I hear the flutelike sound of the wind brushing against the chime I'd hung outside, my mind wanders to the delicate pink crystal hearts I'd hid in the love corner, which happened to be our laundry room—the ones I'd dangled from a nail in the back of the linen closet behind my bulk purchases of tissue boxes and Dove soap. The same gems I'd smashed to pieces last night, feeling like the universe had let me down. I had unflinchingly given all my faith, painstakingly put together a vision board, and religiously chanted my daily affirmations, yet here I was—*alone*. As I'd ripped up every last inspirational photo and motivational quote that I had so carefully pinned to the manifestation corkboard that I had hung over my mahogany desk, I decided it was a sad moment when you realized there really was no magic in this world.

I find Jules and Liam huddled on my couch. "Hey," they say in unison with feigned smiles painted across their faces.

"I'm glad you got out of the house," Jules says as she materializes at my side and gently takes the cup from my hand. "Thanks for this."

"Where's mine?" Liam fake whines, and I shrug.

"Sorry, I didn't know you'd be here," I say as he protrudes his lower lip excessively before smiling. "But I'm really glad you are," I add, hugging him tightly, breathing in the smell of Irish Spring soap.

"It's probably for the best anyway . . . I brought my own comfort drink." He holds up the same flask he had in the bridal suite. For a moment, the night comes crashing back like a wave slamming hard against a rocky coast, but I shake my head slightly to dispel the thoughts and instead conjure a memory of the two of us sitting in the back of a movie theater sipping peppermint schnapps as we laughed hysterically at whatever silly rom-com I'd convinced him to see, always with the agreement that we'd both pretend he didn't love it as much as I did. He reaches down and pulls out a pint of Ben & Jerry's from a plastic Ralph's bag at his feet. "Forget your no-foam soy whatevers. Why don't you join me in *this* kind of comfort?" He holds up the flask in one hand and the carton of ice cream in the other. "C'mon, pick your poison!"

Deciding I'll opt for high-fructose sugar over whatever mystery alcohol he's holding, still nursing a headache from last night's wine bender, I grab the carton of my favorite flavor, Chunky Monkey, from his hand and a spoon from the kitchen.

We sit in silence in a row on the couch— with matched solemn expressions, like three kids waiting for the principal—me stuffing my face with walnut, banana, and chocolate chunks, Jules drinking her mocha, and Liam sipping his liquor. "So I've been thinking," Liam finally says. "What if we make Max pay for what he's done to you the good old-fashioned way—you know, by giving him a nice ass-kicking?"

"Are *you* volunteering?" I ask as Jules and I dissolve in laughter, the tightness in my chest temporarily surrendering. "Because you don't even like to *watch* boxing on TV!"

"Maybe. But that doesn't mean I couldn't take him." Liam balls his hands into fists and jabs his toned arms in the air. "He hurt my girl—that'll help any guy find his inner Tyson!"

We spend the next hour dissecting my relationship with Max, finally concluding there was no way even Jules' spiritual adviser, Jordan, could have seen this one coming.

"I have to admit, Max is the *last* person I thought would do this." Liam kicks his feet up on the coffee table, revealing a sock with a hole in its toe. "You guys seemed way too predictable for something crazy like this to happen."

I wave a spoonful of ice cream at him. "Is that your way of saying we're boring?"

"Not boring." He backtracks, keeping an eye on the clump of chocolate that threatens to fall from my spoon onto his jeans. "But you never seemed to have any problems."

"And that's a bad thing why?" I ask, but don't wait for his answer and look over at Jules, who hides her eyes behind her cup.

"I know you find your own dating situations humdrum if a day goes by without drama, but newsflash, Liam: in most relationships, it's a *good thing* for the two people involved to get along."

"No—I didn't mean that. . . . Jules, help me out here. . . ."

She throws her arms in the air. "You're on your own with this one, buddy."

"What I'm trying to say is you guys seemed like you had already been married thirty years." He laughs awkwardly, and Jules shakes her head at him. "Okay, I'm going to stop talking now," he declares before taking a long swig from his flask.

The truth was, Max and I *were* a predictable couple. We had always gotten along well for the most part—our biggest fight had happened after I backed his new car into a pole and tried to get it fixed without telling him.

My past relationships would usually start out full throttle and fizzle out slowly, like a soda that had been accidentally left out on the counter. My boyfriend before Max had been so moody he once picked a fight over my restaurant choice (he'd wanted dim sum, *not* Japanese) and stormed out, leaving me with the check and a pit the size of a crater in my stomach. I'd told myself I was done bickering over petty things—I wanted someone who wasn't constantly looking for an argument. And then Max had shown up, just when I'd mentally thrown in the towel, Jules squealing about some therapist on *Oprah* who said that's always when you find *the one*, when you're *not looking*. Our relationship built slowly and grew stronger with such ease I had initially questioned it, wondering if it was too good to be true, but Jules assured me I had paid my dues with the other assholes I had dated, that Max was my reward for being patient. And I had believed her, convincing myself that I had finally earned that happy ending that had eluded me thus far.

For months during that period when people's guards are supposed to drop and their "bad" sides start to come out, everything with Max was still so easy—looking back, maybe too easy—that I'd been constantly waiting for the big reveal that Max was just another jerk masquerading as a nice guy. Not that I wanted a cantankerous man like the last one, but I had expected there to be some terse tones or maybe even an eye roll.

When I'd finally asked Max point-blank why he was so mellow, he'd assured me that was who he really was, that he wasn't a closet misogynist like I'd jokingly speculated. He'd said that because he spent his days as an attorney, arguing over tiny details buried in lengthy contracts, if I wanted antibiotic-free milk or to watch a reality show instead of *Monday Night Football,* then so be it. That he didn't want to waste time worrying about the little things. And the system had always worked for us. Or so I'd thought. Now I wonder, did the little things he was trying to ignore pile up so high that they ultimately toppled our relationship, causing it to crash like the falling pieces of a Jenga game?

"So, Max asked me to tell you something," Jules says delicately, her lips turning down slightly as she notices the engagement ring still on my finger. I twist the diamond so it's on the inside of my hand and turn away. I'd ceremoniously removed it in Maui, but kept it close—in a pocket or my purse—until this morning, when something had pushed me to put it back on before I'd left the house. I wasn't sure if it was the fear of my naked ring finger being exposed to the world, or if it was denial or maybe a little bit of both. Hadn't I noticed the barista at Starbucks eyeing it as if she knew it wasn't supposed to be there?

"What does he want me to know?" I finally ask.

"I told him I'd pass it along, but if you're not ready to hear it—"

"You don't have to listen to anything that guy has to say." Liam clenches his jaw. "Fuck him."

I put my hand over Liam's mouth to silence him, his anger with Max threatening to unleash the tears that are clamoring at the backs of my eyes. There was a side to Liam he didn't show everyone, a part that took time to find, like a shell you finally unearth after digging through the sand. On the exterior, he was a guy's guy, slapping high fives when Hanley Ramirez hit a grand slam or when Liam went for a layup on the basketball court like he was still twenty-one years old. But underneath, he could be sensitive, like the time he'd grabbed my hand and sat silently beside me as I wailed like a toddler after my favorite TV show was canceled, something he could have told me wasn't import-ant, but he didn't because he understood it mattered to me. And I was the only person who knew he'd cried while reading *The Notebook*, a secret he'd made me promise never to reveal, information I'd been proud to protect because it represented my favorite part of him.

Our friendship just worked. I understood him and he got me. We never pushed each other to fix our neuroses. He knew I needed to scrutinize ten nearly identical photos before upload-ing one to Instagram, always willing to weigh in on which picture made my arms look the least fleshy. And in return, I understood he wasn't interested in showing his "secret sensitive side" to the women he dated. The Liam he gave them was the thirty-four-year-old hilarious computer programmer by day who went on acting auditions at night, even landing a couple of national com-mercials, not the man whose parents had divorced when he was ten and whose dad hadn't been in the picture much since, the man who fiercely protected his own heart as much as he looked out for Jules and me.

As I regard him now, a scowl settling into his chiseled face and loyalty blazing in his hazel eyes, I know he'd do anything to take my pain away.

"It's okay. I want to hear what he told Jules." I recognize that familiar feeling that's been rising and falling within me every day since he canceled our wedding—*hope*.

Jules inches her body closer to me. "He wants to talk . . ." She pauses, squeezing my palm, and suddenly I'm picturing my mom's warm hand over mine as she choked back her sobs, telling me that she and my dad were getting a divorce. Was the pain I was feeling only a fraction of what she had experienced? There had always been a part of me that had resented her bitterness. But now I could see why it might be easy to wallow in it.

"Kate?" Jules notices I've drifted away.

"Sorry," I say, snapping my attention back to her.

"I was saying that he wants to talk as soon as you are ready. And he wanted me to tell you *again* that he's sorry."

"Did he sound sincere?" I ask.

Jules presses her lips together in a tight line.

"Jules?" I ask again, sinking back into the sofa's plush cushions, remembering when I'd bought it after the feng shui consultant deemed my old futon full of *bad energy*, feeling excited as the movers unloaded the sofa in the center of my living room, imagining all of the possibilities this new piece of furniture represented. But why had I focused so much of my attention on the good fortune some inanimate object would bring my relationship?

"What a prick," Liam says, his tone a sharp contrast to Jules' motherly inflection. "I can't believe he'd try to get to you through Jules—put her in the middle like this."

Ignoring Liam, Jules finally nods her head. "He did sound

like he meant it. But who cares what I think. You should talk to him and decide what *you* think. I know you're hurting right now, but the sooner you do face him, the faster you can start picking up the pieces."

"Ugh. I hate it when you're right." I release an exaggerated sigh. "And even though he's got his tough-guy thing going on right now, Liam does have a point," I say as he peers at me over the top of his flask, nodding his head in agreement. "It's not fair of *either of us* to make you the middleman any longer."

"Don't worry about me—I can handle him," Jules says. "I took care of two kids with swine flu last winter while Ben was at his annual stockholders' meeting. This is nothing!"

I cringe at the visual of Jules getting puked on and running cold baths. "Believe me, I am *very* aware that you can tackle any situation with the proficiency of a drill sergeant, but you're right. I can't avoid him any longer, especially because he lives here—at least he used to." I choke back the bile in my throat as I think about the cold sheets on his side of the bed. "And there are things to divide up—although I don't even know where we'll begin. I mean, what's the etiquette for dealing with those?" I sweep my hand toward the wedding gifts that are piled beneath a quilt in the corner. Jules had thrown the blanket over them after I'd kicked one of the boxes the night before, the sound of whatever was inside breaking, me praying it was the stupid bread maker Max had insisted we register for. When we'd taken the trip to Crate & Barrel, he'd silently shuffled beside me, nodding absentmindedly as I scanned various items. But then, like an elderly person who nods off after a meal and abruptly wakes up, he'd stopped in the middle of the aisle and pointed, offering a strong opinion about the need for us to be able to make home-made bread. "Like, when are we ever going to use that? I can't even remember the last time I had a piece of toast!" I'd screamed at Jules late last night, right before she took the wine from my hand and guided me over to the couch to go to sleep.

But what I couldn't bring myself to say to my best friends now, even though I knew they'd understand, was I couldn't care less about who got custody of the Vitamix blender or the surround sound system. I needed more answers from Max. I needed to know *why*. Why he waited so long to leave. Why I wasn't enough for him.

"I need to go upstairs and call him." I hold my hand up to halt their protests.

Jules stands and starts to speak, but I cut her off, already knowing what she's about to say. "I'll be fine—I promise," I lie as I look at the circular metal staircase that leads to the master bedroom. *I can do this. One foot in front of the other.*

"Okay, we'll be right here," she says, giving my arm a squeeze and glancing at Liam as if she thinks he can talk some sense into me.

"Kate." Liam stands and envelops me in a hug, his chest warm against my cheek. "He has no idea what he's giving up," he whispers fiercely in my ear.

"Thanks," I say, leaning in closer, the quickened pace of his heartbeat reinforcing his words.

I start to pull back, but he tightens his grip. "We love you exactly the way you are—just remember that. If he doesn't, then he doesn't deserve you."

I smile up at him. "I don't know what I'd do without you guys."

When I walk into our bedroom and see the neatly made bed, a memory comes flooding back. The morning after Max first slept over at the apartment in Venice Beach I lived in before I bought the condo, I'd walked out of the bathroom and found him pulling the sheet taut, then carefully tucking it under each corner, then smoothing the top. After watching him for several minutes, I said, "Hey there, Hospital Corners, you for real? Don't tell me you know how to separate the whites too?"

On the morning we left for Hawaii, did he know it was the last time he'd be making *our* bed?

I sit on the edge of the bed and pull up Max's name on my phone. He answers on the first ring, as if he has been waiting for my call. "Kate."

"Hi," I say, my voice catching in my throat.

"Are you okay?"

"Just tell me why you threw away everything we had," I launch in, the edge in my voice harsher than I want it to be. "I deserve to know."

The four beats between my question and his response feel like hours. The only sound is our neighbor's dog, a Jack Russell terrier named Benji, barking urgently in the background. Always a big fan of Max's, I imagine he's yelling, *Be careful! This is a loaded question!*

I suck in my breath, my eyes moving back and forth over several framed pictures of us on the dresser that are angled in two perfectly straight lines, finally landing on the one in the center, our engagement photo that was taken on the beach in Malibu last summer. Finally, the words tumble from his mouth—he's so sorry, he didn't mean to hurt me, he hopes I can forgive him. He tells me he hadn't been happy for some time, but didn't know how to tell me—describing the last few months as a roller coaster that he didn't feel he could stop. He says something about how he's doing us both a favor, even if I can't see that right now. Then he tells me I deserve better. "And there's something else you need to know. Something I want you to hear from me," he says.

"There's more? Lucky me," I say sarcastically.

"Yes . . ." He trails off.

"Enlighten me," I say, hating that I sound bitter. Hating that it's him who's making me sound this way.

His shallow breaths sound amplified through the phone. "God. I don't know how to tell you this. But I feel like telling you is the right thing to do. I'd want to know if it were me."

But it's not you. I would never do this to you.

"What is it?" What could he reveal that could hurt any more than *I don't want to marry you?*

"I think I'm in love with someone else."

Okay. I was wrong. That hurts worse.

I grip the phone tightly, my body temperature rising so quickly that I have to unzip my sweatshirt.

"Hello? Are you still there?"

"Yes," I finally whisper as a lone tear escapes my eye, travels down my cheek, and drips off my chin before he finally starts to talk again.

I try to rub the tension out of the back of my neck with my knuckles. Max used to do that—I'd sit on the floor beneath him and he'd dissolve the kinks with such ease that I'd joke that if his lawyer thing didn't work out, he'd definitely have another career to fall back on.

"But no happy endings!" he'd laugh. "I'm saving those for you."

"Of course," I'd chuckle, foolishly believing he would never so much as let his eye linger on another woman. Turns out I couldn't have been more wrong.

"I want you to know I never cheated on you, not even a kiss," I hear him say, his words sounding muffled like the sound you hear when you put a seashell to your ear. "We never expected this to happen. That—"

"Who?" I interrupt, but am only met with silence. "Who is it?" I demand again, running through a mental index of the women it could be. That glossy intern at his office? His ex-girlfriend from high school who'd friended him on Facebook last year? Some random girl he'd met when I wasn't around?

"Courtney," Max says, so quietly I think I've misheard him.

"Courtney?" I repeat, the shock of hearing her name smacking me across the face like a hailstorm.

That Courtney? *My* friend? *My coworker?* The one I'd busted my ass with for five years—pulling so many all-nighters at the office she finally brought in her favorite fluffy pink slippers and chenille blanket and I hauled in my Keurig coffeemaker and iPod, us laughing that at least we had the comforts of home, *and each other*. I feel a burn in my chest as I recall the exact moment when our partnership at work transformed into a real friendship. It was one of those long nights—the janitor was cleaning the marble floor and we were lying on the couches in the entryway as we tried to think up a slogan for the athletic socks account we'd just acquired. As I listened to the whirring of the buffer, I burst out, "You know what? This really fucking *socks*! We should be home in bed with our husbands. *If* we had husbands!" And Courtney deadpanned, "Husbands? Who needs men when we're married to our jobs!" and I'd started crying, the really ugly snotty kind. And she'd hopped off her couch and onto mine and thrown her arms around my neck and said, "You and I will have hot human hubbies one day, but tonight we only have each other . . ." She trailed off for a moment and reached down toward her foot, and suddenly I felt a soft fabric against my cheeks. "And our socks," she said, using hers to wipe my tears away.

I heave as all the air is sucked from my lungs like a Shop-Vac inhaling everything in its path as the memory of how Courtney and Max ended up in each other's lives floods through me. How, when a smile had danced across my lips the morning after I met Max, Courtney was the first person I thought of telling after Jules and Liam. But as I'd reached for my cell phone, a part of me had worried she'd be resentful because being single workaholics had been our *thing*. I'd had boyfriends before and so had she, but we'd always known they were just seat fillers until the real thing came along.

And I could tell that's what Max was—the real thing. When he'd walked me to my car at the end of the night we met, I'd tripped over my four-inch heels and fallen, grabbing my fender, my legs doing near splits so I didn't hit the asphalt, but I couldn't stop my dress from flying up and exposing the granny panties I'd worn to the wedding because I hadn't done laundry. I'd looked up at Max in horror and he'd started laughing, tears running down his cheeks. "I didn't see anything. I swear," he had declared as he held up his hands so vehemently that we both knew that he had seen *everything*. And suddenly it was as if I could see the movie of our lives playing out: the third date when we let our hands linger over each other's bodies in a way that said we were ready for more, the meeting of the parents, the first time he whispered that he loved me gently in my ear. I could see a future.

When I'd finally told Courtney—making myself wait until I could tell her in person at work on Monday—her eyes had registered it before I even opened my mouth. Her face immediately softened and she'd hugged me tightly and said, "So when do I get to meet this man who has made you look like you're glowing from the inside out?" and I'd scolded myself for doubting her, for projecting onto her the way I probably would've reacted had the roles been reversed.

Ironically, it had been Max I practically had to drag to meet Courtney the first time because there had been a big basketball game on he'd wanted to watch. But within the first few minutes, he and Courtney had hit it off. An innocuous comment from me about being an only child had spawned a conversation between them about their both being adopted, and I could barely get a word in for the rest of the night. *I brought them together and now they're leaving me for each other.*

So this was why I hadn't heard from her since the night of the rehearsal dinner. I had thought she was just trying to give me space, but had felt slightly hurt that she hadn't so much as sent me a text. Even my grandmother, who had instructions taped to the back of her archaic flip phone on how to use it, had figured out how to do that.

"Yes," Max finally answers, breaking me away from my racing thoughts, his words soft, but the tears in his throat making his voice squeak from his mouth.

Oh, I'm sorry this is so hard on you, Max.

"Fuck you," I spit as I hang up the phone and throw myself on the army-regulation-made bed, pulling the covers apart like a child throwing a tantrum as regret, shame, and aching sadness wash over me at once.

I stare at the ceiling for several minutes before hauling myself off the bed and pulling my laptop open. With a mind of their own, my fingers seem to find their way to Facebook, where I spend the next ten minutes obsessively deleting every photo I'd posted of Max and Courtney, my heart simultaneously racing with anger and breaking in pain every time I click on another picture that reminds me of the times we all spent together. I stop short when I come across a shot of the three of us, taken last month at the happy hour at STK, Max sandwiched between Courtney and me, his lopsided smile giving nothing away as he draped an arm over each of our shoulders. I click the trash icon, wishing there was a way to delete this part of my life too. Wouldn't it be nice if we could get rid of hurtful feelings and memories the same way we so easily send a bad picture sailing into our computer's trash can?

I pull up my status box and type, imagining Max and Courtney's reaction when my update appears in their feeds—hoping my strong statement will show them they can't break me down.

> Thanks for all your kind words—they have meant so much to me. But please don't worry! I'm going to be fine!

I pause before clicking on the post button, the insincerity of my words sitting heavy in my chest. I couldn't recall a time I'd ever written something negative on Facebook, instead focusing on the positive things I wanted people to know—a new account I'd landed at work, a fabulous restaurant where I'd scored a reservation, the roses Max had sent me on our anniversary. Even on days when I felt like absolute shit, I'd found something humorous to say or share, deciding no one would want to hear about my bad morning. Or maybe I just hadn't wanted anyone to know I was having one? I had always thought myself above the Debbie Downers who posted about the (gasp!) problems in their lives—the ones who weren't afraid to highlight unpopular opinions or rant about their kids, the people who didn't fear judgment the same way I did.

But as I sit here now, staring at the candy-coated status update sitting on my computer screen, I wonder if those Debbie

Downers have been onto something when they tell it like it is. (Well, except the ones who post about government conspiracy theories—those people are just cray-cray.) Obviously, always trying to make my own life look like a Norman Rockwell painting wasn't getting me anywhere. Maybe it was time to be real.

I quickly delete the disingenuous words I'd just written and type a new status, hitting send before I can talk myself out of it.

Thank you all for thinking of me. I'm devastated that I'm not getting married. I wish I could do the past month over. Please DM me if you have access to a time machine.

CHAPTER FIVE

....

Be careful what you wish for, people. You just might get it.

The high-pitched beeping of the alarm jolts me awake from a dream—I was standing on the balcony of my bridal suite, watching Max and Courtney making out on the beach as the soft waves lapped over them. I tried to yell at them—to find out what the hell they thought they were doing—but no sound could escape my throat. I attempted to move but my feet felt like they were glued in place. I had no choice but to watch helplessly as they laughed in between kisses, Courtney biting Max's lip playfully.

"Fuck you both!" I scream into my pillow, where a pool of saliva has formed.

"Good morning to you too!" a voice says—one that sounds identical to Max's. But it can't be him. He's probably entangled in Courtney's floral bedspread. And she's probably biting his lip just like she was in my dream.

I bolt upright to find Max wrapped in the sheets beside me, rubbing the sleep from his eyes. "What the hell are *you* doing here?" I demand.

Max cocks his head to the side and frowns at me. "I live here, remember?"

"Not anymore you don't!" I hiss, trying to figure out what happened last night—how Max ended up in my bed. My head throbs like it would from a hangover, but I couldn't remember having any alcohol. My mind foggy, the last thing I recall is talking to Max on the phone and melting down after.

I flinch as Max puts his hand on my arm. "Honey? Are you okay?"

"Oh, I'm about as fine as anyone would be after what you did!" I jump out of bed and back away from him. "Did you slip in here last night after I was already asleep? I didn't think I'd need to change the locks. I think you'd better leave—*now*. I'm sure your girlfriend is wondering where you are. She wouldn't be too happy to find you back here with me."

Max rolls off the bed and steps gingerly toward me, as if I'm a wounded animal he wants to help without getting bitten. "It's me, Max, your *fiancé*. Last time I checked, you're my only girl-friend. One I plan to marry in a month."

The room starts to spin and I grab the edge of the dresser to steady myself. *Had it all just been a terrible nightmare?*

"That's not possible. It's already July 1."

"Okay, now you're really scaring me . . ." Max inches closer, his plaid pajama pants hanging loose around his waist, expos-ing his tight abdomen, and I picture Courtney running her hands over it. Then I imagine cutting her hands off with the ginormous twelve-inch chef's knife we had registered for at my insistence.

I shudder and yank one of his white T-shirts out of the drawer and throw it at him. "Could you *please* put this on? I can't think."

He pulls the cotton V-neck over his head. "There—*now* will you listen to me?" He eyes me cautiously. "Look at your finger. You're still wearing your ring."

That proves nothing. I still wore it after you left me.

I stare at the diamond for a moment. "This doesn't prove anything. You need to do better than that to convince me that we're still engaged," I say, crossing my arms over my chest.

Max grabs his phone off the nightstand, drops it on the floor, and kicks it over to me, probably afraid I'll start foaming at the mouth like a rabid dog. "Check the date. It's *June* 1."

I feel his eyes on me as I inspect his phone. The date does say June 1. I quickly check his texts—there are ones that I'd sent him thirty days ago, the last asking if he'd pick up orange chicken from our favorite Chinese place on his way home. "How did you do this?" I ask.

"Do what?"

"Change the date on your phone. Delete all my other texts from the month of June. Was it Rafael? Did you put him up to this?" I ask, referring to his best man, who is an IT expert. "And if so, why? It makes no sense why you would go to these lengths to get back together with me. You made it clear how you felt."

Max takes a deep breath. "Katie, I swear, I have no idea what you are talking about. Is the stress from the wedding getting to you? Is that what's going on?"

I race down the stairs without answering him.

Where had all the wedding presents gone? The ones that had just been piled in the corner under the blanket Jules had tossed on top of them.

"Max!" I yell. "What did you do with the wedding gifts? They were right here," I say as I stand in the empty space where they'd been. "We need to send them back!"

Max comes to the top of the stairs. "What presents? You were just saying yesterday that you were surprised none had arrived yet."

I press my eyes shut. "Max, I have no idea why you're doing this," I say as he slowly descends the staircase, his hand making a squeaking sound as he slides it down the wrought iron railing. "Listen, the jig is up!" I tug the handle on the refrigerator door, expecting to find only half a bottle of chardonnay and a tub of I Can't Believe It's Not Butter. But the shelves are stocked and right smack in front is the Styrofoam carton from Chin's. The same container full of orange chicken that we'd eaten thirty days ago. *Or last night, depending on whom you asked.*

"What the hell?" I say as I open the lid and smell the chicken, the aroma still fresh.

"My sentiments exactly!" Max walks up and pulls me into his chest, and I drink in his familiar scent.

It must have all been a nightmare. Thank God.

"Seriously, babe. Are you okay? Do you need to go back to sleep?"

"No," I say, and pull Max closer. "I'm perfect." I give him a deep kiss, letting the heartache drift from my body as we touch lips. "I just had a *really bad* nightmare."

"Obviously!" He blinks several times as if trying to reason away my strange behavior. He flashes his uneven grin, reminding me of the selfie I'd deleted off my computer. Or *thought* I'd erased. Or thought I had taken in the first place. *I'm losing it.*

I think back to the look in Max's eyes when he told me he couldn't marry me, the shame I felt as we broke the news, the anguish that stirred inside of me when I came home to an empty condo. The sound of his voice cracking when he told me he'd fallen in love with my friend Courtney. "It really was. You have no idea!"

"I've never seen you like that. You sounded so—" Max rests a bag of Sumatra beans on the counter.

"Crazy?" I offer.

"I was going to say psycho." Max turns and a smile plays on his lips and I feel the knots in my shoulders loosen. "Do you want to talk about it?"

I look at him now, taking in his wavy hair that always sticks up at the cowlick when he wakes up in the morning, the way his right dimple appears just when you've forgotten about it, the slightly chipped tooth from a childhood hockey game that he refused to have fixed because he thought it gave him character, and decide to keep the details of the nightmare to myself. Knowing Max, it would only make him feel bad to hear that he'd been such an asshole, even if he'd only done it in my dreams. That's the kind of guy he was.

"I'm so sorry for jumping all over you like that—you didn't do anything wrong. It felt *so real*—I've never had a nightmare like that before. I just need to shake it off and I'll be fine," I say definitively, even though I'm still able to recall every nuance, every pain, every single last moment. I'm not sure I'll ever forget any of it.

"You sure?"

I nod.

"Okay, why don't you go up and take a shower?" Max suggests. "And I'll make you some of *this*," he says, pointing to the bag of coffee. "Extra, extra bold, just the way you like it."

"Thank you," I say, leaning my head against his shoulder and wrapping my arms tightly around his body, not wanting to let go.

Max hadn't left me. Thank God.

As I head up the stairs, I still feel the bad dream pushing on my chest—a small burn reminding me how devastated I'd felt only minutes before. I scrub my body hard in the shower, trying to wash away the emotional residue the nightmare has left on me, but it refuses to disappear, like one of those hand stamps you get at a theme park. Giving up, I finally push open the glass door, the steam enveloping me as I wrap my robe snugly around my body. I rub the foggy mirror in a circular motion so I can see myself, and as I take in my wet, stringy hair, I wish I had gotten that blowout yesterday. I absolutely despise blow-drying my hair—so much that Jules and I have a pact: if either of us wins the lottery, we will hire the other a full-time stylist.

I slide my laptop out of my computer bag and perch on the edge of the bed, pulling up my Facebook page, the photo I'd posted where I was mischievously sticking my head out from behind the dressing room curtain when I was at the boutique for my final wedding dress fitting filling the screen. I close my eyes for a moment, calmed by the memory of the feel of the organza gown hugging my body as I twirled in front of the three-way mirror, tears springing to my mom's eyes as she'd watched.

This wedding is still happening.

Then Courtney's face appears in my feed, and I click on a picture she'd taken after her appointment at Drybar—the one that I hadn't joined her for. A shiver runs through me as I study her chestnut-colored eyes. I know now that she hadn't really stolen my fiancé, but for some reason I still felt inexplicably angry with her, a raw rage that I'd never experienced before—one so intense it compelled me to want to find her and pluck every last silky hair out of her scalp.

I click back over to my own page, desperate to get away from Courtney's perma-grin, her row of perfectly even beauty pageant teeth making my stomach hurt. For a split second, I consider grabbing my phone and pointing it at the bathroom mirror, capturing my hair as it looks in this moment, soggy and limp, half straight, half wavy, framing my face and making me look like a poodle that's just come in from the rain. Then I'd upload it to Facebook and write:

> The wet dog look is severely underrated.
> #whoneedsblowdryers

But of course I can't do that. The only pictures I post have been taken by someone I've instructed to hold the camera far above my head and angle it just so. By the time I edit and upload the picture, I look like the latest celebrity on the cover of *Vogue*, like a plastic version of myself.

Glaring at my blow-dryer resting on the edge of the black-and-white tile countertop in my bathroom like we're in a standoff, I know I've already lost this battle. The dryer and I both know I need him. I don't care what those magazines say. A little mousse combined with a few zaps of my hair through the diffuser does *not* give me beachy waves. I quickly type my status.

> Thinking of the time we'd all save if we had hair that
> would magically blow-dry itself. Is that possible?
> #wishingformiraclehair

• • •

When I look up again and see my reflection in the mirror, I jump back, my arm inadvertently knocking the blow-dryer off the counter and sending it cascading down to the floor. I blink several times, but when I look at myself again, nothing has changed—the wet, stringy hair I had just moments ago has been transformed into smooth strands I'd never been able to achieve on my own.

Am I still dreaming?

I peer over the top of the stairs to see if Max is still in the kitchen. I spot him just where I'd left him, now pouring coffee into his favorite mug—the one with a picture of a bull and the word España printed on the side in bold block letters that he'd bought before we'd boarded our flight home from Barcelona last year. *We have to get something! Even if it is a cheesy airport souvenir,* he'd joked.

If this is a dream, how do I get the hell out of it?

I punch myself in the leg. Pinch my ear. I even kick that part of the bed that sticks out just far enough for me to stub my toe on it regularly. It hurts like hell, but still, nothing changes.

I try to think, letting out a gasp when I finally put the pieces together.

It was my status update.

Reaching for my laptop again, I check what I'd just written—that I'd wished for miracle hair. The ceiling starts to swirl as I remember the update I posted last night—or at least what I had thought had been last night—the one where I'd wished I could do the past thirty days over again. Had my last two status updates actually *come true*?

"It can't be," I say to myself.

"What can't be?" Max asks as he strides into the bedroom holding out my favorite mug, lime-green with a huge chip on the rim that I refuse to get rid of, even though my lip brushes against the sharp edge each time I take a sip.

"Nothing," I say quickly.

"Wow, your hair looks great—I didn't even hear you turn on the blow-dryer!" Max says.

Because I didn't!

"I got a new one—it's the *as seen on TV* one. You know, *perfect hair while you barely lift a finger,*" I say, deciding I'm being sort of honest as I quickly recall the infomercial I'd seen late one night and the blow-dryer I'd come very close to actually buying.

Max smiles as he grabs a towel from the closet. "I never thought that stuff really worked. Now maybe I'll have to buy that Grill Daddy they've been advertising?"

"Maybe," I murmur. "Hopping in the shower?" I ask hopefully as I quickly grab the evidence proving I wasn't being truthful, the lemon-yellow blow-dryer I've had for years—and slide it under the sink before Max spots it. If this was really happening—if my status updates were actually coming true—I needed to test it again to be sure. *Right now*.

"The last grill-cleaning tool you'll *ever* need," Max says, mimicking the deep tone of the announcer's voice from the commercial as he brushes past me and clicks the bathroom door shut.

My eyes dart around the room the minute the water turns on. What is something simple I could wish for? Something Max wouldn't notice? Oh, God—did I really believe this was happening? Jules and Liam would have a field day with this—I imagined telling them the story over drinks, Jules rolling her eyes and Liam spitting out his whiskey after I uttered the words *time travel*, asking me if Doc was waiting for me outside in his DeLorean. "Only one way to find out if this is real," I whisper as I bring my shaking fingers to my keyboard.

I write an update about wishing I'd bought those gorgeous new wedges last week and count to three before stepping into the large walk-in closet that Max and I share. Sitting next to the ivory satin heels I planned to wear on my wedding day are the strappy gold sandals I had drooled over when I'd spotted them at Nordstrom, finally walking out of the store without so much as trying them on after convincing myself that I'd already spent more money on the wedding than we'd planned.

"Holy shit," I say under my breath. *My Facebook statuses are coming true.*

I have no idea why or how. All I know is they are. And not only am I the proud new owner of a glorious pair of shoes and hair so beautiful that it begs to be taken out to dinner, but I have gone back in time, which means my nightmare isn't just an ugly dream, it is real. And in just one month, Max is going to break my heart all over again at our rehearsal dinner. And then he'll start his new life with Courtney, leaving me to pick up the pieces. I rub the skin between my eyes where a sharp pain is throbbing, not sure I can handle having all of this happen to me again. Or maybe this is an opportunity for me to change the course of my life?

Tears fall as the questions start to fill my mind. Is Max already plotting our relationship's demise? Has he already fallen out of love with me? And the most important of all: Can this be fixed?

Max had sworn he had never cheated on me with Courtney. If that were true, then maybe I could alter our course. Maybe I have been sent back in time because I'm *supposed to* alter our course. For some reason, I've been given the power to make any wish come true. I could make myself ten pounds lighter, become the owner of that pale green Craftsman beach house in Malibu that I've always drooled over, or I could make Courtney as bald as CeeLo Green. The world has just become my oyster. The question is, where do I plan to start?

CHAPTER SIX

....

A true best friend loves you even when it seems like you've
gone off the deep end.

The quote I posted on Facebook this morning is on my mind as I
watch Jules compute what I've just told her. "I'm sorry, but you're
going to have to repeat that," Jules says as she expertly kneads a
mound of pizza dough between her fingers. "*Very* slowly."

As soon as Max left for work, I'd raced to Jules' ranch-style
home tucked into the hills of Studio City so I could tell her everything. And as I watch her make the pepperoni pizza for that
night's dinner, I repeat the story of Max breaking up with me in
Maui, finding out he was in love with Courtney, and traveling
back in time. As the details spill out of me like a dam that has
burst, Jules never blinks as she furiously flattens the dough with
a rolling pin while also fielding questions from Ellie and Evan
as they get ready for school. *Where's my backpack? Do we have a
stapler? Where is my other pink shoe?*

She throws out her answers with precision—*the hall closet.
Yes, but we're out of staples, just use a paper clip. In the garage next
to your rain boots*—while never losing her focus on the dough or

me. Finally, her eyebrows furrow together tightly and she wipes her floury hands on a red-and-white-striped dish towel, and for a moment I think she believes me—that she's going to hug me tightly, maybe call me a little crazy, but say we should jump into her Volvo, find Courtney, and slap her silly. But instead she sighs loudly.

"Are you doing okay?" Her question hangs heavy in the air as she slides onto the bar stool next to me and I feel all the hope I had inside evaporate like pool water that's splashed onto hot pavement.

If my best friend doesn't believe me, how will I get through this?

"You've been really stressed from work lately, and the wedding planning has you frazzled . . . I know I've dropped the ball on a lot of my matron-of-honor duties. Between Evan's soccer schedule, the math tutor we had to hire for Ellie, and my demanding hours at the restaurant since it was written up in *Los Angeles* magazine, I've been overwhelmed. I'm sorry. You've clearly needed me and I haven't been here for you," she confesses.

"Jules," I say, firmly squeezing her hand and taking *the tone*, the one we reserve for each other when we have to be painfully honest—like when she had to tell me that I should not, under any circumstances, *ever* wear anything with an empire waist unless I wanted to appear six months pregnant. "I need you to hear me right now, even though I *know* how this all sounds—but it's real. *Very real.*"

"Okay, you have my attention . . ."

"Mom!" Evan runs through the kitchen. "I can't find any paper clips."

"Did you look in the—" Jules stops herself and holds her index finger up to let me know we'll continue this in a minute.

She smiles, but as she swivels her stool toward her son, I catch her eyes rolling back slightly and I'm not sure if it's in response to Evan's incompetence in locating paper clips or my insistence that I've time traveled.

When I'd arrived at Jules' house earlier, I'd knocked a few times, and when no one answered, I'd let myself in, figuring she was busy with the kids. As I'd rounded the corner to the kitchen, I'd heard Ben's voice first.

"We've been over this. My workload more than doubled when Eric left."

"Can't they replace him?" Jules' voice was small.

"Budget cuts." Ben let out an exasperated sigh, as if he'd said those two words more times than he'd wanted to. "I'm lucky they didn't cut my position too."

"So now you have to take on *his* travel schedule on top of everything else? You are gone all the time as it is. Now you're never going to see the kids . . . or me." Her voice was almost a whisper as she'd said *or me,* and I'd felt my heart lurch. I had no idea she and Ben had been fighting about this. She's never breathed a word of it to me. And in all my wedding planning, I had never thought to ask how she was doing.

"Listen, we've been over this. I have to work. It would be great if we could live on your salary at the restaurant, but the reality is that we can't."

"What's that supposed to mean?" Jules' voice elevated slightly, but vibrated as if she was trying to control it. "Forget it," she snapped.

"I've got to go. Remind the kids of who I am if I'm not home to tuck them in tonight," he joked to break the tension, and even though I couldn't see Jules' face, I was absolutely sure that she didn't think it was funny.

I'd quickly ducked into the bathroom and closed the door, not wanting Ben to see me. Overhearing this conversation made me feel awkward, as if I was viewing hidden-camera footage of them in their bedroom. I'd never heard them argue over anything more serious than who was going to call the sitter to ask if they could stay out longer and have another cocktail. I'd waited a few minutes after the front door slammed, then made my way into the kitchen, where I'd found Jules lost in thought as she kneaded the dough. I'd wanted to hug her tight and tell her that Ben didn't mean to be hurtful, that he was probably just tired, but then I'd have to admit I'd been eavesdropping.

"Auntie Kate, Auntie Kate—do you like my pink shoes?" Ellie's high-pitched voice jars me out of my thoughts as she appears by my side with her American Girl backpack slung over her arm, balancing on one leg while holding her other foot out to me.

"They are gorgeous," I say, reaching down to run my hand over the sparkly texture.

"My friend Megan has the same pair, but they are purple. We are going to be twins today."

"That's sweet," I say just as Jules comes back into the room.

"Ellie, did you brush your teeth? Megan's mom just texted me, she's going to be here in five minutes." Ellie reluctantly heads toward her bathroom.

"So *if* this is true—and I'm not saying I think it is—then that means I have to accept that Max did this to you—and with Courtney? I just can't believe it—" She shakes her head, her eyes rimmed with concern. I can also see the strain in them, the extra concealer she's using to disguise her shadows, and how her dress is hanging on her thin frame.

"Jules—are you doing okay?"

"Am *I* okay? Me? You're the one who's apparently"—she leans across the sink and whispers—"traveled back in time, and you're wondering how *I'm* doing?"

"You just look a little tired. And when did you lose so much weight? Not that I'm not jealous as hell, but you're turning all Twiggy on me."

She grabs a dish towel and flings it at me. "So you're saying I look like shit? Thanks a lot," she scoffs, then presses her lips together into a half smile. "Anyway, I'm fine! Things are just crazy right now. I mean, whose idea was it for Evan to join club soccer anyway? Do nine-year-olds really need to practice three times a week? It's not the World Cup, for God's sake!" She points to the calendar on the refrigerator. "We have six tournaments this summer. Six! When am I going to get anything done? And don't tell anyone, but I actually bought one of those chairs that has an umbrella built in."

"You didn't!" I cry out. "I thought we made an agreement that we'd never become soccer moms."

"Hey, you'd be surprised at the things you start doing when you have kids." She starts to busy herself with the dough again and I decide not to press. I can tell by the way she's slightly arching her back and gripping the rolling pin that now's not the time to push her.

"So this thing with Max. It's the real deal?" she says again.

"Yes . . . and it's going to happen all over again unless you help me. What can I do to get you to trust me on this?" I grip the edge of the countertop.

Jules thinks for a moment. "So you can really wish for *any-thing* you want?"

I nod. "Yes—case in point!" I exclaim, running my hand through my hair.

Jules gathers her own blond strands into a ponytail then lets it fall loose around her shoulders. "I haven't changed my style since before Ellie was born."

"You don't need to—you always look beautiful."

Jules rolls her eyes. "Please. J.Crew called and it wants its cover outfit from the 2005 catalog back." She tugs at her pale yellow dress and blue-and-white-striped cardigan sweater. "I'm in such a rut lately. Like I could use a serious update—starting with this." She frowns as she points at her hair.

"Like cutting bangs?"

"No! Don't you dare wish me those. Bangs are *never* the solution." Jules shakes her head as if a shiver has just run through her. "You should know that better than anyone," she says, reminding me of when I'd lopped off the front of my hair into what a magazine had described as *blunt fringe* when I got my job at the advertising firm, convinced it would make me look *edgy*. It did not.

"Point taken," I laugh. "So what do you want, then? Because I'll wish you a hot boy toy if it means you'll believe me."

She raises her eyebrow, but the doorbell rings before she can answer. Jules calls to Ellie and Evan and ushers them quickly out the door, her body visibly relaxing once it shuts.

"I cannot tell you how glad I am that it was *not* my day to carpool. This is going to be so much more fun!" She rubs her hands together. "Okay, so I'm ready. Do your thing—wish me a makeover!"

Heart pounding, I pull out my phone and quickly type a status on Facebook, silently praying that this will work:

Not that she needed one, but Jules looks amazing after her makeover. She's a hottie!

She grabs my arm and pulls me into the bathroom, giggling like a tween at her first concert, and I can't help but join in as we lock the door.

"So what's this going to feel like?" Jules says tentatively. "Will I go through some kind of transformation à la *Teen Wolf*? And what will people think when they see your status? There are going to be questions."

"Hopefully no one will be growing facial hair and fangs in this scenario!" I laugh. "And so far, all the posts I've written have disappeared as soon as the wish has been granted," I say, thinking about how I had searched my timeline frantically after I'd written the status asking for the strappy sandals, but it was nowhere to be found. "Let's just close our eyes and count to three and then turn and look in the mirror."

"One, two, three," we say in unison, then cautiously we swivel around and face our reflections.

"Oh. My. God." Jules screams, clasping her hand over her mouth. "I'm fucking hot! Ben is going to shit his pants when he sees me." She turns around, scrutinizing herself from every angle.

Jules has never lacked in the looks department, with straight blond shoulder-length hair and round green doll-like eyes that are only accentuated by mascara on special occasions. But now her hair is shaped into a layered bob with sharp edges and golden highlights, and her skin is dewy and glowing. She lifts up her shirt and lets out a yelp. "Look at my stomach. I have abs again! Feel them." She puts my hand on her abdomen and laughs.

I shake my head. "I draw the line at feeling you up—but *now* do you believe me?"

"Hell, yeah!" She laughs. "Can you give me some liposuction on my ass too?"

I smile, slapping her butt. "You do not need that! If anything, the makeover gods should've given you a little more junk in your trunk!" I study her body, still as thin as it was before I wished her a makeover, but I had to admit the wish had created an air of sophistication that looked good on her. We lock eyes in the mirror. "How are you going to explain this to Ben?"

She waves me off. "It won't be a problem." Jules turns away from her reflection to face me in the half bathroom and hits the towel bar as she awkwardly brings me in for a hug. "I'm sorry I doubted you, Kate. But I'm with you now—one hundred percent."

"Thank God. Because I'm kind of freaking out. And I need you."

"Okay, so you have this amazing power. But how should you use it?"

"I obviously have to figure out how to stop history from repeating itself," I say, sitting on the toilet, the image of Max's resilient face as he broke the news to me at the rehearsal dinner still burned in my mind. "But first, I need you to be brutally honest with me about something."

"Like when you told me the belly band wasn't working after I had Ellie?"

I nod. "Although I still feel bad about that. You were so hormonal that I hated that you made me go there. You were only a few months postpartum."

She laughs. "It's fine. I already knew the truth. I just needed to hear it. So what do you need to know?"

"You really think Max and I are good together? That this relationship is worth fighting for?"

"Of course!" Jules says without hesitation.

"Even knowing what you do now—about his feelings for Courtney?" I say. "After it happened, Liam confessed that Max and I had seemed really predictable." I scrunch up my nose as if the word has its own stench. "Do you think Max was bored?"

"No!" Jules' hands fly up in front of her face. "I honestly think he just freaked out about the whole 'rest of your life' thing!"

"Really?" I push, her opinion holding so much more weight than she knows. If she thinks my relationship with Max is worth saving, then maybe it is. I hadn't realized the power of that question until I'd heard it squeak from my mouth.

"Absolutely—I *know* he loves you," she says, and the burden I've been carrying, the part of me that wondered if I had misread my entire life, instantly lifts off my shoulders. "And now you can stop him from leaving again. Do you have any idea how many women would kill for an opportunity like this—to keep their husbands from going down the wrong path? To be able to reconnect before it's too late?" She looks down, studying her hands, picking at the flour that's still wedged under her fingernails.

"What about you? Would you fight for Ben? Even if you knew his heart was somewhere else?"

Jules folds and refolds a hand towel next to the sink before responding. "I would—we have a lot of history, and that means something. Plus, it would be a second chance. And this is yours, Kate," she says, perching on the edge of the countertop. "Sometimes even the best couples lose their way, but that doesn't mean they shouldn't be together." She breaks eye contact with me before looking up again, and I wonder if she's thinking of the fight she'd had with Ben earlier. "Listen, I know you. You're a problem solver. So I want you to understand this is not about anything being wrong with *you*." She shakes her head. "Max stumbled for whatever reason, which happens sometimes, even in the most solid relationships, and she was there at the right time. But that doesn't make her the right girl."

I nod, but say nothing—it feels good to hear Jules defend me, to defend what Max and I have together.

I feel my pocket vibrate and frown when I read a message from Courtney.

We still on for drinks tonight at STK?

The baby hairs on my arm stand on end as I consider the timing of her text, and for a split second I forget I'm reliving this day—that she is simply reaching out because she's confirming our happy-hour date for tonight. That the last thirty days as I know them never happened.

"What is it?" Jules looks over my shoulder to read the screen. "Why the hell would *she* think you'd have a drink with her? After what she did to you?"

"She doesn't know I know, remember? It hasn't happened yet. According to her, we are still girlfriends and coworkers—"

"—and apparently women vying for the same man!" Jules interjects.

"Yes, that too—thanks for the reminder." I smile to let her know I'm being sarcastic. "And we're supposed to go to happy hour with Max *tonight*."

"Can you do that? Can you pretend *not to know* what they did or *are going* to do to you? You were so cool about it when they became good friends . . ."

"What?" I press, the rest of her sentence hanging in the air like a kite on a breezy day.

Jules shrugs.

"Just say it. I was too trusting, wasn't I?"

"No! I was just thinking that it's enviable you were able to be like that. Most women would be jealous." She stops mid-sentence, thinking for a moment. "You know, even Ben got a little weird about Liam in the beginning. I'm not sure if I ever told you that. I laughed so hard when he brought it up because it was Liam. *Liam!* I could never imagine . . ." Jules doesn't finish her thought, but she doesn't need to. The way she rapidly shakes her head at the thought of being intimate with him speaks volumes.

Max and I had discussed his friendship with Courtney *once*, when he'd come stumbling in the door from one of the concerts they had attended a few months after meeting, beer and cigarettes thick on his breath. They were both huge fans of nineties bands, and with my blessing would occasionally see whatever group was passing through town. Before, I had been the one who went to see Toad the Wet Sprocket or Good Charlotte with Max. But to be honest, I had been relieved to be off the hook, much preferring to stay home and curl up with the latest issue of *Entertainment Weekly* than bobbing my head with feigned enthusiasm as I listened to songs I didn't particularly love when they were originally on the radio.

"You smoked?" I said to Max, recoiling slightly at the sound of my own voice, a voice I'd only heard inside my head, the voice that had started once the clock ticked past 1 a.m. My mind had involuntarily drifted to an image of the two of them dancing, their plastic cups of booze held high in the air above their heads, having so much fun together that time had slipped away. I'd made a vow that I wouldn't confront him when he got home. I was simply feeling anxious because I couldn't sleep, and in the morning I'd feel better. But when Max had gotten into bed well after 2 a.m., the smell of smoke triggered the insecurity I'd been trying to bury. When she was just my friend, Courtney's model-like face and body never threatened me, but that night, it was the first time I had wondered if he'd also noticed her exquisite beauty.

"Courtney bummed one from some guy and I took a drag, but it was awful." He mock coughed and suddenly I'd imagined him with his arm around her waist, leaning in and gently removing the cigarette that was dangling from between her lips.

"Should I be jealous here?"

"Don't be ridiculous!" Max laughed, grabbing my face between his hands and planting a drunken kiss on my lips.

"Just tell me I have nothing to worry about," I said as I pulled back from his grasp and searched his glazed eyes for the truth.

"You have nothing to worry about," he repeated, kissing each of my fingers softly, then, after a few moments of silence, adding, "Let me put it this way—you would never think of Liam like that, right?"

When he said those words, it was like everything clicked—I wasn't being fair. Of course he could have a friendship with a woman if I could have one with a man. And if he felt the way about her that I did about Liam, I really had nothing to worry about. He'd rolled to my side of the bed and curled his arms around me, and I'd put the whole incident aside, burying the uncertainty so far down that I could almost pretend it was never there.

• • •

Jules rubs her temples. "This whole situation is like some kind of crazy brainteaser. It hurts my head."

And it hurts my heart.

"I don't know if I can go to the happy hour tonight," I answer honestly, feeling like the one time I agreed to run a 5K with Max, the finish line seeming so far away.

"If anyone can do it, it's you," Jules says, and I raise my eyebrow at her.

"Really?"

"How do you not see how strong and smart you are? You drive me nuts, girl!"

"Well, it's especially hard to see my strengths when my fiancé has just told me he's upgrading to someone else."

"Did he say that?"

"No . . . not exactly, but why else would he be leaving me for her?"

"It might not have anything to do with you—like I said, he was probably just scared to commit and looking for an easy way out."

"If I didn't know better, I'd think you were secretly watching *Oprah* again."

"Hey, that was a short-lived phase after Evan was born—but I did learn a lot." Jules smiles.

"Okay, Ms. Armchair Psychologist, how do you suggest I handle not only going to drinks with my fiancé and his secret love interest, but also my working relationship with her?" I know I will have to fake it everywhere—especially at the office. Simply asking to be reassigned to different accounts so I don't have to brush shoulders with Courtney every day will never work. I can picture the disapproving frown forming on my boss Magda's thin lips when she realizes my agenda—I'm trying to distance myself from Courtney. She will demand an explanation, one I won't be able to provide. Disappointing my boss couldn't also be part of this arrangement.

"Don't ask me. I watched O, not Maury Povich!"

I jokingly push Jules in the shoulder. "Seriously! I need your advice here—you know I've never been good at masking my real feelings."

"Okay, okay. Sorry! Start by remembering something. This

isn't just about her. To really fix this, you need to figure out what went wrong with you and Max." When she sees my face fall, she softens. "Don't worry, I have no doubt you will—you and Max are great together."

"You mean *were* great together."

"No—I mean *are,* as in present tense. You said it yourself—they don't know you know. So use this do-over you've been granted as an opportunity not only to get Max back, but to distract Courtney." She winks. "And you know what I'm thinking?"

I can almost see the wheels turning in Jules' mind.

I shrug.

"Instead of doing a makeover on her, let's do a make*under*. Do something awful to that gorgeous hair of hers!"

I try to imagine Courtney's blond locks transformed to a deep shade of blue, but it still doesn't make the uneasiness inside of me disappear.

"Why are you frowning?" Jules asks.

"I know I'm lucky to have this second chance, but it feels weird—like I'm cheating."

"You are *not* the one who cheated here." Jules narrows her eyes. "And as far as I'm concerned, you deserve every crutch, cheat sheet, and crystal ball you can get."

"Okay, so what are the Cliffs Notes on how I can stay professional at work when all I'm going to want to do is kick her ass?"

Jules smiles. "That would be something to see, but you know it won't help you get Max back. Just stay focused on your goal—that means business as usual with her. Plus, you can use time to your advantage. What are you always saying? How you and Courtney are always in competition to be on Magda's good side? That a compliment from her is as rare as—"

"—a California condor sighting," I offer.

"Right—remember that you don't only know about Max and Courtney, you also know what's already happened at work. So use that information to your advantage with Magda. Save a deal that's going bad or fix a mistake before it happens. Overnight, you'll be the star."

"Again, cheating—"

"So what! This is your life! Remember that."

CHAPTER SEVEN

....

If only Jules had been right. It turns out living a day for the second time isn't necessarily an advantage, especially when you have to pretend you don't know your close friend and trusted colleague is planning to steal your fiancé. When I first arrived at work, I nearly collided with Courtney as I'd tried to duck into the bathroom. I studied her face for a moment, searching for signs that she was in love with my future husband, but there was nothing that gave her away. She'd offered me a warm smile and asked if she could grab me a coffee. I'd stammered something about already being overcaffeinated and proceeded to hide in the bathroom stall, trying to catch my breath until Magda's assistant came looking for me, relaying a message that I was already five minutes late for a meeting about the Calvin Klein campaign we had landed the month before.

And the day didn't get any easier from there. By the end of it, my tongue was sore from biting away the details I already knew but couldn't share: that the start-up wedding website was going to fire us after lunch and there was nothing we could do to change their minds; that Magda's latest boyfriend was going to break up with her right before a hugely important conference call; and that we were going to discover a major accounting error that was going to cost the firm thousands of dollars.

Then there was the idea I'd pitched to Magda for the spa we were trying to acquire as a client—a concept I *knew* would secure us the business, even though Magda's perfectly arched eyebrow and patronizing stare more than suggested she felt otherwise. She'd given me the same disapproving look she'd given me thirty days ago, the one that launched us into the same argument today, me defending my *Come find your happy ending* billboard idea and Magda scoffing at it, her ill-fitting jacket accentuating her emaciated body—something she took a great deal of pride in, grinning wildly when a homeless man had called out to her to *eat a cheeseburger already* as we'd strolled by. But what I'd forgotten was that thirty days ago, when I'd pitched this campaign the first time, it had been *Courtney* who'd swooped in, taken my side, and won Magda's praise for being more convincing about my own idea than I'd been.

As Courtney defended my intuitiveness and raved about how I always knew what the clients wanted, I'd wondered how I could be so in tune with the people I did business with yet so clueless about those closest to me—*like her*. When Courtney had backed me up last month, I'd shot her a smile and stage whispered that I'd buy all her drinks later that night when we went out with Max. But this time, I could barely force a smile, reluctantly swallowing the rage I felt toward her.

As we'd walked out of the glass-walled conference room, Courtney had laced her arm through mine and I'd stiffened in-voluntarily. As she pulled me down the hall toward our offices, my mind kept wandering to what Courtney would look like if her eyebrows were "suddenly" shaved off.

I dialed Jules' number as soon as I got inside my office. "I need a lifeline," I whined as soon as Jules said hello.

"I always wanted to be your *phone-a-friend*!" Jules exclaimed, both of us remembering how we used to fantasize about being contestants on *Who Wants to Be a Millionaire*. "You would've called me, not Liam, right?"

"Of course!" I laughed.

"So what's going on? Because I know you're not sitting there with Regis Philbin."

"It's just that being at work with her is even harder than I thought it would be," I'd lamented. "Especially when she's *nice* to me."

"Well, of course she's laying it on thick. She feels guilty about harboring feelings for *your man*."

"That's why she was kissing my ass so hard in the weeks leading up to the wedding," I'd said after giving it more thought. "She was constantly swinging by my office with an extra Starbucks coffee or bringing me the latest *People*, even offering to stay late so I could go home and work on my wedding to-do list. To think I believed she wanted to help me because she was my friend, when she only wanted to relieve her conscience." I rested my forehead in my hand. "This all feels hopeless."

"You need to pull it together," Jules said sternly. "Where's the girl who graduated at the top of her class from Occidental? Where's my best friend who held my hand during seventeen hours of labor? And most importantly, where's the woman who *originally* captured Max's heart? *She* would be able to do this!"

"I just wish I knew what went wrong between us, then at least I'd have a place to start."

Jules sighed into the phone. "Do you have any ideas?"

We'd experienced a few tense moments in our premarital

counseling. I remember bickering about which parent's house we should spend our Christmases at or if we should have a joint checking account, but we'd eventually compromised on both. I couldn't think of an issue between us that we hadn't been able to work through in the past three years, something I'd always considered one of our greatest strengths. But how would we work through this?

"Remember that 'what-if' game we played at your house that time?" I asked Jules.

"How could I forget? A few relationships almost ended that night!" Jules started to release a laugh then stopped herself.

"Do you recall the card Max pulled—the one about cheating?"

"Oh yes—"

"He said he was *so sure* he'd want to work things out if his spouse was unfaithful—"

Max had drawn the card with the question: *What would you do if your spouse cheated on you?* He'd thought about it for not even a split second before swiftly responding, "We'd work through it." The room had erupted, everyone's opinion flying through the air. I'd righteously thought, *But neither of us would ever do that.* And even though Max had sworn up and down that he didn't actually cheat with Courtney, he had still betrayed me emotionally, even if their lips had never met. And instead of attempting to work out whatever problems we'd had, he'd simply chosen her.

"I don't think anyone knows how they'll really behave in situations they've never been in before. I think people would like to believe they'd act a certain way, but you just never know . . ." Jules' words became softer, eventually disappearing.

"Obviously," I scoffed. "But he didn't even give us a chance to work on our relationship."

"But remember, you have a rare opportunity here—to pin-point where things went wrong," Jules argued. "So you can try to fix it before it gets too far."

"True. But I would never have expected this to happen *now*. You always think there's a chance down the road, maybe ten years in, but not *before* you even say *I do*."

I'd felt an instant spark when I met Max at our mutual friends' wedding—after Jules had spotted him, I'd let my gaze follow hers and they'd landed on a man with olive-green eyes, dark brown hair that was slightly long on the top, and a strong jaw lined with stubble. He'd grinned as he recognized Jules, and as his mouth opened, he'd revealed the dimple that to this day remains hidden unless he smiles just a certain way—a feature he only brings out when he wants to charm executives, my mother, and probably Courtney too.

After she introduced us, we'd sat outside on the patio and talked for hours—Max throwing his jacket around my bare shoulders the moment I shuddered from the cool breeze that had begun to blow. After our first date, he'd insisted on walking me to my front door, where he'd given me a warm hug and gently brushed my cheek with his lips. Before I'd closed the door, he'd thanked me for a night of stimulating conversation. Max's atten-tion had felt so pure, so transparent; he had genuinely seemed interested in what made me *me*. In the past, I'd always felt as if I had to find a new way to sparkle to keep my date interested, but with Max, I could finally let go of the breath I always seemed to be holding. On our fourth date, I'd pushed aside the Chinese food that had just been delivered and pulled him close, whisper-ing I had something else in mind. He hadn't argued.

Somehow we'd found our way from there to here. What hap-pened to the people who would watch an episode of *Top Chef* and then try, usually unsuccessfully, to re-create a dish that didn't look *that hard* to make, musing that Padma would criticize us for our lack of salt? Where was the couple that dressed head to toe in Lakers garb and cheered on Kobe in our living room, often laughing that we should probably just buy a ticket to the actual game already? And what had become of the Max and Kate who I had thought were such a perfect fit that I'd had a silly puzzle made from a picture of us and given it to him last Christmas?

I wondered if Max had started to pull away during the wedding planning. I was more opinionated than Max was in general—especially when it came to the details of our nuptials—but that didn't mean I wasn't willing to take his feelings into consideration. In the days after he proposed, I had asked him a million questions as I scoured TheKnot.com with a fierceness that rivaled my approach to preparing for final exams in college, searching for the style of wedding we might want—backyard country or hotel chic? I'd wanted to know: Did he prefer I walk down the aisle to a popular song or to a harp? Did he think we should have a band or a DJ at the reception? Ahi or salmon for dinner? But had I only asked him to weigh in because I knew he'd wave me off, that he'd tell me that he trusted me to make the decisions? I knew my behavior was often commanding, and I'd always thought that was something he found endearing, but now my newfound gift of hindsight left me questioning if I had ever known anything at all.

"I think I might know where we went wrong," I said to Jules as I rocketed up out of my desk chair.

"What? Where?" She'd asked.

"I need to give him control—let him plan the wedding however he wants. Make him feel more involved!"

"But it's only a month away."

"I don't care. Whatever he wants, he can have it. I'll change anything."

"Even yourself?" Jules said carefully.

"Yes, if that's what it's going to take. Just trust me, Jules. I got this," I said as I'd hung up the phone and grabbed my purse, deciding if I was going to suffer through drinks with Max and his girlfriend tonight, I'd better look damn good doing it.

CHAPTER EIGHT

....

"You ready yet?" Max calls up to me.

Will I ever be ready for this?

I wonder again how I will be able to stomach sitting at the same table with Max and Courtney tonight. It had been hard enough hearing that Max thought he was in love with her, but now I'll be watching their clandestine relationship unfold right in front of me. I'll have to sit in silence as they tease each other, something I used to view as harmless, but now every smile shared between them, every *accidental* brush of their hands, every look—will feel like a spike into my heart. And even though they may not be in love *yet*, I know it's coming, and the process of waiting will feel like a Band-Aid being slowly peeled off my tender skin. *Unless I can stop it.*

"Just a sec," I yell to Max as I post my status on Facebook, deciding that what I've wished for isn't *that bad*. My broken heart might never be mended, but Courtney's hair *will* grow back. *Right?* I can hear Jules cheering me on, reminding me that the future of my relationship is at stake. *Plus, it doesn't hurt that Max is a sucker for long hair, does it?* she'd said when she'd heard my plan.

Twenty minutes later, my head is pounding, practically drowning out the music booming through the speakers as I scan the crowded lounge for Courtney, waiting to see the results of the status I'd written:

I'm shocked that Courtney chopped off all her hair.

"Is that her over there?" Max asks, and I swivel my head in the direction he's pointing in.

"Wow," I say under my breath as I spot her—her sandy-colored hair has been hacked off into a pixie cut. I feel queasy as I look over at Max, who's staring at her with his mouth slightly open. She looks even better than she did before. *How the fuck is that even possible?*

As we approach her table, Courtney's hand flies up to her head. "Oh my God, it's *so short*, isn't it? I literally just left the salon," she says, biting her lower lip as if waiting for our approval. "I went in for a trim right after work and came out looking like this." She throws her arms up. "At first I was furious with my hairdresser, who claimed the scissors *just seemed to take on a life of their own*," she says, rolling her eyes. "Seriously, it was almost as if I blinked and it came out like this. . . . But now I kind of love it!" She squeals and claps her hands together like a seal.

"It looks good," I say reluctantly. *Really damn good.* I sink into the chair across from her, deducing that I must be suffering some sort of karmic payback for wishing something bad to happen to another person. But maybe her hair looking good is just a fluke. She already has a pretty—make that beautiful—face, so I probably could've wished her bald and she still would've ended up looking amazing. I'd have to write a more impactful status next time—less about her looks and more about *her. But what?*

It was one thing to hold this power in my hands. It was a whole other thing to use it properly.

"You totally pull it off," Max says, jarring me from my thoughts as he takes Courtney in his arm easily, placing a small kiss on her left cheek, no different than he's done in front of me a dozen times before, but this time, watching it sends a ripple of panic through me as I wonder if his kiss has ever spread to her supple lips, her red lipstick leaving its mark on his mouth.

"You think?" she says shyly before turning my way. "But look at *you*," Courtney purrs as she eyes me. "That is one hot dress, mama, is it new? Did you sneak out of work and hit Nordstrom without me? Meow." She holds her hands up as if they're claws.

"Thanks," I say, deliberately not answering her question. The truth was, this outfit was courtesy of a status I'd posted earlier. I'd wished for a dress that would *make me look two sizes smaller and six inches taller and accentuate every curve—without the use of Spanx*. I'd mused at the time that due to my newfound magical powers, I'd never again have to go through a dozen outfit changes to escape the frumpiness I was feeling. But I still felt inadequate now and also hadn't succeeded in getting Max's attention earlier. He'd barely looked away from *SportsCenter* as I'd descended the stairs. And now he only glances over at me briefly before burying his nose in the menu, asking if we want to order the spinach dip.

As I watch Max flag down the waitress, I decide that even though my wish for Courtney backfired, I am still the one with an engagement ring on my finger. I need to remind Courtney of something I had with Max that she couldn't compete with— *history*. *We* took the trip to Barcelona last year and sat in a café on that quaint cobblestone street and talked about how many kids we'd like to have. *We* had registered for the chef's knives and the Dutch oven and the waffle maker because *we* like to cook together. And *we* had fallen in love that night in Big Bear as we'd sat in the ski lodge and sipped hot toddies while sharing stories about our childhoods—me confiding how I'd let my mom's insecurities become my own; Max revealing that he was adopted, and even though his parents had been everything he could ever ask for, he still often wondered why he hadn't been good enough for the woman who gave birth to him.

I turn to Max. "You know what I was just thinking about?"

"What's that?" he says.

"That time we went to Big Bear—we should go again."

"What made you think of that?" he asks, and a flicker of concern flashes in his eyes so quickly I tell myself I must have imagined it.

I press on anyway. "Well, with the wedding only a month away, I've been working on my vows and was remembering where we first said I love you." I smile. "Sorry to get all sappy in front of you, Courtney!" I say, resting my hand possessively on top of Max's arm.

Courtney hides the beginning of a frown by taking a huge gulp of her mojito.

Okay, so clearly she already feels something. But what was Max feeling?

"So what do you think?" I ask Max. "I'll book us the cabin we stayed at—remember, it had the most gorgeous view of Big Bear Lake and we had those delicious crab cakes at that restaurant in town?"

"Sure," Max says noncommittally and takes a long drink of his scotch. I bite my tongue so I don't make the sarcastic remark sitting on the edge of my lips: *You seem about as excited as a guy going in for a vasectomy.* But realizing it's going to take more than one day to snap him back to *our* reality, I decide to change tactics—and focus on Courtney instead.

"So, Courtney, tell us what's going on with that guy James you've been dating," I say after our waitress sets down our appetizers. "You were all giddy about him—I think you even called him dreamy? Didn't you go out on your third date last week?" I ask, refusing to look at Max, afraid I might see jealousy reflected in his eyes. But hoping this will remind him that Courtney isn't sitting at home quilting every Friday night. That she is actively dating *other men*.

"That guy?" She laughs as she plays with the mint leaf at the bottom of her now-empty glass. "I was *so* wrong about him—found out he was seeing, like, three other girls after telling me he wanted to be exclusive."

"That must have really hurt. To have someone betray you like that," I say, wondering if she hears the irony in my words.

"Not really—I hadn't known him very long. He did me a favor actually—I'm done going out with guys I meet at the gym or at a bar or"—she wrinkles her nose—"on Match.com. They're all the same. I've decided that I'm just going to focus on work. Don't they say the right guy comes along when you least expect it?" She giggles.

I swallow the words at the base of my throat—the ones I wish I could scream at her—at *them*.

Max is not the right guy for you. He's the right guy for me.

But before I can so much as shake my head, she leans in and asks Max about an acquisition his device company has been feverishly working on. I suddenly feel like a third wheel as I listen to him tell her about the stent they are attempting to license from a small German company. Courtney nods her head vigorously as Max explains that this small mesh device, used to treat narrowed arteries, has the potential to revolutionize angio-plasties and shows great promise in its phase 3 trials.

"This could be huge for us," he says, before taking another drink. "Send the stock prices through the roof!"

Last time we'd all met for happy hour, I vaguely remember the details, having tuned out around the time he walked us through the step-by-step process of how arterial plaque forms in the artery, instead turning my attention to my Instagram account. But this time I forced my eyes open with interest, ignoring the buzzing of my cell phone, trying to keep pace with Courtney, who to my dismay looked genuinely interested.

It wasn't that I didn't find Max's work compelling, I did. His analytical mind is one of the things that had drawn me to him from the beginning. But there was only so much clinical infor-mation I could handle, Max often joking that he knew I was far more interested in discussing whether the basketball players should've U-turned the divorcées on *The Amazing Race*. Had I made him feel like his work wasn't important? That his stories were no longer interesting? Was that where I'd gone wrong?

The rest of the night feels like a boxing match, Courtney and me in the ring, each trying to win a round of "who can hold Max's attention longer?" And if there had been a referee, I think he would've called it for Courtney. By the time we get the check two hours later, I'm so exhausted that it feels like I've run up and down all 170 steps of the Santa Monica Stairs a dozen times. I fall into bed the second we get home, the three mojitos I con-sumed sending me into a quick, but restless sleep.

I wake up a few hours later, one question still nagging at me. *Were they already in love?* I couldn't tell if I was imagining things at dinner based on what I knew, or if the subtle nuances I'd noticed were real. I eye Max's cell phone resting on the edge of the dresser next to his wallet and car keys. I could check it—just to find out if they'd been texting or emailing about more than Hootie and the Blowfish's latest album.

Sliding out of bed, I tiptoe over and grab the phone, freezing when Max turns over on his side. Finally, when I'm sure he's still asleep, I shut the bathroom door silently behind me, shaking.

I warily slide his phone across the countertop. Before this all happened, I'd never so much as glanced at one line of an email that he'd left open on his computer, and now I was about to look through his phone. This wasn't me. But considering what I now knew, talking myself out of it was harder than convincing myself not to rip the plastic off that second row of Thin Mints. Just as I'm about to give in to temptation, a woman Liam dated briefly last year comes to mind—one with serious jealously issues who constantly accused him of seeing other women behind her back. (He had been, but in his defense, he'd never told her they were exclusive.) Whenever he talked about her, he'd make the sounds from the shower scene in *Psycho*. When I'd prodded him about why he stayed with her, he'd claimed the sex was great, but that he was also glad he didn't own any bunnies for her to boil.

The relationship had come to a crashing halt when she'd gotten ahold of his phone. Although he'd been diligent about deleting everything, even texts between Jules and me, she'd used the search feature to access texts from the trash. Liam had told us the story over drinks one night, describing how she accused him of having threesomes with us—something we had all found both horribly disgusting and incredibly hilarious.

I sigh and lean back against the bathroom door. I should just put the phone back where I found it and figure this thing out the old-school way—by using my instincts instead of going all

Fatal Attraction on him. But I only knew how this story ended—I didn't know which chapter we were on. Before I can change my mind, I pull down the search box and type in Courtney's name. The only text exchange I find is from after we'd left the restaurant.

Courtney
You okay? You seemed a little off tonight.

Max
I'm fine.

Courtney
Okay. Know that I'm always here for you.

Max
Thanks. I just have a lot on my mind. I'll be okay.

Courtney
Kate's a very lucky woman—I hope she appreciates you.

I check for a response from Max, but there isn't one. Rage rises to my throat as I try to push the image of Glenn Close holding a butcher knife from my mind. I rack my brains, trying to remember if I'd ever given Courtney the impression that I'd been taking Max for granted. Had I somehow made it seem to her like he wasn't my number-one priority? But more importantly, had I made *him* feel that way?

"I have to do something about this," I whisper to myself as I open the door and place Max's phone back on the dresser and grab mine. "Right now."

I climb back into bed, the sound of Max's breathing comforting, reminding me that what I'm about to do is for *us*. Courtney needs a distraction. And I have the power to give her one.

I gulp my tears away as I pull up Facebook. I had always believed Courtney was a true friend—someone I could trust with *anything*. But now I knew she should never have been given that kind of access to my private thoughts. To my life. To my fiancé. And I couldn't allow her to take another step toward the line I knew she'd eventually cross with Max.

I think back to tonight—how she'd talked over me as I'd tried to share something funny our wedding planner had said, how she'd stolen glances at Max when she thought I wasn't looking. And then I remember a remark she made to me after Max sent me chocolate-covered strawberries to the office a couple of months ago with a note that said, *just because*.

"How did you find such a great guy?" She'd sighed as she slid the card back into the envelope. "I hope you know how lucky you are!"

How long had she plotted to take Max from me?

Finally, I type the words and let the tip of my index finger linger over the post button before closing my eyes and pressing it down hard, feeling a sliver of relief that Courtney will never read it because the status will disappear like all the others, but my heart still pumping in overdrive because I've just wished for the one thing that Courtney *and I* fear most.

It's so sad that Courtney can't get off Magda's shit list no matter how hard she tries.

CHAPTER NINE

....

I feel the jersey fabric of the sheets, still warm after Max has left for his run the next morning, and silently pray that ours will be the only bed he will sleep in again. At least a hundred times, I've considered wishing for Max to be hopelessly in love with me—to have not one single doubt about spending the rest of our lives together—but I don't want to use my power to *make* him feel that way. I want his heart to lead him there on its own. Because if it's not his decision, then I'll always be left wondering—had he been given the choice, would it have been me?

My head throbbing from the mojitos last night and the text exchange I'd discovered between him and Courtney, I grab my laptop and head to the kitchen to take care of a few chores that have fallen by the wayside since I traveled back in time. With a few clicks of my mouse, I wish for the laundry that is piled high next to the washing machine to be washed, dried, folded, *and put away*; for our dry cleaning, which had been sitting across town for a week, to be picked up; and for my upper lip to be waxed—*without pain* and without leaving the embarrassing red mark that taints my fair skin for hours afterward and screams to the world, *yes, I just got hair removed from my upper lip, how are you?*

But as I pull the plastic off Max's freshly pressed shirts and slacks that are now hanging on the back of the chair next to me, I wonder—no, *I know*—that I'm being too frivolous with my wishes, that I should probably be helping others, not just myself and Jules. I could hear my mom scolding me now. *Why didn't you wish for a cure for a disease or to end hunger in third-world countries?* And she'd be right. Why hadn't I?

I think back to last Christmas, when I'd found so much joy from adopting a family in need, spending hours carefully choosing their gifts and wrapping them beautifully with the biggest bows I could find. Or when I'd given up a chance to attend the live *Survivor* finale to stay home and care for Max when he threw his back out playing flag football. Sure, I'd been known to forget to replace the toilet paper roll on more than one occasion, but I was definitely someone who always wanted to do right by other people.

Like right now. Excitedly I type, *I can't believe they've found a cure for cancer,* and hit post. I click over to CNN.com, expecting the website to be flooded with the news. *Nothing.* So I try again. This time I ask to end hunger in the world. But still, *nothing.* I quickly delete them both off my page before anyone can start peppering me with questions about why I'd write such a thing. It didn't make any sense. I could give Jules a flatter stomach and eff with Courtney's hair, but I couldn't help starving children in Africa? Why do certain wishes come true and not others?

The sound of the front door opening startles me. I hear Max walk in and quickly slip the dry cleaning into the front closet, not prepared to lie about how it had ended up in our house. It was the same reason I wasn't wishing to win the lottery or for a new car. After Max questioned me about my instantaneous blowout,

I realized how hard it would be to explain even the smallest of things, especially when I had always been a terrible liar.

"How you doing?" Max says, kissing my cheek and grabbing a carton of orange juice out of the refrigerator. He pours himself a glass, then leans back to drink it, his quads showing the results of running over ten marathons. It was Max who'd introduced me to running, although I'd never felt as passionate about it as he did, only running occasionally, barely completing one 5K last year. Maybe I should start being more consistent? See if he wants to help me train?

"I'm okay, how are you? How was your run?"

"Really good," he says, rinsing his glass out in the sink and putting it directly into the dishwasher.

As I watch Max put detergent in the tray and push start on the machine, Courtney's text to him crosses my mind for the thousandth time.

I hope she appreciates you.

I need to show him that I do. I need to prove that I value his opinion and care about the things that matter to him. Maybe that's what's making him feel connected to Courtney. I think back to the analytical questions she'd asked Max when he was talking about his job—the thoughtful follow-up questions that would never have crossed my mind. Magda has always said Courtney and I worked well as a team because Courtney was OCD and I was ADD. And interestingly, I have always had a similar dynamic with Max—our differences seemed to smooth out each other's edges. But now I wonder if he has been craving someone more like-minded.

"Hey, so I was thinking about the wedding—"

"Oh?" Max smirks. "I know that look," he says, stepping closer to me. "What is it? You want to switch out the color of the flowers again?"

"No! God, you make me sound so frivolous," I say, hoping he'll correct me. But instead he pulls a container of cottage cheese out of the refrigerator and starts to spoon it into a bowl.

I shake off his silent agreement and continue. "Anyway, I wasn't thinking about the gerbera daisies, silly. I was thinking about you. I feel like I've been planning this without you and it's something we should be doing together. I want it to feel like *our* day, not just mine."

Max offers me a small smile. "It *is* our day. And it's fine that you've taken the reins. You know what you want and I want you to have that—I want you to be happy."

"Great. Then you want to know what will make me happy?" I press on before he answers. "Let's call Stella and toss out everything and start over. Let's plan this party together."

"You feeling okay? First you had that crazy dream and now you want to scrap the ideas you've been planning for a year and start over? With only"—Max looks at his phone—"twenty-seven days to go? Is that even possible?"

Yes, anything's possible when the rest of your life depends on it.

"Don't worry about that. Just tell me, what would *you* do if it were up to you?" I walk over and kiss his neck. "Because your wish is my command," I say with a smile, Max having no idea how true that statement really is.

"You really want to know?" he says, frowning slightly and studying my face.

"Yes," I say, excitement brewing inside of me as I watch his eyes start to animate.

"Okay. Here it is. I don't want to wear a suit. And I don't want the groomsmen to either. It's too stiff for Maui. Let's be casual. Maybe even wear flip-flops."

Oh, gawd.

"Okay," I say, forcing my head to bob up and down.

"And forget the hoity-toity rehearsal dinner on the roof—let's have a pig roast with a couple of guys juggling torches. That will be much better on my parents' budget too."

I'm beginning to remember why I didn't push him to be involved.

"Great." I smile.

"Really?" He squints at me.

"Really," I say firmly. If buying some linen pants and burying a pig in the ground is going to get my man back, then so be it.

• • •

I nearly collide with the UPS deliverywoman later that morning as I'm rushing out the front door, digging through my cluttered purse for my sunglasses, worried I'll be late for my meeting with Magda. I bend down to pick up the boxes that dropped and read the Williams-Sonoma return label. *Our wedding gifts are arriving.* Our eyes meet as I stand back up and I realize she looks familiar, her caramel-colored curls sparking a memory as they glisten in the morning sunlight. But I'm sure she's never delivered anything here before. "Tom out sick?" I ask, still trying to place her face.

"Something like that," she answers cryptically as she readjusts the packages in her hand.

"Wait! I know. You work at Starbucks, right? Remember me?"

She tips her chin toward me. "How could I forget that loud sigh of yours, Kate?"

Something about the way she says my name makes me pause

as I awkwardly hold an unusually heavy box to my chest—*could it be the ice cream maker I couldn't wait to try out?* Finally, she adds, "In fact, not only did I make you a kick-ass latte, I also gave you the power to change your life."

I take a step back and stumble over a Macy's box I hadn't seen resting at my feet, the stranger grabbing my elbow before I fall. "H-how . . ." I stammer. ". . . how do you know about that?" I whisper, glancing back toward my front door, not wanting Max to overhear us. Knowing I'll never be able to come up with a believable story to explain why I'm in a heated discussion with the UPS driver.

She smiles, revealing a small gap between her front teeth. "You've just found the person who holds the key to all the questions you have, and *that's* what you want to ask me?" She leans her head back and laughs before glancing at her watch and heading back toward her truck.

"Hold on!" I cry. "I have a better one. Why me?"

"You needed help," she says simply as she hops behind the wheel and begins to buckle her seat belt, extending a handheld computer toward me. "I'm going to need you to sign for those right here." She winks.

I scrawl my signature. "Why do some come true and not others?"

She smiles sweetly. "You want to bring peace to the world?"

I nod.

"One thing you must understand, Kate. All wishes must lead back to you and your journey. So no wishing for the cure for cancer or for the end of poverty, even though that would be nice," she says, and turns the ignition, which comes alive loudly. "And remember, every choice has a consequence," she calls out over the engine. "So be careful."

"What does that even mean?"

"You'll see," she says cryptically as she taps her watch. "Gotta run. These packages won't deliver themselves!"

"Wait," I ask, feeling desperate for her to stay a few minutes longer. "What's your name? And how will I find you again?"

"I'm Ruby. Don't worry, I'll track you down," she says right before pulling away from the curb, the exhaust choking me as she speeds down the street.

• • •

"Come in and shut the door," Magda says as soon as I arrive at the office, still reeling from my run-in with Ruby.

"Good morning," I say, and smile. "I love your necklace," I lie, the large baubles looking far too big around her birdlike neck. But flattery goes a long way with Magda.

"Thank you," she says briskly, and then waves me toward a white leather chair in front of her desk. "Have a seat."

"What's up?" I ask casually while wiping my wet hands on the cushion, wondering why she called me at home to ask me to meet her, praying she's just going to unleash one of her usual rants, like I'd used the wrong font in an ad or she hadn't liked the outfit a model had been wearing in the proofs she'd seen.

"I'm having a lot of problems with Courtney's work," Magda says plainly, and I hold my breath as she rattles off a series of mistakes she thinks Courtney's made. She tells me she woke up that morning with a change of heart about Courtney's attention to detail and work ethic. Everything Magda says sounds nothing like the Courtney I've worked with for five years—who may be the kind of woman who would steal your fiancé, but at work, always played by the rules. She worked hard to make sure every *I* was dotted and every *T* was crossed.

My first instinct is to defend her, but I remind myself that I wished for this. And maybe struggling at work was just what Courtney needed. She'd been spending far too much time focusing her attention on Max and needed to pour more of herself into her job. And if there was one thing that would capture Courtney's full attention, it would be attempting to please Magda.

I nod as Magda tells me she's going to call Courtney in next and tell her how disappointed she is and shift her responsibilities until she feels she's worthy of managing an important client again.

"So you're talking to me before her?" I ask. "Why?"

"Because I need you to take over Calvin Klein."

I swallow hard. Courtney had been working on landing that account for almost a year. She'd wined and dined them until they'd finally signed on. This would devastate her, and possibly them. They adored her. The part of me who understands how hard this job is, who gets just how important it is to have an account like Calvin Klein on your résumé, starts to protest. But I think of Max—how Courtney had pretended to be my friend until the very end, even texting me the day of the rehearsal dinner to tell me she couldn't wait to see me. Even when she knew what was about to happen. No, she doesn't deserve my sympathy. Maybe it was time for her to lose something she loved too.

CHAPTER TEN

. . . .

Oops I did it again. #MaybeBritneywasontosomething

I hurry into my office and close the door tightly behind me, anxious about crossing paths with Courtney, not sure what I'll say when I see her. *Um, sorry, I wished you a demotion* didn't exactly top the list. Despite what she'd done to me, I didn't love myself for stooping to her level. Jules kept reminding me of the old adage, an eye for an eye, but I'd never operated that way—preferring to take my grandmother's advice and always choose the high road. Until now. Presently, I am driving 150 miles per hour down the low road.

I kick off the heels that are already cutting into the flesh across my toes, making a mental note to make a wish for gorgeous four-inch stilettos that *never hurt*, telling myself there's nothing frivolous about a woman wanting comfortable *and* sexy footwear. As I start to dig into the mound of work that's piled high on my desk, my computer dings with an email from my mom. I flinch when I see her name, wondering what she could possibly want after our marathon chat on my way to work this morning. Although, in her defense, she might have been able to tell I was only half listening. My mind was swirling with questions I still had for the only person who seemed to hold the keys to unlocking this mystery of why some wishes came true while others didn't.

My mom had called on my way to the office and I'd picked up without thinking, my shoulders tensing when I heard her voice. Not that I didn't want to talk to her, but it wasn't a conversation I was prepared to have this morning. She'd already left me a half dozen messages in just two days, and before I could even get the words *how are you?* out of my mouth, she launched into a tirade about everything from not wanting to stay on the same floor of the hotel as my dad and *the wife* to wondering what they were getting me as a wedding gift—hoping they weren't going *off registry,* which would be so *like her.*

As I'd listened to my mom rambling on, I knew she was just working through the stress she was feeling about spending several days around the very people she'd spent years avoiding. Even though I knew weddings often brought out just as much family drama as joy, I needed her to stop. Because the more I listened to her rants, the more I was starting to worry about my own future with Max. Even if I were able to fix things with him, would he still eventually leave like my dad did? And then would I spend years being resentful that I hadn't moved on after I discovered he had doubts about us?

To my relief, my mom's email turns out to be a link to several mother-of-the-bride outfits she's considering and I quickly click through them and select my favorite, and write back that we should get together for breakfast soon. Deciding that when I see her I'll delicately broach the subject of dating. *She needs a man.*

An hour later, I've barely made a dent in the stack of press releases that need to be approved when my cell phone buzzes with a text message from Liam.

Thai tonight?

I write back without hesitation:

Absolutely!

Then I fire off another:

Our usual place?

Yes! 6:00?

Perfect! Craving spicy noodle soup and Thai Elvis!

I laugh to myself as I send off the last text, thinking of the Elvis impersonator who performs at our favorite Thai place, knowing I can count on his solid rendition of "Hound Dog" to bring some levity to my day.

As I'm humming the tune to myself, there's a knock and I stiffen. "Come in," I say, already knowing it's her.

"Hey," Courtney says, pushing the door open, her eyes wet with tears.

"Hey," I echo, trying to steady my shaky voice.

"So I guess this is all yours now." She hauls a large cardboard box across the room and drops it in front of my desk. I flinch when it hits the floor.

"I don't know what to say—" I start.

"Do you have *any idea* why she's doing this to me?" She

slumps down on my sofa. But before I can respond, she keeps going. "Because it feels so out of nowhere. She's saying that I've been dropping the ball and making mistakes, and when I asked for examples, she gave me dozens. But, Kate, I don't remember doing any of the things she's accusing me of!" Her eyes fill with tears again.

"You know Magda, she gets her mind set on something and it's hard to change it. She'll come around," I say, trying to stick to truthful statements. Hating to lie any more than I already have.

"Can you even handle all this with the wedding coming up? There's a lot going on with Calvin Klein."

Fortunately, I've already lived this month. I know about the embarrassing typo we miss on that vineyard's press release; I have a plan for how to correct the major faux pas we make with the powers that be at Whole Foods; and I am going to avoid Magda's meltdown by not letting us screw up the pitch for the up-and-coming vodka brand like we did last time around.

I nod. "So what will you be doing now?"

"Filing, photocopying, and answering phones! She's treating me like an intern. Why doesn't she just fire me?"

Because I didn't have the balls to wish for that.

"Maybe it won't be such a bad thing to get back to basics," I offer. *Because I need you spending time in the copy room, not with my fiancé.*

"Maybe." She doesn't continue her thought, and I see that familiar sparkle in her eye—the one she gets when she's considering an opinion that's not her own. It's a quality that's helped her secure more than one client as she compromises without losing the upper hand. It's also a characteristic I've been envious of—I could often be shortsighted and stubborn. "I guess I could use a little downtime. I've had a lot on my mind lately."

"Oh? Anything you want to talk about?" I ask lightly.

"No, but thank you." She frowns and strides toward the door, somehow looking even longer and leaner with her new haircut.

"Because *I'm always here for you if you need me*," I call after her, wondering if she catches that I'm using her own words to Max.

• • •

I walk into Palms Thai a few minutes before six and immediately spot Liam sitting at one of the long wood tables in the back. He holds up a bottle of Singha and smiles and I practically run across the restaurant, both excited to see him and eager for a drink after what feels like the longest day of my life. I slide into the chair next to him without speaking and lay my head against his shoulder as he wraps his arm around me.

"Hi," he says, kissing the top of my head.

"Hi," I say back and chug half of his beer.

"Rough day?" He smiles, signaling to the waitress that we'd like two more.

"You have no idea," I say with a sigh.

"What's going on? You look like hell!"

"Thanks?" I laugh and pick up the menu, Liam watching me with amusement in his eyes. "You wouldn't believe me if I told you."

"Try me," he says, leaning forward.

"I'm going to need a beer and a fried wonton first," I say as a server passes by with a tray full of barbecued chicken and pad thai, the rich smells making my stomach rumble.

After we order our appetizers, Liam tells me that he just started dating a new girl, a brunette with "legs for days," he says as he stretches out his arms and I picture the woman he brought to my wedding.

"Pouty lips, porcelain skin, tiny waist," I murmur.

"How did you know that? You haven't met her." He furrows his brow.

"I have—Angie, right? Nice girl, doesn't say much though. You brought her to my wedding."

"What are you talking about? You aren't married yet."

"Well, that part is true. In fact, I don't get married at all. Well, not the first time around anyway," I say after the waitress delivers our wontons and beers. I grab a wonton and dip it in sweet-and-sour sauce as Liam frowns at me.

"Okay, you're going to have to speak a little bit slower for this country boy because I'm not following what you're saying," he says in a mock southern drawl.

"It's all part of the story you'll never believe." I take a drink of my beer.

"Okay. This is getting weird. Start talking." He points to my mouth as I'm swallowing another bite.

After I tell him the whole story, he stares at me for a full minute before finally speaking.

"Are you shitting me?"

"No—and believe me, I wish I were," I say as the Elvis impersonator swaggers onto the stage in his tight rhinestone-encrusted white jumpsuit.

"Does Jules know?"

I nod my head.

"And?"

"She believes me," I say as I pop the last fried wonton into my mouth. "Well, she might have been a bit doubtful at first, but then I wished her a makeover and, well, have you seen her?"

"But Jules did *not* need a makeover," Liam says protectively.

"I agree! And it wasn't anything major. But there are certain things that need a little firming up after you have kids." I smile.

"Would you stop with this! She's like my sister—I don't want to think about her naked!" Liam presses his eyes shut as if he's trying to block out the mental image this is giving him.

My mind drifts back to a night in college when Liam and I had stumbled home from a party. He'd been walking me back to my dorm and I'd tripped. He'd tried to grab my arm and we'd both nearly fallen into some rosebushes near the student center. In a romantic comedy–like moment, we'd drunkenly looked into each other's eyes and he'd leaned in to kiss me. "Stop! You're like a brother to me, silly!" I'd said, giving him a fun-loving swat against his chest.

"I know how you can convince me this is real!" he says now, still looking almost exactly like he did in college, a mop of brown hair that's always in need of a cut, with just a few more lines around his eyes. "How about telling me tomorrow's winning Powerball numbers. Or better yet, who wins the NBA finals? I'll put some money on it."

As I stare at the doubtful look on his face, I begin to deflate, my shoulders sagging as I realize that Liam, a skeptic who is always the first to punch a hole in any story, wasn't going to be as easily convinced as Jules. "Forget it. I'll just let you see for yourself when he leaves me at the rehearsal dinner," I say, my cheeks damp with the tears I didn't realize were waiting to fall. I take the back of my hand and wipe them away, but they keep coming.

"Hey, don't cry. It's okay. Just swear on Thai Elvis and I'm in." His lips start to curl into a smile and I know we're both thinking of the last time we were here, when Elvis pulled me on stage and made me sing a line of "Jailhouse Rock," Liam laughing so hard he'd spit out his beer.

"You're tough," I say as I hold up my hand. "Fine. I swear on his blue suede shoes."

He reaches over and hugs me. "I can't believe Max would do that to you. What a prick," he says.

"That's what you said after it happened. You were so pissed at him!" I say into his chest, and he looks at me as if he wants to say more, but doesn't. "So do you *really* believe me?"

He exhales deeply. "I believe that *you* believe it," he says carefully, keeping a solid grip around me.

I pull my head back. "I can prove it."

Liam shakes his head. "It's okay, you don't have to *prove* anything to me."

But I did. Liam had always been my rock—he'd always understood me without explanation or justification. I couldn't go through this month with him just humoring me, bobbing his head up and down when I needed his support, but rolling his eyes when he thought I wasn't looking. I wanted him to be *all in* like Jules. I pulled my phone out of my purse. "So this new girl, Angie? You into her?"

He takes a beat before responding. "She's okay. For now," he says before leaning in. "But she doesn't appreciate *fine dining establishments* like this one," he says sarcastically, clinking his beer bottle against mine. "And that may turn out to be a deal breaker."

I shake my head. Typical Liam. Each girl he dated was just one minor fault away from being dumped. There was Andrea who liked cats but not dogs. Then there was Emily who liked dogs but not cats. And who could forget Hailey, who was allergic to both. I had begun to think Liam was allergic to serious relationships. And often wondered why he really was so hesitant to let himself fall in love.

"What about Nikki Day?" I ask, referring to the actress Liam had crushed on since they filmed a commercial for oatmeal, playing the mom and dad of a toddler who would throw a tantrum unless he ate sugary cereal for breakfast. Well, that is, until he tried Oats for Tots and "forgot" about his addiction to high fructose. Nikki had just been cast as a brainy blonde in a sitcom they were calling the next *Big Bang Theory*, and was recently listed in *Us Weekly*'s "30 Under 30 to Watch"—I had to pry the magazine out of Liam's hand at the pool the day of the rehearsal dinner, shaking my finger in his face as Angie slept beside him.

Liam puts his hand dramatically over his heart. "What about her?"

"What if I could make that happen for you?" I ask, a smile playing on my lips.

"You mean you could make a wish that she'll go out with me? Please! Her last boyfriend was on the Olympic swimming team! She'd go from that kind of guy to *me*? I mean I know I'm a hunk and all, but she barely even said hi to me when we shot that commercial. And now she'll be my girlfriend?"

"Not girlfriend—*date*. I'll wish for her to say yes to a date with you, but then it will be your job to work that famous Liam charm on her," I say, thinking again that no one should be forced to feel anything they don't actually believe in their heart.

Liam rolls his eyes.

"Listen, I get that it sounds like I've gone cuckoo for Cocoa Puffs here, but do you really think I could—*or would want*—to make this stuff up?"

"You're in advertising, isn't that your thing?" he taunts.

"Do you want a chance with Nikki Day or not?"

"All right. I'll bite."

I pull up Facebook on my phone and type:

Wow—Did y'all hear that Liam and Nikki Day are dating?

I turn so he can see the screen. "You think you can handle this?" I say, and pray that the universe will consider my request even though it's not technically *for* me. But it had worked with Jules and I had a strong feeling the powers that be would grant this one too—these were my best friends, and what happened to them affected me as well.

He pulls the phone out of my hand. "You're actually saying that's going to happen?" He points to the words I've just written. "As soon as you hit post, poof, I'm hooking up with the hottest actress on the planet?" He laughs nervously.

"If you think this is all bullshit, then it won't matter, right?" I challenge.

Liam stares at me for a minute before reaching over and posting the update. "Why the hell not? Let's test this sucker out," he says, just as Thai Elvis belts out the first line of "Love Me Tender."

CHAPTER ELEVEN

....

"The green is my favorite," I declare as I fan the assortment of men's neon briefs on the conference table, trying to focus my attention away from Courtney, her glossy lips turned downward in a pout as she buries her nose in her cell phone, only half listening as Magda and I debate the shade of underwear the Calvin Klein model should wear in the billboard ads, Magda arguing that pink will pop more against the black-and-white background, and me pointing out that Hanes just used a similar shade in a recent print advertisement. The junior associates and interns watch us lob arguments back and forth like we're playing a tennis match.

As Magda clamors on about how hot the color pink is this year, I can't seem to force my gaze away from Courtney, surprised by her insubordination. If Magda had demoted me, I'd be doing everything I could to win back her favor—even the assistant-like duties she's been assigned. Which is what I thought Courtney would do—throw herself into her work and claw her way back to the top. Instead, she seems to have given up, her attitude like that of a senior in high school who is already imagining herself on a college campus somewhere far away. Courtney's cell vibrates and a sly smile forms on her lips as she reads a message. As her cheeks flush, I feel a burn in my chest—*is she texting Max?*

"Courtney, what do you think?" I ask suddenly, grabbing the briefs and dangling them in front of her, a silence falling over the conference room. The staff members pivot their necks quickly, no doubt curious how she'll respond, since the news of her "reassignment" had traveled quickly through the office, tons of rumors swirling about what had *really* happened between Magda and Courtney—the one about a secret lesbian love affair being my personal favorite.

Courtney stares at me for a moment, barely glancing at the underwear between my fingertips. "Either one," she finally says, ignoring Magda's sharp look from across the table. "*You're* in charge now. Whatever *you* want—" She squints her eyes at me, then whispers, "Boss."

"Okay, then," I stammer. "Let's suggest to the client that we do some test shots before we make a final decision."

Magda purses her lips and gives me a quick half nod—her equivalent of a yes—just as Courtney releases a quiet laugh after her phone vibrates again. As everyone starts to file out of the room, frantic thoughts speed through my mind like sprinters rushing to the finish line of a hundred-yard dash, and I envision the texts that she and Max could be exchanging.

I imagine him and Courtney bantering about the Soul Asylum concert they were seeing at El Portal in North Hollywood tonight. Shooting texts back and forth like:

Think they'll play "Somebody to Shove"? I don't know, but I will shove someone if they don't! ☺

An involuntary shiver runs up my arm as I remember the insecurity I'd felt about their relationship the night he'd stumbled into the bedroom drunk, that feeling I'd buried forcing its way up like a geyser. But even after that surge of jealousy, I had never considered that Courtney might be attracted to Max. Although he was objectively attractive, he was nothing like the men she dated—with chiseled stomachs and movie-star good looks. Max was more boy-next-door cute than soap opera handsome. Not to mention she'd always sworn she'd never be caught dead dating anyone under six feet, and with Max barely clearing five foot eight, I never in my wildest dreams thought he'd be on her radar.

Last night, I'd stayed up long after Max fell asleep, going through old pictures and souvenirs I'd saved from our special occasions together. As I'd sifted through the plastic bin, I came across a few ticket stubs from concerts I'd seen with him. I ran my thumb over the one from Jesus Jones, remembering one of our first dates. As we'd noshed on calamari, I'd asked Max to share something I didn't know about him.

"That's easy! I'm a huge fan of old-school bands—especially from the nineties. And I love seeing them play live."

"Like Pearl Jam?" I'd offered.

"Sure, I mean they're not in my top ten, but yeah."

Not in his top ten? Then who was? I'd wondered.

I'd always justified that it was healthy for us to have interests independent of each other—I was a voracious reader and loved going to book signings to meet my favorite authors. Max had joined me once, waiting patiently next to me in line for forty-five minutes to get my tattered copy signed. He hadn't even complained that he was the only human being with a Y chromosome in the room. But still, I hadn't missed both the forced smile when I asked him if he was having fun or the not-so-subtle glances at the ESPN home page on his phone while the author read from her novel.

• • •

I grab the front-row-center tickets to Soul Asylum that I wished for earlier and smile, feeling confident that tonight would be critical to getting Max back. Ruby had made a brief appearance at the Thai restaurant the other night, showing up to bus our table after Liam excused himself to use the restroom. As she'd stacked our empty beer bottles and dishes on a tray, she'd sternly warned me that my wishes weren't unlimited. She'd nodded in the direction of Liam as he made his way back toward us. "Be careful what kind of wishes you make from this point forward, because they are going to run out—*soon*."

"When?" I'd called after her, but she disappeared into the kitchen without so much as glancing over her shoulder.

But even with the knowledge that the wishes I had left were finite, I had decided tonight was critical to getting us back on track, recalling again the sloppy smile that was painted on Max's face when he arrived home the last time he'd seen a concert with Courtney. Plus, music is one of Max's greatest loves, and *I* should be the one sharing that with him. So I hope this will be the night I reclaim my spot not just next to him in front of the stage, but also in his heart.

As I slide the tickets into my tote, I breathe a victorious sigh remembering Courtney's face after I'd casually mentioned I'd be joining her and Max as we walked out of the Calvin Klein meeting.

"We'd love for you to come," she'd said, smiling sweetly. "But it's sold out. Maybe next time?"

I bet you'd love that. Because you're hoping there won't be a next time—that by then he'll have made you his permanent concert date.

"I was able to score five front-row tickets!" I exclaimed, re-membering Jules and Liam both telling me I owed them one after I begged them to come as my reinforcements.

Courtney's mouth had transformed so swiftly from a frown into a smile it was as if someone had just told her to *turn that frown upside down*. "Fantastic," she said slowly. "But I thought you hated Soul Asylum. What was it you said when Max and I said we were going? That your ears might bleed if you got within a ten-mile radius of El Portal?"

I shrugged. "I guess you could say I had a change of heart."

She looked at me skeptically. "Okay, but you'd better not make Max leave before all the encores!" She laughed, but under-neath it, I heard the edge.

"Oh, don't you worry about that," I said as I ducked into my office, shutting the door and leaning my back against it.

"I'll be there for him until the very end," I said to myself, and prayed that I was right.

• • •

Several hours later, I squeeze Max's hand as he helps me navi-gate my way out of the back of the sleek Escalade limo I had or-dered—*not* wished for. I step out onto the sidewalk and catch my reflection in the window. I'd spent two painstaking hours in front of the mirror, simultaneously watching YouTube instructional videos and applying eye shadow, mascara, and blush until I was semisatisfied. And exercising more willpower than I did when I agreed to do the five-day master cleanse with Jules, I resisted my newfound impulse to wish for a new outfit, instead choosing my favorite little black dress, hoping it would be enough.

Relief washed over me when I heard Max's whistle as I walked out of the bathroom. "Don't take this the wrong way, because you know I always think you look good, but you've been looking extra hot lately." He pulled me in for a kiss. "What's going on?"

"I just want to make you happy," I said, the truth of my words bringing tears to the back of my eyes. I squinted hard to hold them in. *Keep it together, Kate.* Before he could respond, the doorbell rang, signaling the arrival of the limo, Max running to answer it.

"Do I make you happy, Max?" I whispered before following him, not sure if I knew the answer anymore.

• • •

"Nice ride." Courtney walks up as Max is shutting the door to the Escalade. "And you couldn't pick me up because?" she asks lightly, but there is an accusation in her voice. I've seen the confusion in her eyes when I gave her my clipped answers or brushed past her in the kitchen at work this week—and she had probably chalked it up to prewedding stress. Little did she know *she* was my prewedding stress.

I put my arm around Max's waist possessively. "We needed some alone time," I say as I wink at her, hoping she'll assume we'd gotten down and dirty on the way here. The truth was Max had taken a phone call from his boss and had spent most of the ride discussing something about trial results as I Instagrammed pictures of the limo and caught up on my Trivia Crack games.

"Let's head inside," Max says, pulling my arm toward the entrance as Courtney falls in step beside us.

"Wait—Liam should be here any minute." My phone buzzes in my pocket. "This is probably him."

The text is from Jules, the third she's sent in less than a

minute, profusely apologizing for canceling. She writes that she wants to kick her babysitter's ass for coming down with strep throat even though she's quite sure Ellie gave it to her. And that she wants to kick Ben's ass for traveling all the time. I text her back immediately, the words from the fight I'd overheard still ringing in my ears, wishing I could help her get some adult time or that I could make Ben get home to her.

It's FINE! You know I *wish* I could wish for a new babysitter! But I need to be more careful with my wishes—I don't know how many I have left.

As I wait for her response, I bite my lower lip, understanding but hating at the same time that she won't be by my side tonight—needing her to tell me it's all in my imagination when I notice a look or smile shared between Max and Courtney. And wanting her to stare down Courtney with the look of death that she usually only reserves for people who cut her off in traffic or after she wastes her precious free time by watching a bad episode of *Nashville*.

I understand—but at least Liam will still be there! I told him he could have my ticket and he said he's bringing a date! I want the SCOOP.

I look around. Liam and his mystery date are late. And if he cancels on me too, I'm not sure how I'll get through this night.

I turn to see Courtney and Max waiting near the door, the matching looks on their faces telling me I am screwing up their preconcert mojo big-time. "Sorry! Just a minute." I hold up my finger. There is no way I am sending them inside without me.

I scan the people walking up from the parking lot. *Come on, Liam.*

He rounds the corner a moment later, his broad shoulders blocking the woman behind him, a dopey grin on his face. When he reaches me, he leans in and whispers, "It worked, Kate. It fucking worked—look who I'm with!"

I glance beyond Liam, where a crowd has already formed around Nikki Day—she's smiling and signing a man's arm but shoots Liam a pleading look. "You better go save her," I say with a laugh, and pull the tickets from my purse.

Once we're seated, Liam properly introduces us to Nikki. I wince when she compliments Courtney's new haircut, saying she's wanted to get the same one, but the producers of her new show won't let her. "It's fabulous," she reiterates as she reaches up to touch it, Courtney blushing modestly.

As I sit sandwiched between the two couples, sipping my Corona, it's hard not to feel like a fifth wheel, with Liam barely able to tear his eyes away from his date, while Courtney and Max jokingly argue over whether Soul Asylum will play "Without a Trace" or "Runaway Train" for their final *final* encore song.

"'Runaway Train' would be appropriate for this train wreck of a night," I mutter to myself, wondering what the hell I'm doing. I've painted my face, I've shown interest in what Max loves, I even brought him here in style. But I *still* can't pull his attention from Courtney.

And Liam seems to have conveniently forgotten that he's here to help me, not hang on Nikki's every word like he's her lapdog. I narrow my eyes at him, him mouthing sorry and quickly shifting his body toward mine.

"So, Max," he says, raising his voice over the preconcert music playing. "Can't wait until the wedding, bro!" He reaches over and slaps him on the back—hard, Max's eyes opening wide in surprise. "Only three and a half weeks before you marry the girl of your dreams." Liam holds his gaze as he says the last part, almost daring Max to break eye contact. "You are one lucky man."

"Yeah, it will be great." He smiles and squeezes my knee.

I smile my thank-you at Liam, wishing his words to Max were making me feel better, wishing that I was convinced that Max really did feel lucky to have me. But the only thing I am sure of anymore is that I have no idea what is going on inside his head.

"And, Courtney, can you believe Kate hooked us up with these killer seats?" Liam presses as she stares straight ahead, waiting for the band to take the stage, her eyes boring into the microphones and equipment like a hawk waiting for its prey.

"They're amazing," she answers honestly as she catches my eye. And for a split second I miss her. Because I see the Courtney I thought I knew—the one who I believed was sincere and painfully honest. The one who never felt right exaggerating information about our firm when we were trying to land a new client. The one who would simply smile if Magda asked if she liked her newest two-sizes-too-big pantsuit.

Suddenly, she jumps up as the band walks out, Max springing up beside her, them bobbing their heads in unison to the beat of the opening chords, and the nostalgic hole in my heart is quickly closed.

"Oh my God, they're starting with 'Misery'—I can't believe you were right!" Courtney punches Max in the arm.

As the words *Put me out of my misery* fill the air, I can't help but agree.

Liam grabs my wrist and pulls me up too. "Get your head

in the game," he scolds into my ear. "Your fiancé is acting like he's on a date with another woman and you're sitting here like a zombie!"

I immediately force a smile onto my face and wedge myself between Max and Courtney as they dance, hands in the air, singing the words to each other. I mimic them, flinging my arms toward the ceiling and moving my lips, pretending to know the words to songs that I hadn't even listened to the first time around.

I loop my arm around Max's waist, bringing him in for a kiss between each song, holding on to him not just literally, but figuratively too. All while trying to block out Liam, who is treating Nikki like a mirage that might disappear at any moment. She's been friendly enough all night, but there is something about her that's been bothering me, something I can't quite put my finger on. Maybe it is the whole celebrity thing, I'm not sure. But Liam seems happy—in fact, I haven't seen him act like this around a woman he was dating before. Not to mention he now believes that I am telling the truth about traveling back in time. So I decide to brush aside my feelings about Nikki and concentrate on the task at hand.

I bite my lip through the *three* encores, trying to hide my disdain as Max tells Courtney she owes him a beer for guessing the order correctly. *God, I had been so blind.*

I lean my head against Max's shoulder once we're back in the limo, exhausted from pretending all night. Pretending to care about Soul Asylum, pretending I didn't notice the stolen glances Courtney threw at Max, pretending that I was still sure I could fix my relationship with him. Maybe it had been a mistake to come back—to try to rewrite fate. But Ruby had said I'd been given this power because I needed it. So what did I need it for if it wasn't to make things right with Max? Because I seriously doubted the universe gave a shit how my hair looked or if Jules had washboard abs.

"Did you have fun?" Max asks as we pull away from the curb.

"It was fantastic!" I lie enthusiastically.

Max tilts his head slightly. "Really? I wasn't sure."

I pull my head off his shoulder and look him in the eye. "What are you talking about? I danced all night. I didn't even sit down!"

What did I have to do to prove it to him? Rush the stage? Start a mosh pit? Get Soul Asylum *tattooed across my chest?*

"I know you did," Max backtracks. "And don't get me wrong, I love that you came, that you got us great tickets and the limo—" His voice falls off.

"But?" I ask.

"It's just, I don't know. Never mind. I'm drunk." He laughs and kisses me. "Forget I said anything."

But he didn't have to finish his sentence. I already knew what he was too scared to say. That although I had been there with a smile pasted across my face, he could tell that my heart wasn't in it. A knot forms in my throat as I realize he had seen right through me.

"I'm sorry," I offer.

Max sits up and pulls me back into him. "Don't be! It was a great night. And, Kate?"

"What?"

"You don't have to pretend to like Soul Asylum for me. Just be you."

I tried that the first time around and it didn't work.

"What gave me away?" I say sheepishly.

"Let's just say it was pretty obvious you had heard of, maybe, one of their songs. And I hate to break the news, but I don't think a career in lip-synching is going to work out for you." He laughs and kisses me deeper, his hand finding its way under my dress as he raises the privacy window. "But I love that you tried," he breathes to me between kisses.

As he takes me right there, like we're a couple of rock stars on the way home from the Grammys, I feel a glimmer of hope. Maybe I hadn't put on the best show, but he seemed happy that I'd made the effort. And for now, that would have to be enough.

CHAPTER TWELVE

....

"You want to do *what*?" Stella, my wedding planner, asks, releasing a high-pitched cackle into the phone.

"Make a few changes," I repeat.

Stella lets out a long breath, and I imagine her tugging on one of her short, bouncy curls, her cheeks flushing a deep red as she considers what I've just told her—that I want to rethink how we've planned everything: the rehearsal dinner, the wedding ceremony, and the reception. "You're not just suggesting switching out gerbera daisies for roses, Kate. I've just written down"—she pauses and I hear her counting quietly—"at least twenty things you want to do differently."

After Max gently used the word *hoity-toity* to describe the event that I'd spent almost a year planning, it had felt like a punch in my gut. Even though I'd asked him to tell me honestly what he'd change, I was surprised when he'd had such specific ideas, wondering why they were so different from my own. In fact, they couldn't have been more opposite. I hadn't pushed for his involvement, only because I had assumed we were on the same page. Or maybe I had just chosen to assume that, taking off with the planning like a horse running free from the barn—never looking back. *Until it was too late. Almost.*

Maybe *I had* gotten carried away with things that didn't matter—like the ice sculpture, the chocolate fountain, and the customized dinner menus. The truth was, it wouldn't kill me if we made things a bit more casual or if we embraced the local culture. At this point, I'd consider letting Thai Elvis marry us at city hall if that's what Max wanted—if that would make him happy.

"A pig roast, really?" Stella's question snaps me to attention.

"Yes, a pig roast," I say more curtly than I mean to, just as Courtney passes in front of my office door, shooting me a questioning look.

Stella continues. "I mean, luaus are very popular here—*obviously*. And hula dancers and flame throwers and all that Hawaiian tradition you're now considering is what a lot of people want. But it just doesn't sound anything like you—"

"Look, I can enjoy a fireball being tossed in the air just like the best of them, okay?" I snap.

"Of course. Of course you can," Stella says. "Let me get my head around all of this and see what I can figure out. I'll give you a call back with a plan by tomorrow. Okay?"

"Yes, thank you—and sorry I barked at you," I say.

"Oh, that was nothing!" Stella chuckles. "On a scale from one to ten of bridezilla moments I've dealt with, I'd give yours a negative five! You should've seen the bride who screamed at me like a banshee when the door of the dove's cage got stuck and the birds couldn't fly into the sky at the end of her ceremony! Or the one who hurled a platter of strawberries across the room because she *claimed* she'd told me to cover them in dark chocolate, not white." She laughs again. "The bitchy 'tudes are all part of the job. That's why I charge so much!

"So how did you calm them down?" I ask, shaking my head as I imagine the scenes she's just described—realizing my stuck-zipper situation must have severely paled in comparison. "Sounds like you need to raise your rates even more," I add, laughing. "I mean after *my* wedding."

She giggles. "Maybe so. But in the meantime, let's just say there's no situation a shot of tequila and a piece of wedding cake can't solve."

Mental note: give Max tequila, not champagne, at the rehearsal dinner.

After we hang up, I rest my head against the back of my chair, hoping Stella is able to pull a miracle out of her ass and change my entire wedding with only a little over three weeks to go. I tell myself that I don't need to intervene, that this is her *job* and, after hearing her crazed-bride stories, one she can clearly handle. In fact, I'm now starting to think that Stella could probably arrange the ceremony atop an active volcano if she put her mind to it. I pray Max won't ask for that next.

"Knock-knock!" Courtney says as she hovers by my door. "So last night was fun, huh?" she says unconvincingly.

Yeah, about as fun as a colonoscopy.

I bob my head up and down once because technically I did have fun—but it was only in the back of the limo on the way home from the concert. "What's up?" I ask, shuffling some papers around on my desk. "I have that meeting with the vodka people in twenty minutes."

"I was just curious—did I hear you talking about a pig roast?"

"Yeah, why?"

"Oh, I was just going to ask if that's for your wedding."

"Yeah, we're making a few changes."

Why am I telling her this?

Courtney smiles as if she's thinking back on something.

"Why do you ask?"

"I just think that's awesome! I have always wanted to get married right on the beach, not even wear shoes—maybe just flip-flops or even go barefoot. And then have a party on the sand—a luau with the whole nine yards. The flame throwers, hula dancers, and a pig roast—I mean, how cool would that be, just being super laid back with those you love the most? Without all that hoity-toity stuff?"

"Why did you just use *that* word?"

"Which word?" Courtney asks, her eyes widening.

"Hoi . . . ty . . . toi . . . ty." I drag out each syllable dramatically, never unlocking my gaze from hers.

Has she been talking to Max about this?

"I don't know. That's just how I'd describe most weddings . . . Sorry, did I upset you?"

"That word really just popped into your head? You didn't hear it from someone else?"

Like my fiancé?

"No . . . I swear!" Courtney gives me a bemused expression. "This is the first I'm hearing of your wedding having any changes to it at all. The last time you and I talked, you were trying to decide if you should serve chocolate fondue at the reception."

I stare at her for a moment, searching for any signs of deception, then almost laugh out loud because how would I even know if she was telling the truth? She'd already fallen for my fiancé right under my nose once; what's to say she wouldn't lie to me now? But there was still something about her reaction, which seemed so raw and unrehearsed, that made me believe her. She really did want to wear a damn coconut bra on her wedding day. Which meant she shared the same opinion as Max did *just because*—another thing they had in common. No-frills weddings and bad nineties bands. What was next? I didn't want to find out.

"I swear, Kate, you've been acting really strange the past few days. One second you're up, the next you're down. Are you okay?"

No, I'm not okay! And you are the reason why!

I swallow the urge to accuse her of having serious feelings for Max. To ask her why, when there are a gazillion other guys on the planet, she would want *mine*. Why she threw what I thought was a solid friendship away. But I can't. I need more time. Because the last thing I'd want is for my accusations to throw them closer together.

"I'm just freaking about how the wedding will turn out," I say, because it's the only truthful statement I can think of.

• • •

I toss my car keys to the valet at The Grove and run to meet Jules just as the sun is setting that night. Already twenty minutes late, I pull open the door to the Tommy Bahama store and find her sitting on a wicker chair with her arms crossed over her chest.

"Yeah, this is exactly how I wanted to spend my evening— staring at sixty-year-old men modeling Hawaiian shirts and fisherman sandals for their wives." She motions her head toward a man griping about not needing a second pair of silk pleated pants, his wife rolling her eyes. "Not help you find something for Max and his groomsmen to wear for the wedding."

"Sorry I'm late. There was horrible traffic."

"You could have solved that problem with a few clicks," she says matter-of-factly.

"I can't, because, like I mentioned in my text the other night, I have to be more conservative with how I use—" I lower my voice as a sales associate walks by. "How I use this power."

I fill her in on my run-in with Ruby at Palms Thai and she eyes me skeptically.

"So then why did you wish up Liam the hot new girlfriend?"

"She's not *that* hot," I say.

"Sure, if you don't count her tiny waist and gorgeous Angelina Jolie–like face."

"Anyway," I say as I start to sift through a pile of linen shorts. "I asked for that for Liam *right before* Ruby told me the wishes were going to run out eventually. I have no idea how many more are left—she was cryptic, only saying they were finite."

"So that means you still have the ability then?" Jules asks, a faraway look in her eyes.

"Why are you acting like I'm a drug dealer and you need some of my crack?" I say, sliding down in the chair next to her. "What's going on with you? Wasn't the makeover enough?" I ask. "You look amazing."

"Thanks. And I don't mean to sound ungrateful. I guess I just thought that it would make me feel better than it did—that Ben would notice it more."

"What was his response?"

"He told me I looked hot and then fell asleep when I ran upstairs to turn off the kids' lights," she says with a groan. "Then he left again this morning for Orlando, or was it Omaha?"

"So then, when he gets back home, put the kids to bed early and wait for him in the bedroom and *make him* take notice. The kids can sleep with the lights on!"

"It's not that simple. He's just so tired all the time." She looks away and adds quietly, "I'm tired too."

"Oh, come on! You're telling me you guys can't down a Red Bull one night to make the magic happen?" I joke, then stop as I notice Jules' eyes fill with tears. "What is it? What's going on?"

"Nothing, I'm fine. You're right, I need to try harder."

"I'm sorry, I wasn't saying you aren't trying. And what do I know anyway? I couldn't even keep a goldfish alive, let alone raise two kids while working."

Jules smiles and wipes her eyes. "True. You wouldn't last a week." She smiles.

I lay my hand on her arm. "Hey, why don't we shop another time and go grab a glass of wine and talk?"

Jules' face closes up. "No! Your wedding is practically around the corner and you're changing *everything*. This shopping trip has to come first. Now let's find the boys some linen!" She marches over to a rack and starts pushing hangers to the side as she looks at each shirt.

"Jules," I say quietly. "Tell me what's going on. All this other stuff can wait."

She swivels around quickly and shakes her head, clasping a red, short-sleeve shirt with embroidered white flowers in her hand. "It's nothing for you to worry about. I'm just feeling over-whelmed."

Her words seem forced. "Are you sure?" I ask, wondering if I should tell her I heard her and Ben fighting the other day. That I was worried for them.

"Yes! But I do have a really important question to ask. And I need you to be honest."

"Promise," I say, and lean in.

A smile plays on her lips. "So you're really okay with this Maui-wowie bullshit?"

"This is what Max wants." I force a smile.

"Okay, I get that. But what about what *you* want?"

"I want Max."

"I know you do," she says slowly, in a way that reminds me of when she once had to break the news that my favorite velour sweat suit was no longer in style. "But I just wonder—to get him back, why do you have to let him dress like Jimmy Buffett? For your *wedding* ceremony?"

"First of all, he doesn't want to wear a Hawaiian shirt like *that*—I think my dad has that one." I laugh. "He just wants to be casual beachy, and this is the only place I could think of."

"That's not what I mean," Jules says as she tugs on the silk fabric. "I'm just worried that you're losing yourself a bit—"

"Why wouldn't I give him what *he* wants for a change?" I say, cutting her off. "Hasn't our relationship always been about me? Isn't that the problem?"

"You're being too hard on yourself, Kate. It's not like you had the guy in a choke hold. There were definitely plenty of times when he put himself first too. What about how he always takes his mom's side when she's picking on you and then tells you after that he's sorry but it's just easier than dealing with her rants? Or when he turned down that promotion at work without even asking for your opinion? It's easy to look back and only remember the perfect parts, but you need to think about *all* of it—including the bad. Because, believe me, that's what he's doing."

"Ouch."

"I'm sorry. That came out wrong. You know I care about Max, but *you* are my best friend and I hate to see you blaming yourself for everything that's happened."

"I want to do this for him—okay? Can you please just help me pick some pants and a shirt?" I plead, my eyes welling with tears as I lean against a table covered with straw hats. "I don't care what he ends up wearing, I just want him to be donning it while he says I *do* to me."

Jules tosses the shirt she's holding to the side and walks over to me. "I get it, really, I do. But the concert, the island wear . . . I think you might be focusing on the wrong things here," she says.

I pick up a leather flip-flop from a shelf, remembering Courtney's words about wanting the same kind of low-key wedding Max did. Which might be true. But she didn't know him the way I did. She'd never nursed him through the stomach flu or cried with him when his grandfather died. Max and I were engaged to be married for a reason—and for the first three years of our relationship my lack of knowledge about the band Smashing Pumpkins hadn't been a deal breaker for him. Courtney had simply been in the right place at the right time when Max was questioning our future—and she'd distracted him. I needed to take him away from unnecessary detours like her so we could focus on each other. Because when was the last time we'd done that?

"Okay, I know what I should be focusing on," I say slowly, and Jules raises an eyebrow. "I'm going to surprise him with a weekend away to Big Bear—where we fell in love."

"And if that doesn't work?" Jules asks carefully, the look in her eyes saying more than she can.

"Then I'm going to wish Courtney off to a deserted island!" I say confidently, even though I know I won't—because it won't solve anything. But I grab Jules' hand and we laugh together anyway, our laughter masking the worry I know we're both feeling inside—that I might already be too late.

CHAPTER THIRTEEN

....

Orange is NOT the new black #justsaying

"Do you have this in orange?" I ask the salesgirl, trying not to cringe as I finger the delicate fabric of the comforter Max had pointed out as he looked over my shoulder at the Pottery Barn catalog last night, mentioning that he had always thought we needed this color in our neutral bedroom. My mouth gaping open, I asked, "Since when do you care about interior design? Are you the same man who didn't know what a duvet was when we moved in together?"

"What? You're the one who always makes me watch HGTV with you—I saw it on an episode of *House Hunters*," he'd replied, his face turning crimson. "It looked really cool."

"Really? HGTV?" I had asked, careful to keep my voice even. When I started urging him to tell me what kind of wedding he *really* wanted, it was as if I'd opened the floodgates. Suddenly he was asserting his opinion about everything, from the type of cottage cheese we should start buying (large curd!) to his admission that he was tired of watching reality TV and wanted me to start watching more sports with him. While I was happy to finally hear what was on his mind, it had shocked me yet again that his opinions were so different from my own.

I lay awake again last night, sleep proving more and more elusive with each passing day, patiently waiting for Max's steady breathing to arrive before sitting up and staring at the contours of his face, wondering again how we had arrived here. I thought back to what Jules had said at the store—was winning Max back still a victory if it meant I was losing myself in the process?

The Pottery Barn saleswoman nods before disappearing to the back, returning with the orange duvet cased in plastic. "You're sure?" she asks when she sees my face. Much to my chagrin, the shade of blood orange did *not* look better in person than it did in the glossy pages of the magazine. It was a shame; the crushed chiffonlike fabric was light and airy, and I had practically drooled over the ivory one on display, imagining pairing it with bold red and pale gold accent pillows. But waking up each morning wrapped in Max's arms was what I wanted. So as I hand the cashier my credit card, I remind myself that it's the people under the duvet, not the duvet itself, that matter.

As I make my way back to work, I feel lighter as I embrace the new dynamics of my relationship with Max. Sure, maybe I'd have to be more open to change, but at least I'd finally know the *real* Max—his opinions and feelings, everything. Maybe this would end up being the best thing that ever happened to me, and to us.

Holding the comforter under my arm, because I planned to FaceTime with Jules and show her, hoping she'd tell me the color didn't resemble a prisoner's jumpsuit, I use my hip to push open the door to our office entrance, nearly colliding with Courtney, who is awkwardly balancing a large box and her even larger striped tote.

"What's going on?" I ask, catching my breath as I spy her

favorite picture, a framed print of the Brooklyn Bridge at dusk, peeking out the top of the box. *Was she fired?*

"I quit," she says simply.

"Wait, w-what?" I stammer, a thousand emotions rushing through me—feeling ecstatic, guilty, and evil all at the same moment. Happy she would be gone and most likely distracted by an intensive job search, guilty for the part I played by wishing her onto Magda's bad side, and evil because my master plan was working.

"When did this happen? Why didn't you tell me?"

"It wasn't planned. Magda pulled me off the PumpedUP energy drink account and I just snapped. Remember how hard I worked to get them to sign on? The things I did?"

I think back to Courtney challenging the CEO to a drinking contest—if she could outlast him, then he would hire us. He happily agreed, thinking that there was no way a 110-pound girl in black jeggings could drink him under the table. But she did as we both looked on in awe.

"Anyway," she continues. "Something in me just cracked as I stared at her god-awful red lipstick and birdlike face. I told her to fuck off!"

"You what?" I smile despite myself, having imagined doing the same thing several times. When Magda took credit for the work we did, when she bit our heads off about things we couldn't control, when she refused to acknowledge we had been right about something she didn't agree with.

"Yep. It felt great, Kate. You should try it sometime." Courtney grins widely, and for a moment I almost forget that she's my enemy. That Max is her latest challenge. A flash of regret slices me. Now I'd have to deal with Magda all on my own.

"Maybe," I say quietly, glancing around to make sure that

Magda or her tattletale assistant aren't within earshot. "What are you going to do now?"

"Have a cocktail!" A carefree smile lights up her face. It's the same one I saw her repeatedly flash Max at the concert—the grin that made my stomach hurt, especially when I saw how he'd smiled back. "Want to join?" she asks hopefully, then quickly adds, "You know we haven't hung out in a while. You know, just you and me."

"I can't. I'm sure Magda is waiting on me," I say, holding up the comforter to indicate I've already spent enough time out of the office.

"I understand," Courtney says sincerely as she eyes the duvet. "Oh my God—did you just buy that?"

"Oh, this?" I say, pulling the bag to my chest, embarrassed. "I know, it's—"

"—totally awesome!" she finishes, setting her box down and pulling the duvet out of the shopping bag as if it's a pile of money. "They're saying orange is the new black. It was all over Fashion Week!"

"Really?" I say weakly, a hard ball of anxiety lodged in my throat. How is it that she and Max agree again—and about something so random? "It's for our *bedroom*." I deliberately linger on the word as I study her reaction.

She flinches slightly as she leans over to pick up her box. "So I guess this is good-bye," she says as she stands up, a look I can't read now flitting in her eyes. "For now, anyway. I'll call you later, okay?"

"Sure," I say as I watch her glide to the elevator, her feet barely grazing the floor.

• • •

Predictably, Magda spends the rest of the day on a rampage, her protégée telling her off and quitting in one fell swoop clearly not sitting well. Even though I had wished Courtney onto Magda's shit list, the truth was she had always been Magda's favorite and I knew, even with my interference, it was only a matter of time before she reclaimed her special place in Magda's heart. But then she'd quit—throwing everything off. I was dependable and consistent, but Courtney had that extra something I didn't. It was her flashes of brilliance when she knew just how to handle our cranky art director so we could meet our looming deadlines, or when she thought of a fresh idea after hours of brainstorming. Despite how Magda had *thought* she'd been feeling about Courtney's work, there was no doubt we were all going to feel the gaping hole her absence would leave.

Magda raged on about an innocuous mistake a junior associate had made, making me confirm details about a campaign we'd already gone over ad nauseam, and snapped at me when I missed a small typo in a memo *she* had sent out. As the day wore on, I felt a slow anger burn inside my chest toward Courtney, the image of her practically skipping to the elevator stuck in my head. Angry that once again I was left to deal with a mess she had created. Sure, maybe I had been the one who had set all this into motion, but still. The bottom line was that, so far, my wishes seemed to be creating more problems for me than solutions.

• • •

"Hey," I say as I walk into our living room, immediately noticing Max's silhouette on the couch, watching the Dodgers game on mute. "You'll never guess what happened today." I throw my purse on the table and slide myself into the crook of his arm.

"I have some crazy news too," he says. "You first."

"Courtney quit," I say, trying my best to twist the expression on my face into a mix of equal parts serious and contemplative. "I hope she'll be okay."

Max breaks into a grin. "She's going to be just fine!" he declares with more confidence than he had when he convinced me that bungee jumping on my thirty-third birthday would be a great idea.

Panic rises inside of me. "What do you mean? How would you know that?" I glance at my watch. "She's been jobless for half a day."

"She's not unemployed anymore," Max says cryptically.

I squeeze my eyes shut, not wanting to hear where this is going but unable to control my impulse to find out. "Care to elaborate?" I ask, trying unsuccessfully to control the clipped tone in my voice.

"Well, it was a crazy coincidence," Max starts, his eyes glimmering with excitement. "But long story short, she was hired at my company—in the marketing department. She's going to be a product manager!"

"What the fuck?" I blurt.

"I know, right?" Max says, mistaking my shock as happiness instead of frustration.

"Okay," I say, trying to catch my breath. "How did this happen?"

Max tells me how he ran into Courtney while grabbing lunch. He was dining with the senior product manager for an ear implant device they'd just licensed, who had been lamenting to Max that even after two rounds of interviews, they still hadn't found any suitable candidates for their opening in the marketing department. Courtney just happened to be sitting at the bar, sipping vodka and soda with a twist of lime—a detail Max gave me, although I wasn't sure I needed it. Apparently, Max had *literally* bumped into her as he was being escorted to his table—something about the hostess dropping her menus and Max stumbling, which had sent him flying into Courtney. Seeing how down she looked, he invited her to join him and his colleague, and by the time their crème brûlée was served, she was also being handed a job on a silver platter.

"She starts tomorrow!" Max finished.

Of course she does.

I nod my head and bite my lip as Max talks about how it must have been fate that they ran into each other. That it was meant to be.

That's what I'm worried about.

"Listen," I say later after dinner, after we've rehashed yet again how lucky Courtney is. How she had charmed the hell out of the product manager. How fortunate they were to have her on the team. "I know this is last minute, but I think we should try to get away one last time before the wedding."

Max raises his eyebrows. "But isn't the wedding a getaway?"

"Yes," I say patiently. "But we'll be surrounded by other people there. I really just want some time to ourselves." I reach over and grab his hand and lock my eyes with his. "I'm worried that we're drifting."

Max breaks eye contact for a split second before forcing his eyes back to mine. "Okay."

"Remember I mentioned Big Bear the other day?" I say, watching his face intently.

"Ah." He smiles and places a soft kiss on my lips. "The place where it all began."

"Yes," I say, relieved. "So, can we? Leave Friday afternoon? I've already called and booked it, hoping you'd agree." Because it was the off-season, I had been able to secure the same cabin we'd stayed in early on in our relationship, when Max had told me he loved me as we sipped hot toddies while cuddled up next to the crackling fire. It would mean I'd have to work until midnight every night before we left to get all my work handled, but I'd decided it was worth it.

"Sounds fun," Max says as his phone buzzes on the table, Courtney's name flashing across the screen. Max looks guilty before saying quickly, "She's just checking in about tomorrow."

"I understand," I say. *I understand that she'll be using this opportunity to get closer to you.* Courtney hadn't even bothered to text me with her good news. Was it because I'd been shutting her out? Or had she not reached out because now that she worked with Max she didn't need me?

I make a noise that's a cross between a snort and a guffaw, picking up the new *Us Weekly* to distract me from Max's text banter with Courtney. "She has a lot of questions," he says as his fingers fly across his phone.

"I'm sure," I say as I take out my frustration on the magazine, turning the pages aggressively until a picture stops me. It's Liam and Nikki Day, locked in an embrace in front of BLT Steak in West Hollywood, the caption reading "Nikki Day's New Hottie!"

I can't tear my eyes away from the picture, Liam's arms wrapped tightly around Nikki's Barbie doll waist, her hands in his hair as they lock lips. Max finally looks up from his phone and grabs the magazine. "Is that Liam? Holy shit!"

"I know, right?" I say, pulling the tabloid back from him and staring at the half-page picture again, scanning the story underneath that spills the details of their courtship. How much of this was true, I wondered, as I read about their *instant connection,*

Nikki supposedly telling friends Liam was so different, in a good way, from anyone she'd dated before.

"He looks pretty cozy. Maybe he's finally ready to settle down."

"Maybe," I echo, feeling exhausted. Why did it seem like everyone around me was moving forward while I stood still? Courtney escaped Magda without a scratch, Liam finally found a girl who made him happy, and Max seemed to be slipping out of my fingers no matter how hard I tried to hold on to him.

"I'm going to head up to bed," I say, standing up. "Want to come?"

"In a bit, babe," Max answers, and I involuntarily look at his phone. Did he want to stay up so he could keep texting with Courtney? My feet feel heavy as I march up the stairs, holding back my tears as I make the bed with our new orange duvet before lying down and pulling it tightly around me, still seeing the bright color in my head when I close my eyes.

CHAPTER FOURTEEN

....

Max is fumbling with his necktie when I come out of the bathroom the next morning. "Want some help with that?" I ask, but start adjusting the silk into a wide knot before he can answer. I glance from the dark gray tie into his eyes, our chests almost touching as I straighten the fabric, trying to muster the confidence to ask him what I spent last night's sleepless hours thinking about—a question I'm still not completely sure I want the answer to.

"Thanks," he mumbles as he studies something on his phone. "I'm in a hurry . . . need to get into the office—it's a big day."

Because it's Courtney's first day?

I raise my eyebrow but let his mention pass. "Speaking of *big days* . . ." I pause, watching Max pull on his nicest navy-blue suit jacket, the one that changes the color of his eyes into a deeper shade of green. Had he selected that for her?

"Have you seen my keys?" Max rushes out of the bedroom to hunt for them, his eyes still glued to his phone.

"Max—before you go, I wanted to ask you something." I take the stairs two at a time after him, my fuzzy pink slippers making a squeaking sound with each step.

"Yeah?" he yells back as I hear him sifting through a drawer in the kitchen, cursing under his breath.

"Where did you last see them?" I ask. It wasn't like him to lose anything—*ever.*

"In the ignition when I was driving home last night," he snaps, then stops his ransack of the junk drawer and gives me a sorrowful look. "Sorry—can you drop me off on your way out?" he says, his tone softer.

"Just take my car," I answer without thinking and dangle my keys in front of him, watching the stress disappear from his face like the foam dissolving into a hot latte as he folds his hand around them.

"How are you going to get to work?"

"I'm sure your keys are around here somewhere. I'll find them and take yours," I assure him. "And I know you're in a rush, but before you go, I have a quick question."

"Shoot," he says, but starts striding toward the front door and I trail behind like a puppy dog clamoring for a treat.

"You said today was a *big day,* which got me thinking about, you know, *ours* and those very big vows we need to write. I just wanted to check in and see how yours were coming—" I clasp my hands behind my back as I wait for his response.

"They're done!" he says proudly. "Been finished for a while now."

He has them written? He had something to write? Maybe I haven't lost him yet.

"Wow, I'm impressed!" I break into an uncontrollable grin as the pendulum swings back toward hope again. I lightly kiss his lips, tasting his peppermint toothpaste.

"You seem surprised," he remarks as he grabs his messenger bag and slings it over his chest.

I reach over and push a flop of hair away from his forehead. "No—well, yes—but only because I haven't even started mine."

"Have you met me? Have you met you?" He laughs, and for a moment, I feel like *us* again as we banter. "Of course I'm done and you're not, Ms. Perfectionist!"

He was right. I was often paralyzed by projects. My overwhelming desire to make them perfect caused me to fall behind as I considered all the ways I could tackle them. And Max was always ahead of schedule—he was the guy who filed his taxes by February 1.

"I can't wait to hear them!" I say quickly before I can pull the words back, watching his face for any signs that I might not ever get that opportunity. But his expression is unreadable.

"No peeking!" is all he says as he strides out the front door.

"Of course not," I lie, heading straight for his journal the moment he's gone.

I run my hands over the soft brown leather notebook that conceals Max's inner thoughts, flipping it back and forth in my hand, debating whether I should open it, whether I should be reading the words he's written. Even though they are intended for me, it feels wrong. But this could be my only chance to discover what is in Max's heart leading up to the wedding—and that outweighs the guilt. I peel back the cover and my eyes fall on his familiar loopy handwriting. When I'd first seen his signature, the even shape of his letters reminded me of the words I'd traced in the fourth grade when trying to achieve my cursive license. "You write like a girl!" I'd exclaimed, letting out a cackle, then throwing my hand over my mouth. He'd smiled, his eyes laughing with me as he'd grabbed a Sharpie off his desk, a piece of paper out of his printer tray, and wrote *I love you, Katie* in his big, curvy scrawl. I still have it.

Kate,

Everything with you has always been so easy. From the night we met, I've known our relationship was special, that you were different. When I look into your eyes I know we have the solid foundation we need to stand the test of time—that we will go as far as we want in life, that we can do anything together. There's a comfort in knowing I can count on you, I can count on us. That we can go the distance—that we're built to last.

I love you more than words can say.

I set the notebook back in the bottom drawer of his desk, his words stinging my heart, even though I'm not sure what I had been expecting. Max has never been the most romantic guy, always choosing to let Hallmark do the talking for him on special occasions, his name signed firmly at the bottom of the card. And it's not like what he'd written was *terrible*, but it had felt like reading one of those greeting cards—with all the right things printed inside of them, but they were not *his* words. I had always been confident that he loved me, and had come to accept that like many men, he struggled with translating his feelings onto paper. But as I'd read his vows, I wish he could've dug a little deeper just this once, could've tried to come up with something that was intimate between us, that didn't feel so generic. Unless this was the best he could do—saying he was comfortable, that we were built to last. Making me sound more like a Subaru than his future wife.

• • •

With the vows imprinted in my mind like a message written across the sky, I'd tried to concentrate on finding Max's keys. I'd tossed the couch cushions, searched the laundry hamper, and even checked the freezer, but still couldn't locate them, finally giving up and calling a cab. I knew the keys were probably dangling right in front of me, but I was too distracted. I was bothered, not just because the vows felt stiff, but because I wasn't sure I could do a better job with my own. Max didn't know this, but on the night of our rehearsal dinner, my vows still weren't written. I'd spent months thinking about what I should say, but I couldn't decide what combination of words would properly encapsulate *us*. And now I wonder if there was a deeper reason why the pages in my own journal had remained blank. Did I not have the right words because *we* weren't right?

The yellow taxi pulls up and I slip into the backseat. The driver swivels her head around and smiles at me, revealing the familiar gap between her teeth. "Where to, Kate?"

"It's you," I say as one of her toffee-colored curls slips out from under her tweed driving cap. I quickly recover from the surprise of seeing her. "I'm meeting my mom at Grub on Seward Street for breakfast."

"Sounds good," she says, and makes a U-turn.

"I'm so glad you're here—I have a million questions I want to ask you!" I exclaim.

"You can ask one."

"Just one?" I whine.

I meet Ruby's eyes in the rearview mirror and she narrows them at me. "Fine," I concede.

As I take several minutes to collect my thoughts, staring out the window at the 10 freeway, I realize there's only one issue that's been pressing on my mind. "Why do my wishes keep pushing Max and Courtney closer together instead of driving them apart?" I ask, my heart thudding as I wait for the answer. I have my own theories, but I pray that none of them are right.

Ruby pulls the taxi to a stop in front of Grub and shifts her body toward the backseat. "Fate's a lot like Mother Nature. Sometimes you just can't mess with it."

"So are you saying I can't use this power to get Max back—my life back?" I ask.

"That's another question." Ruby looks at me sympathetically.

"Please," I plead as I grip the back of her seat. "I can't keep fighting if I know it won't change anything."

Ruby holds my gaze for a minute before answering, ignoring the person in the brightly colored wrap dress standing impatiently outside my door, waiting to get in. "You do have the power to change things, but not everything is as simple as you want it to be. Just have a little faith." She reaches over and puts her hand over mine. "Now, please, get out before this person loses her mind." She laughs as the woman throws up her hands in frustration.

Still in a daze from Ruby's cryptic message, I find my mom sitting at a small table in the back of the restaurant, her face glowing from her day spent at the spa yesterday. I'd cringed when I'd read her post on Facebook:

My masseur didn't believe my real age. I had to show him my ID! Talk about happy ending for me! Wink, wink!

She'd posted a picture she'd taken of herself clad only in a white cotton towel with her arm flung around the man who'd just massaged her.

"Hey," I say, sliding into the seat across from her.

"Sweetie, it's so good to *finally* see you. I took the liberty of ordering for you," she says, and I glance at my phone. Less than ten seconds and she's already giving me a guilt trip. That has to be a record.

"I know—I'm sorry it's been a while. Things have been really hectic—"

"With the wedding planning? Do you need help?"

In more ways than you could possibly know.

I shake my head. "Stella has everything under control," I say as I imagine her scrambling to find the Samoan fire-knife dancing team that Max just added to the list.

My mom's face brightens at my answer. "I saw on Facebook that your wedding gifts were starting to arrive. You posted that adorable picture holding the oddly shaped package, asking everyone to guess what they thought was inside. I still think it's a Roomba!" she says, clapping her hands together.

I think back to the photo I'd made myself post yesterday, wanting so much to live my life as if I didn't know what was around the corner. Last time around, I would've blissfully held the box with a smirk on my face as I tried to guess its contents, excited to see what funny items my friends would speculate could be inside. But this time, the whole thing felt forced.

As my mom laughs at her own guess, her pale blue eyes close slightly, exposing the fine lines around them. Lines I think make her more beautiful, but that she's been considering eyelid surgery to remove. I'd argued when she'd first announced her plans, trying to convince her that the collagen fillers she'd already been getting in her upper cheeks and forehead were unnecessary. I was worried that one cosmetic surgery would lead to another and she'd end up looking like one of those Botox-addicted Real Housewives. But I couldn't tell her that—since my dad left, she'd been convinced he married Leslie so he could have a young trophy wife on his arm.

Courtney comes to mind. I had always confided in Jules about how deep my mom's denial ran when it came to my dad.

Now I wondered if I was going to follow in her footsteps, clamoring for something that had already disappeared right before my eyes. "Can I ask you something?"

She nods, sipping her coffee.

"What was it about Dad—why did you want to marry him?"

"He was *everything*," she answers immediately.

"What do you mean?" I ask, mixing a packet of sugar into my latte.

"He was everything I'd ever wanted—all of the good parts of someone rolled up into one." She smiles, but it quickly shifts into a frown. "Well, before he met *her*."

I've often wondered if my mom even remembers the marriage as it actually was or if she's become a revisionist historian since Dad left, not wanting to accept that his love for someone else could ever be deeper than his love for her.

"Why do you ask?" My mom eyes me suspiciously as the server sets down a fruit plate in front of her and a plate of scrambled egg whites in front of me. I look around as if the rest of my order is going to arrive—the bacon and hash browns I would've requested. But I knew better. My mom eats like a bird and wants me to as well.

"I came across Max's vows . . . and, I don't know, they just didn't make me feel all warm and fuzzy inside," I say, suddenly thinking of my furry pink slippers that I'd had since college and wore year-round because they were comfortable. That's the same word Max had used to describe us in his vows. Was he right? And if so, was that even a negative? What was wrong with a relationship that was safe and easy?

"Warm and fuzzy?" my mom scoffs.

"I guess when I read them I thought they would show that he *gets me*."

"*Gets* you?" she repeats, cocking her head to the side in confusion as if I've just spoken Japanese.

"I just expected his thoughts to be more personal—and he'd laugh and maybe even cry as he read them, because they'd include all these nuances that maybe no one else would even understand—our little inside jokes, you know?"

"What else did he write?" My mom leans forward.

I pause, seeing his words scrawled across the page of his journal. "He said we were *built to last.*"

A look of relief passes over her face. "You are! You and Max are solid. He loves you and will take care of you—something that counts for more than you know. Honey, I think you're putting way too much weight on this. There's no rule book for writing vows. You just express what's in your heart. And whatever you read—that's what's in his."

Maybe that's the problem. There doesn't seem to be much in there.

"Wasn't he also supposed to actually vow something?" I ask. He hadn't promised anything.

"Like what? To love you in sickness and health?" She laughs, throwing her head back like she's just delivered a hysterical joke. "I've taken care of you after you got food poisoning—you're not exactly a model patient!"

I roll my eyes. "Let's change the subject," I say, stabbing my eggs with my fork and ignoring my mom's look as I sprinkle them with salt. "What about you?"

"What about me?" She pops a blueberry into her mouth.

"Do you ever think about getting back out there?"

"Please." She shakes her head forcefully. "I'm perfectly fine on my own." She arches an eyebrow, which reveals no wrinkles in her forehead, the skin tight from her last Botox injection.

"Are you though?" I press, and watch her fidget in her chair. She's never been one to delve into emotionally heavy topics, preferring to keep the conversation more superficial, much like her Facebook feed. *This is wonderful! Look at me! I'm so happy!* But in person, I could easily detect the underlying sadness in her that often bordered on bitterness.

"Will you stop—of course I am! I'm retired and living quite well after some savvy stock market investments. Thank you, Google!" She laughs. "Not to mention, I'm in the best shape of my life. Have you seen these guns?" She curls her bicep. "But most importantly, I've got you. What more could I possibly need?"

Love? Happiness that's real, not manufactured?

"What if the perfect man came into your life? Wouldn't you be open to the possibility of a relationship?"

My mom's eyes mist with tears, but she looks away quickly, and when her gaze returns to me, she's composed again. "After the broken heart I suffered, I prefer a life where my happiness isn't up to someone else."

"I'm not saying you have to get married again, Mom—or even fall in love—but you're not even up for having coffee with someone?" I ask, thinking that I could wish for her to meet a nice guy—to give her what I know she's just too scared to do on her own.

"It's never just coffee, honey," she says, shaking her head. "Now back to you. You've got a great thing with Max—a guy that a thousand women would line up around the block to be with. The romance and the fire and all that stuff you wish he'd written in his vows—those aren't the things that ensure you'll grow old together. Just because he's not Robert Frost doesn't mean he's not the right guy for you. Learn from my mistakes, Kate. Don't take your relationship for granted, because one day he could be gone. Or worse, he could end up in the arms of someone else."

The truth of her words strikes me hard. I think of Courtney and her *big day* at Max's company. Her new job that I'm indirectly *or directly* responsible for, despite my best efforts to keep her away from Max. My mom was right, I needed to hang on to him. But I couldn't get the word Ruby had used out of my mind—*fate*. Because what I really needed to know was why the universe had sent me on this journey in the first place—and there was really only one way to find out. I had to stop using magic and let fate take its course—no matter what the outcome.

CHAPTER FIFTEEN

....

"What the hell?" I say as Liam pulls up to the curb in a jet black convertible Porsche.

"What?" he says with a broad smile as I slide into the passenger seat. "It's just a car."

"What happened to Frank?" I ask, referring to the white Ford Explorer I had helped him pick out and name almost ten years ago. "Frank Ford" had always had a special place in my heart, never so much as blinking a headlight when I threw up all over his backseat after my twenty-fifth birthday party in Venice Beach.

"Don't worry, Frankie is just fine—he's resting comfortably in my garage. This baby is just a loaner."

"Let me guess. From Nikki?" I blanch as I say her name. Had she made Liam feel like Frank Ford wasn't good enough to be seen in? I feel offended for Frank *and* Liam.

Liam gives me a sideways look as he pulls into traffic, cutting off a large SUV and accelerating into the left turn lane for the freeway. I had called him for a ride home after Max had taken my car this morning. I had been hoping Max would check in to see if I had found his keys, but I hadn't heard from him all day, causing my imagination to run wild about what was going on between him and Courtney at work. On a seemingly endless loop, images of the two of them flirting flashed through my mind. I saw Max *accidentally* brushing Courtney's arm and feeling an electric pulse shoot through him as he guided her down the narrow hallway to the conference room where she'd meet the others on the creative team. I pictured her making excuses to stop by his office to find out where she could stock up on staplers and hole punches. I could even see Max lingering in her doorway, then casually inviting her to lunch at his favorite bistro just around the corner. Finally, when I couldn't take it anymore, I'd closed my office door, squeezed my eyes shut until darkness enveloped me, and yelled, "Stop!" at the top of my lungs

"I thought you'd be happy. If I recall, you're the one who set this whole relationship in motion," Liam says, raising his voice over the sounds of the freeway. I grab my hair and twist it into a braid to block the wind's effect.

"I'm sorry," I say, boosting my voice to match his. "I am happy for you. I just don't want her to change you."

"To *charge* me?" he asks, an incredulous look spreading across his face. "Why would she *charge* me? She's not a prostitute!"

"*Change* you!" I yell as we pass a semi, the exhaust from its tailpipe stinging my nostrils. "Like this!" I spread my arms wide. "Speeding down the 405 in a flashy sports car? Screaming at each other over the motorcycles and trucks? This isn't you! You don't even like sitting on the patio at the Newsroom Cafe! Because too many cars pass by on Robertson!"

Liam says nothing as he navigates off the freeway, pulling over onto a side street and pressing a button that efficiently brings the top up around us. "Do you really think driving a

Porsche for a few days is going to change me, Kate? You think I'm that shallow?"

"No, of course not," I say with my head down. "It's just, look at you—four-hundred-dollar Gucci sunglasses and, wait, is that a Chanel shirt?" I ask, remembering the Calvin Klein model wearing a similar one when he came into the office. "And you showed up in my Facebook feed today—on the *Us Weekly* page! They were asking everyone what they thought of Nikki's new 'man candy'! How can you say this relationship, as you call it, isn't changing you?" I think about the women in my office who had swooned over the picture of Liam online, me shaking my head as I pored over the comments on that post instead of the mound of paperwork that had piled up in Courtney's absence, each sexual remark about his good looks making me more uncomfortable than the last. When I had made this wish for Liam, I hadn't considered the impact it might have on him or our friendship. If I had, I might not have gone through with it.

Liam puts the car into gear and takes a sharp right at the corner toward my house. "Listen, I get how all this looks, but I'm not the one who's doing the changing." He gives me a pointed look.

"What is *that* supposed to mean?" I ask.

"You know exactly what it means."

"I'm not making *that* many changes," I argue.

"Oh, really? Then please tell me how that hideous ensemble I'm supposed to wear to the wedding arrived at my house yesterday? The Kate I know wouldn't make her worst male enemy wear linen!"

It was true—I had shipped Liam's new best man outfit to his house because I couldn't face him. I had written *Wearing this without question will be considered payment for "setting you up" with Nikki* on a yellow Post-it, but knew I was going to catch shit for it anyway. "It's just a pair of pants and a shirt. I'm just trying to show Max I'm trying. That I care."

Liam parks the car in front of my condo and turns to me, his eyes suddenly softer. "I know how much you want this, so I'm going to cut you some slack. But please, remember something."

"What?" I say, surprised to see two silhouettes through the sheer drapes hanging from my front window.

"If he doesn't want you exactly the way you are, is he really worth having?"

"Spoken by the man in the two-thousand-dollar Chanel shirt." I laugh quietly, but Liam doesn't join me.

"I'm serious, Kate. This isn't a game. This is the rest of your life we're talking about."

"Point taken," I say as I lean over and kiss his cheek. "Thank you. For the advice and the ride."

"You're welcome. And just so you know, Jules and I are not changing a damn thing about your bachelorette party next weekend, and won't be making you sport some ugly-ass Hawaiian getup—even though it is very, very tempting!" He laughs before adding, "Unless it involves a short straw skirt. Hmm . . . maybe that's exactly what we should do." He winks.

"Not likely," I smile. I had been so consumed with all the changes for the wedding I had totally forgotten that my bachelorette party was only a week away. My last one had been such a blast. I had felt so happy as Jules, Courtney, Liam, and I danced the night away, the cheesy veil they snapped into my hair swinging around me like a gymnast's ribbon. I try not to think about what it will feel like this time as we celebrate something that might not happen alongside the person who wants to take it all away from me.

I step out of the car and wave to Liam as he speeds off to dinner with Nikki, an event that will no doubt be chronicled online tonight by TMZ. Before he drove away, he invited me to a *Los Angeles* magazine party in Nikki's honor the week before the wedding. "I'll come if you promise to wear a shirt that costs less than my wedding dress," I had joked, blowing a kiss in his direction as he deliberately gunned the accelerator pedal.

I open the door quietly, still wondering who is inside with Max. I catch my breath as I see him and Courtney cracking open a bottle of champagne in the kitchen, Max motioning the bottle toward Courtney and acting like he's going to shoot the cork at her. I knew this joke well. He had done the same thing to me the night we got engaged.

I drop my bag on the table to alert them to my presence, and they both look up at the same time. I search their faces for deception, guilt, *anything* that will tell me what's really going on between them, but I see nothing. Max doesn't jump away from her like he's doing something wrong, and she holds my gaze as she walks over, gives me a tentative hug, and tells me I'm just in time to toast with them.

"What are we toasting?" I ask through gritted teeth, suddenly remembering the last time Courtney was here, just a few nights before the wedding. I'd invited her over, ironically, to celebrate. We'd just landed a new client and I'd splurged on a bottle of wine that we'd shared while talking for hours on the patio. As I look back now, it's surprising that Courtney never seemed *off* or like her mind was elsewhere. Max had gone for a late run and had come out to say hello, shirtless and sweaty, just as Courtney was leaving. "It's pretty dark out there, let me walk you out," Max had suggested, and I'd been proud to be engaged to such a gentleman. I'd hugged Courtney tightly and smiled as she and

Max disappeared through the front door. As I got ready for bed, my body tingling from the wine and feeling thankful that I had such a great friend and fiancé, had they been outside planning their future?

"Courtney's first day—it went really well!" Max answers, and suddenly it's clear why I never heard from him all day. He was too busy picking out champagne at the corner liquor store with Courtney. "She even wooed Ernie!" he says with a laugh, referring to the notoriously prickly CEO.

"Fantastic," I say halfheartedly as Max fills another flute and hands it to me. "Where did you find your keys?" I ask, pointing to where they are sitting on the counter.

"Oh, I'm so stupid. They were actually in my messenger bag the whole time!" He looks at Courtney and they laugh together as if they're sharing an inside joke, and I imagine him telling her the story as they sipped their coffee in the break room, Courtney batting her eyelashes and giggling at his forgetfulness. "Sorry, honey," he adds, almost as an afterthought.

"No problem," I repeat limply. "Liam gave me a ride home," I add, to no one in particular.

"Oh, good," Max says breezily, clinking Courtney's glass and then mine. I take a seat at the counter and listen as they regale me with every story of the day, from the way Courtney's new boss kept calling her Cathy to the food truck that had pulled up outside their office building with the most *mouthwatering* Kobe beef sliders you've ever tasted. I nod my head at the right intervals and try not to hyperventilate. I had caused this. I tried to tear them apart, but instead I had brought them even closer together. It seemed the more I tried to hold on to Max, the further he was slipping away, like a thread that continued to unravel. And, as I observe Courtney and Max laughing about a painful regulatory meeting they had suffered through, it's becoming harder to believe that they weren't going to end up together. Perhaps this was why people wouldn't want to know when they were going to die. Because how could you truly live knowing the end was coming?

Several glasses of champagne later, Courtney finally heads home, but not before Max offers to carpool with her the next day. "Lovely," I say under my breath as they debate whose iPod they are going to listen to.

"So you like having Courtney at work?" I state the obvious as we head upstairs to our bedroom, Max taking the steps two at a time like a schoolboy.

"Of course," he says innocently. "You know that better than anybody. Aren't you the one that used to say she was the only thing that made your job bearable?"

Yes. That was true. But that was before she blew up my life and took you with it.

"Oh, yeah, she's great," I say, trying to hold back the sarcasm that's been bubbling just beneath the surface all night.

"What's going on with you?" Max sits down on the bed. "You seem annoyed. Is this because I didn't pick you up from work?"

I sit next to him and grab his hand. "No, although that would have been nice."

"I'm sorry. I guess I never really worry about you that way."

"What does that mean?"

"I mean, you're probably the most independent girl I've ever met," he says. "Sometimes I'm not even sure that you need me." He laughs, but his eyes are full of questions.

My pulse quickens. Had I made Max feel like I didn't rely on him? I tighten my grip on his hand. "I do need you. More than you know," I finish, a tear escaping from the corner of my eye as I think about the way he had been *so willing* to walk away from me.

Max wipes the tear from my cheek. "You know, you could have just asked me to come get you. And I didn't mean anything by the independent thing. I was just saying that I knew you'd find a ride home. That's all."

"Are you sure?" I ask. "Because, Max, I want you to know, you can tell me anything. Even if you think it will hurt me. Let's get it all out into the open now, before the wedding."

Max pauses and I can almost see the wheels in his head turning. I imagine him starting to feel the buds of something with Courtney, but he's telling himself that it doesn't mean anything. He shakes his head slowly at me, probably squelching the little tweak in his heart he feels when he's with her, deciding it isn't worth throwing everything we have away—yet.

"Maybe it will be good for us to get away to Big Bear this weekend?" I ask hopefully. The words *I feel like I'm losing you* sit at the tip of my tongue, but I'm too afraid to say them out loud. Here I am, sitting with the man I love, the one I'm supposed to marry, the rest of my life hanging in the balance, and I can't say those simple words—too paralyzed by fear to ask Max how far he's slipped from my grasp. To discover if he even wants me to try to pull him back up. Instead I bury my head deep in his neck, hoping he'll hear the words in my heart that I can't say out loud.

"Yes," he finally says. "It will be good for us."

CHAPTER SIXTEEN

....

While packing for our trip to Big Bear, I thumb the Lycra fabric of my sunflower-yellow bikini, my mind wandering back to the morning we left for Maui. Max had just returned home from his morning run and I'd just reopened my suitcase so I could pack this very swimsuit, along with a matching cover-up and oversized straw hat. He'd found me straddling the black and red Tumi wheeled bag, pressing my weight into it as I attempted to zip it closed. I'd looked up and he was leaning against the doorjamb, his cheeks ashen, not flushed like they normally were after completing a six-mile run.

"What's wrong?" I'd jumped up from the bag and the top had sprung open, revealing the straw hat that was now smashed. I shook my head and pulled it out.

"Just watching you," he'd said, taking a long drink from his bottle of water.

"Oh?" I'd said, still staring at his face, an unreadable look in his eyes.

"You're beautiful, you know that? Inside and out."

"Why thank you. You're not so bad yourself."

"Kate. I love you."

"I love you too," I'd said, confused by his solemn tone. I'd leaned in to kiss him, but missed his mouth because he'd grabbed me, enveloping me in a bearlike hug.

I'd squirmed out of his grasp, the sweat from his chest having created a large spot on my sundress. "What's gotten into you— you know we're going to be late if you don't get in the shower. And now I have to change out of this!" I shook my head at him. "We have a five-and-a-half-hour flight to snuggle!"

He'd smiled and said, "You're right, we do."

But as I'd turned to attend to my bag, a pair of espadrilles having now spilled out from it, I caught Max's expression from the corner of my eye—he looked sad.

As I thought back, it had been another warning sign I clearly hadn't wanted to see. So much so that I'd blocked it out until now—the bikini unlocking the memory. I toss the bathing suit aside and pack a simple black one-piece instead, not wanting to relive that moment, the one where he might have told me he couldn't go to Maui at all, if I'd been paying a little more attention. If listening to him had been more important than how many pairs of shoes I could shove into my suitcase.

First thing tomorrow morning, we'd be driving up the winding road toward the city at the top of the mountain where we first fell in love, the large green pine trees whirling by, the expansive canyons overwhelming, and hopefully the silence in the car wouldn't be deafening. In the past few days, our conversations had been limited, us becoming more like ships passing in the night as our work schedules became increasingly demanding so we could each take the two weeks off for the wedding and honeymoon. Max's devotion to work didn't concern me—last time around, he'd spent the same amount of hours in the office and Courtney wasn't working there. And even though she was now a fellow employee, I got the sense that she'd been in training most of the time and they only saw each other occasionally in the halls or the parking lot, that I had maybe let my imagination get the best of me. But it did concern me that when I did see Max—passing each other as one of us stepped out of the shower and the other into it, or in the kitchen as we'd silently eaten from our Styrofoam take-out containers—our exchanges felt stilted. I felt out of the loop in his life, wishing he'd give me more details about his days, more information about how he was feeling. As I'd complained about how Magda now wanted *me* to find a replacement for Courtney, he'd moved his head up and down as if he was listening but offered nothing more. I worried that he was keeping *everything* bottled because he was scared that if he uttered even one word, every thought he was having would cascade out of his mouth. Including his doubts about me. So I hadn't pushed, hoping that our trip to Big Bear would organically inspire us to talk the way we used to—and maybe remind him of who we used to be together.

• • •

"Kate, when will you have candidates for me to meet?" Magda's piercing voice barks through the phone later that day while I'm nestled in my office, listening to my relaxation playlist on my iPod. I hold the receiver away from my ear as she hollers about how bad this gap in our executive staff is going to make our firm look to our clients.

The truth was, I hadn't found anyone who even halfway compared to Courtney. Her work ethic, the blend of humor and heart she injected into her pitches, and her innate awareness of what clients wanted were incomparable. I hated to admit it, but I missed her. Not the part of her that wanted to take Max from me, but the part that made my work life easier. I stare at the résumés on my desk, the endless stream of people who would kill for this job, none of them coming close to having the experience or talent Courtney does. "Are you sure you don't want to rehire Courtney?" I hear myself asking.

"No fucking way!" Magda cries.

"Okay, then," I say evenly. "I'll keep looking."

"Try LinkedIn," she screams as she hangs up the phone.

"Gee, thanks for the hot tip," I say into the dial tone.

I stare out the window and wonder what my life would be like if I'd just accepted that Max wasn't the man I was supposed to marry. There were so many things I'd never know. Like if I'd still be working at the agency with Courtney or if one of us would've quit because the tension between us would've been insurmountable. Or if Max and Courtney would've ended up in a relationship or quickly discovered that once their secret feelings were revealed, the excitement was gone. And there was also no way of knowing if I would've been miserable without Max, or, after experiencing some time alone, would've discovered I was happier without him. But I'd never find out if that was the case because, for whatever reason, I was given a second chance. And it's this opportunity that has been the sliver of hope I've been clinging to—that tiny ray of light shining through the crack that reminds me there is still a chance. That the universe has made a mistake and is trying to right itself.

My phone buzzes with a notification. Callie Trenton from college has commented on my oddly shaped wedding gift picture. *It's definitely a cake pop maker! They're all the rage!* I click over to her page and there's a series of pictures from her latest family vacation to the Bahamas. As I scroll through her album, I feel that twinge of jealousy in my chest and it slowly builds until I finally have to close out of Facebook completely.

"She's only posting the best parts of her life," Jules says adamantly when I call her and tell her about the pictures—the last was of her swollen belly, revealing that she's expecting her third baby.

"She has a lot of 'best parts,'" I remark.

"How old are her kids again? I can't remember," Jules asks.

"I don't know."

"You practically stalk this woman's page and you can't even ballpark it? Come on!"

"Okay—maybe they're eight and ten?"

"Oh, honey, let me tell you something. That is definitely an oops baby!" Jules squeals.

"How do you know?" I ask, my mind flashing back to Callie's hands wrapped around her slightly protruding belly, the sun setting behind her making her look almost angel-like, the caption "Heaven on Earth" seemingly fitting.

"I'm looking at her page now and I'm just telling you that there is *no way* she and her husband looked lovingly into each other's eyes after eight years and said, *You know what? Our life is just a little too easy right now. We are sleeping through the night, everyone's potty trained and can basically fend for themselves, so, hey, let's go through the newborn and toddler hell all over again!* That would be like Ben and me getting pregnant right now. I love my two children. But three? No thank you. I can't even fathom adding a pet to our household! I can't be held responsible for one more living thing—not even a goddamn houseplant!"

"Aren't you being a little harsh?" I ask with a laugh, caught off guard by Jules' tone.

"I'm just saying that no matter what the *real* story is with that baby, Callie has the same bullshit in her life we all do. She's just not posting about it. The same way I'm not and you're not.

I mean, look at your mom. We both know she's bitter half the time about something that happened twenty years ago, but if you believe only what she writes on her Facebook feed, she's the most secure woman in the world." Jules giggles. "Like that one from today—"

I sigh, remembering my mom's most recent post that laser hair removal was the best thing since sliced bread.

"So, Big Bear tomorrow! You excited?" Jules asks, and I'm thankful she's changed the subject, although this one is no less painful.

"I'm nervous. I feel like this is it. That if I can't get through to him this weekend, it's over."

"You will. You just need some time alone together," she says, and pauses, and I can sense her unspoken words hanging in the air.

"What?" I ask. "I can *feel* you thinking over there. Just say whatever's on your mind."

Jules exhales before answering, as if trying to decide if I can handle her internal dialogue. Finally, she breaks the silence. "Marriage is hard, Kate. *My* marriage is hard. Even when you get off on the right foot, you have to always keep fighting for it. The minute you stop, it starts to slip away from you again. So if this is what you want—"

"It is," I interrupt.

"Then fight like hell for it, and then whatever happens, you can walk away without any regrets."

I pause, letting her words settle—knowing they aren't just for me. Now that I had seen the cracks that existed in her marriage, I wondered how long they had been there. Maybe if I had looked just a little harder, paid a little more attention, if I hadn't been so self-consumed, I would've seen her distress sooner.

"Jules, you know you can talk to me about anything, right?"

"You've got your hands full with your own problems, girl-friend!" She laughs, but I hear her voice break slightly.

"True." I echo her laugh. "But, seriously, Jules, I was so wrapped up in myself that I didn't even notice my fiancé was falling for one of my closest friends. So I'm here to tell you that my head is officially out of my ass. And I don't want to miss anything else important that could be going on with someone I love. So I'm here for you. Okay?" I pause, hoping she'll quickly fill the silence with the story of whatever she's been going through—that as her words spill out of her, she'll feel an instant release and she won't feel so alone. That just talking to me will help.

I hear her take a deep breath. "Don't worry, my problems will still be here after we solve yours—we can deal with them then, okay? Oh shit!" she cries out.

"What is it?" I exclaim.

"I have to go—my cheese soufflé is about to collapse. And I'm late to pick Evan up from piano. Or is it soccer? Dammit! Good luck this weekend! Love you!"

"Love you too," I say after she's gone, and hope that the cheese soufflé is the only thing collapsing in her life.

• • •

"It's exactly the same—they haven't changed a thing," I say, dropping my weekender bag on the auburn-colored chenille chair in the corner and pulling open the curtains to reveal the dark blue water of Big Bear Lake. The ride up the mountain had started off slow but then had gone quickly, me peppering Max with intelligent-sounding questions about the latest product his company was working on, thanks to the incessant Google searching I had done the night before.

I feel Max wrap his arms around my waist and rest his chin on my shoulder. "It is spectacular. Are you up for kayaking?" He holds out a pamphlet that he must have grabbed from the lobby.

I can think of about fifty things I'd rather do.

"Maybe . . . I was thinking of popping this open first." I reach into my bag and pull out a bottle of wine. "And then opening these." I grab the waistband of his jeans and guide him toward the bed, pushing the colorful quilt onto the floor, trying not to search his face for the same desire I'm feeling, not wanting to read into his every touch. But to my relief, Max engulfs me with an urgency I hadn't seen in months, his teeth grazing my ear as he throws me down onto the bed, not even bothering to undress me, instead just pulling my skirt up around my waist and sliding inside me, both of us calling out when we climax together a few minutes later before collapsing onto the floor, still entangled in each other's arms. For the first time since I had been given my power, I forgot about Courtney and what happened at the rehearsal dinner. I forgot to be scared that Max might do it to me again. For those brief wonderful moments, I forgot myself.

"Don't take this the wrong way," Max says, brushing a strand of hair away from my face. "But that was amazing—it felt new, like it used to, in the beginning."

"I couldn't agree more," I say as I nuzzle up to him.

"I can't believe I wanted to go kayaking instead of this!" He laughs and runs his hand down my leg, sending ripples of excitement through me.

I rest my head on his chest, and as it rises and falls, my own breathing syncs with his. *This is us. This is who we are—two people who aren't predictable, just in sync with each other,* I think as I fall into a deep sleep.

I wake a few hours later just as the sun is setting. I pull

Max's shirt on and look out at the lake, a speedboat passing by, its wake causing waves to lap against the rocks along the shoreline.

"Hey," Max says, his voice thick from sleep.

"Hey."

"I'm starving," we say in unison and smile, our eyes locked, and I feel my mouth start to move—to curve to create the words I need to say so we can really move forward. To ask about Courtney. I want to tell him that she might be making him happy *right now*—at a confusing time for him—but I'm the woman who will make him happy *for life*. But instead I say, "I made a reservation at our place," referencing the restaurant where Max and I had dined for hours last time we were here, finishing two bottles of wine, my mouth salivating as I remember the sweet butter sauce that I had drizzled on my lobster.

"I'm definitely getting the rib eye." He sits up and pats his abdomen, and my gaze lingers on his navel.

"Can I help you?" Max teases, noticing my stare.

Without responding, I tug his shirt over my head and straddle him, kissing him long and hard until he's inside me again, my need to consume him overwhelming. I hold him tightly after we finish, threading my hand through his hair, trying to memorize the way his strands feel between my fingers.

"Look at us, you'd think we were a couple of newlyweds or something," I say without thinking, and quickly panic, not wanting to see his face contort at the mention of going through with our wedding.

"We will be soon enough!" Max says and kisses me gently on the mouth. "Not a problem for me that we're getting started early."

As he steps into the shower, I realize this is the first time since I can remember that he's talked about something that would happen between us *after* our wedding. I let the knot in my stomach loosen slightly, thinking of Jules' words. *I'm winning the fight.*

• • •

When the hostess seats us at a table by a window that overlooks the main street in the quaint downtown, I notice Max seems more relaxed than he has in a long time. After the server pours our wine, he holds up his glass. "I'd like to propose a toast," he says, the gold flecks in his eyes shining from the candlelight.

I raise my glass and wait.

"To us," he says, tapping his goblet against mine.

"To us," I mimic, then add, "To being us."

"So, Kate, I want—I need—to talk to you about something," he says slowly, and I feel my stomach twist back into a knot as I watch his face tense. Had I misread the entire situation?

"Okay," I say carefully, hoping he can't see the fear in my eyes.

"I know I've been a little distant—okay, make that *a lot* distant—lately and I owe you an explanation."

"Okay," is the only word I can manage.

"Would you two like to hear about the specials?" Our server interrupts and we must have matching looks on our faces that scream *no*, because he nods his bald head in our direction and scurries off.

"So, anyway, Kate. I've been confused. We've been so caught up in all this wedding stuff. It started to feel like"—he looks down at his glass—"like it was more about what wine we were going to serve than about us starting our life together. I began having doubts. And then, well, something happened. And I think you deserve to know."

No. I can't believe this is happening—again. Even sooner this time. My eyes fall to the black linen napkin in my lap as I try to press back the tears.

"Kate? You okay?" Max asks.

I look up and nod because I'm still too afraid to open my mouth.

"Oh, God, do you already know?" He takes a big drink of his wine.

Yes, I already know, but I will sit here patiently as you break my heart all over again.

"Max, just tell me whatever it is, please," I finally say, bracing myself for the sting of the words.

"Courtney kissed me," he says, his voice barely a whisper.

"What? When?" I ask, my voice rising. I press my mouth closed to keep from screaming.

"I did *not* kiss her back—I swear to you," he says adamantly, and I believe him. Why tell me and then lie about the details?

"Why did she kiss you?" I ask, even though I already know the answer.

"I think I might have given her the wrong impression. Not that I'm making excuses for her, but there was definitely a connection between us. I felt something in our friendship shift recently. And I'm not going to lie—it was really confusing. I started wondering if that meant there was a problem with you and me. I started thinking that if it was so easy for me to connect with someone else, then maybe that was a sign that you and I weren't meant to be." He shakes his head.

"So what happened?"

"A couple of nights ago, we were both working late, and she came into my office to ask me something about the health care plan I was enrolled in, and one minute I was telling her about why I went with a PPO instead of an HMO, and the next second, she's got her mouth pressed against mine. When I didn't kiss her back she stood there, almost shell-shocked, then stammered an apology and raced out in tears." He pauses and looks at me, but I stay silent, so he continues. "After she left, I sat there for a long time. It was almost like her kissing me lifted this heavy fog that I'd been surrounded by. I had thought my confusion was about Courtney and how I might be developing feelings for her, but then I realized it was about us. That I'd felt so disconnected from you lately. You felt it too, right? I'm not crazy?" he asks, his eyes pleading.

"It's not just you," I say quietly, trying to absorb his words. *Courtney had kissed him, and he's choosing me. Max wants me.* "I felt it too," I add, the warmth from my chest rising to my cheeks. It was here in this restaurant that we had begun. How ironic that it would also become the place where we might get the chance to start over.

"But something changed. You've been so different and we felt right again. And that's what I want—I want you. I want us." He looks at me, anxious for my response. "Kate, do you still want us?" he finally asks.

I imagine Courtney primping in the mirror of the ladies' bathroom before heading to Max's office, her heart thudding in her chest as she swiftly unbuttons the top snap of her blouse before walking through his doorway. She makes a little small talk, asks her bogus insurance question, then puckers her lips, her pink gloss shimmering as she leans in toward Max, believing her kiss will be returned, that they will get their happily-ever-after. Maybe the first time around, she got a fairy-tale ending. But this time, it was my turn. Fate had led Max back to me.

"I do," I finally say, reaching across the table to grab his hand, deciding that this is the moment when I won't let Max slip away. *Not again.*

CHAPTER SEVENTEEN

....

It's interesting how differently people can react to bad news. Some cry, some seem almost catatonic, some even laugh. I've always found the way our mind and body works to protect us from pain to be fascinating. Like after my dad left, I never saw my mom cry—not once. In fact, as his U-Haul pulled away, us both watching from the window, my mom had chuckled. Then she'd clapped her hands together and proclaimed that we should go get hot fudge sundaes at Baskin-Robbins. I hadn't known what to make of her reaction then, so I'd just followed her lead, biting back my own tears as the truck—and my secret hope that my dad wouldn't go—disappeared. And now, after hearing about Courtney's betrayal all over again, even though my heart had fallen to my feet so hard my chest actually felt empty, I wasn't going to let Max see my pain. Because I knew even though it hurt like hell right now, I'd get through it. And in the end, it meant that Max and I would be together.

Relief spreads across Max's face as he watches mine. "I—I didn't think you'd react this way. I thought for sure . . ."

"I'd be upset?" I ask, thinking the old me would've been.

The old me would've wanted to rip Courtney's plump lips right off her perfect face and then kick Max where the sun don't shine.

Max nods as he takes a long drink of his water, the color slowly returning to his pale cheeks. *He really wants this to work with me.*

"Well I'm not exactly doing cartwheels over here . . ." I pause, trying to block out the image of Courtney sitting on the edge of his desk, waiting for her chance to lean in and make her move. "But I'm glad you told me. You have no idea how much it means that you were honest." I smile, my eyes locked with Max's, feeling like I'm seeing the man I fell in love with for the first time in a long while. I remember just yesterday how my own words had sat silently inside of me when I was too afraid tell Max the thoughts that swirled around in my head. "I think the lesson learned here is we need to communicate better."

Max reaches his hand across the table and covers mine. "I agree . . . and I'm sorry."

"For what? You told her *no*. You stopped it."

Max starts to say something, then forcefully clamps his lips shut, reminding me of a puppet.

"Courtney is the one who should be sorry!" I say a little too loudly, and an elderly couple at the neighboring table look over sharply.

We both reach for a piece of warm garlic bread that the server has just set on the table before running off again, us chewing, me waiting for Max to agree, Max's brow deeply furrowed—the way it does when he's thinking hard. And I know he wants to choose his next words carefully. "She crossed a line, for sure. But we can't put it all on her. Like I said, the lines of our friendship had been temporarily blurred. I blame myself for maybe leading her on unintentionally. And I'm sorry to you—*and to her*—for that."

Max's confession sends a shiver through me as I realize how clueless I had been last time. He told me nothing had happened between them before he called off the wedding and I believed him. In fact, I can't shake the nagging feeling that somehow me knowing about their "relationship" this time around seems to have fast-tracked it. That Courtney kissed him because she could feel that I was checked in, that I wasn't going to let him go.

"I want you to know that I'm sorry too—"

"*You?* For what?" He arches an eyebrow.

"For not making us a priority. For planning the wedding instead of our life."

"Thank you for saying that, but honestly, I'm going to say something weird here and I don't want you to take it the wrong way . . ." He pauses, waiting for me to promise I won't.

"Okay, I'm listening."

"I can't get rid of this weird feeling that this needed to happen. You know, for us to make it."

I think of Ruby and her declaration that things weren't quite as simple as I wanted them to be. Maybe this is what she had meant—that the status of *all* things in my life would have to first get messy in order for them to get better.

"I think it did too."

I watch Max as he relaxes his shoulders and lowers his gaze to study his menu, feeling the tension in my neck and back fade away. I wait for a few minutes, pretending to scan the specials— the lobster ravioli, the gnocchi with sage and butter cream sauce, the filet mignon with garlic mashed potatoes—knowing I still need to broach one more subject. "So," I say delicately. "We should figure out what we're going to do about Courtney. Obviously some things need to change."

Max's brow creases, a desperate look overtaking his face. "Kate—I can't get her fired."

I chew on my lower lip, thinking of the wish I'd made, realizing now how poorly I'd handled the power I'd been given, acting like a mean girl on the playground who uses her social status to push down her classmates.

"I'm not suggesting that! She earned that job—and from what you've told me, she's a natural at it."

Max presses his lips together and nods slightly, not wanting to give Courtney too much of a compliment, even though I can tell he would under other circumstances.

"But, my friendship with her is over," I proclaim, shocking myself a little as I take my memories of her and shelve them in a box in the corner of my mind—the late nights after work when we'd grab a drink at a dive bar on Sunset just to shake off the day; the times we'd laugh so hard I'd swear I was going to pee my pants; when she found me crying in my office after my mom had told me that the clock was ticking down and I needed to find a man, not leaving until I'd promised her ten times over that I was fine.

I wait for Max's reaction, but he doesn't offer more than an attentive stare. "And yours will be too, right?"

He exhales loudly, running his fingers through his hair. "How do I do that? With her working at my office now?" He rubs his temples. "Even the past two days have been awkward, me avoiding her like the plague."

"You obviously have to be professional, but no more concerts, no more champagne parties in our kitchen." I raise an eyebrow.

"No way—strictly business," he says simply.

"And if she does corner you about it—just tell her that you feel it's better you don't have a relationship that exists beyond the walls of your office building." I pause, thinking again about how I basically got her the job there. "Or she can just call me if she has any further questions."

Max gives me a pointed look. "What about you? How are you going to handle things with her, *really*?" he asks.

I take a second to think. I'd been so focused on winning Max back that I'd never considered what it would mean for my friendship with Courtney when I finally did. The betrayal I felt even before she'd kissed him chipped away at my heart every day, but I hadn't let myself take more than a few moments to acknowledge the pain that came along with it. Saying good-bye to Courtney would mean I'd have to confront not just her, but what she'd done to me. Because even though she did a terrible thing, she had been my friend for many years, and there was a part of me that would mourn that loss, a void that would remain long after we parted ways. "I will talk to her on Monday and disinvite her to my bachelorette party and the wedding," I say forcefully, even though I'm dreading the conversation. "Now, can we get back to us—no need to waste any more of our weekend talking about her, right?"

Max nods in agreement, then shakes his head.

"What?" I ask.

"I just can't believe how close I came to ruining everything," he says as he grabs my knee under the table.

I just smile wryly and shove a piece of bread into my mouth so I don't have to tell him I'm glad it happened, that I'm so happy he got things right this time.

• • •

The rest of the weekend passes by quickly, Max and I swallowed up in each other like we were when we first started dating, strolling hand in hand in town, sharing an ice cream sundae as we sit on the wooden bench outside of the parlor. We even get out on the lake in a kayak, me not complaining when it tips over and ruins my blowout. For the first time in as long as I can remember, our conversation flows freely, although I am careful to engage Max in topics that he is interested in and avoid the subject of wedding planning. That can wait.

I had texted Jules and Liam the second Max fell asleep the first night to let them know that we were officially "back together." Liam's response was hard to read—the same way he'd been since he started dating Nikki. He'd simply written *great news*. I'd stared at his response, wanting more, mentally urging him to add to it, to tell me that he was happy for me—that this was how it should be—*anything*. Even though he had only been with Nikki a short time, I still felt a difference in him, something I couldn't shake or reason away no matter how hard I tried.

Jules' reaction was much more enthusiastic. She'd sent a series of emojis of champagne glasses and hands clapping, then immediately asked if I could now use my remaining wishes on her. I had laughed out loud, causing Max to change positions in bed. As I watched his eyelids flutter, curious as to what he was dreaming about, I wondered how I would use them now. My whole goal had been to get Max back, and now that I had, did I still have the power to wish for more changes in my life? Did I even want to?

• • •

Waking up Monday morning back home in our bed, I lean into Max's solid body nestled against mine, his arm slung protectively around my waist, and feel a wave of emotions. A swarm of butterflies dance inside my abdomen as I think about marrying him at the end of the month, as I realize my breath will no longer catch in my throat with the fear that I won't. But I'm also nervous and, honestly, sad about the conversation I must have with Courtney. I knew that there was a part of me that would miss her. I just hoped that Max didn't feel the same way.

I pull up to Max's building at 6 p.m. sharp, when he said I would probably catch Courtney walking out. We'd texted more today than we had in a long time, ironically bonding over his time spent avoiding her. He'd confessed to spending half the day holed up in his office, terrified to run into her in the kitchen. It had felt great to banter with Max again—me joking that it must really be awkward if he was suffering caffeine withdrawal in order to avoid her. But behind our playful teasing, I still felt anxious.

I see Courtney push through the front door, her lips turned down in a frown as she glances at her phone. I fight to keep my composure, my heart racing so fast I have to take long breaths just to get my mouth to form the sound of her name. I finally call to her, and she does a double take when she sees me. She hesitates and looks in the direction of the parking garage, no doubt pondering her escape before realizing she's trapped—forcing a smile and walking hesitantly toward my open window.

"Hey," she says carefully. "Here to see Max?" she asks casually, but there's a sliver of sadness in her eyes. She pulls her sunglasses down from the top of her head to hide it.

"No," I say evenly. "I'm here to talk to you."

Courtney glances at the phone still gripped in her hand. "Oh?" she asks, clearly caught off guard. "I wish I could, but I really have to get to—"

I cut her off. "I know *everything*."

Her eyes blink rapidly behind the tinted lenses of her aviators. "I can explain."

"Good," I say as I reach over and push open my passenger door. "I can't wait—get in."

She pushes her sunglasses back up as she sits down, her eyes pooled with tears. They begin to trickle slowly like the water from a leaky faucet, then, as she starts speaking, they speed up like rainwater cascading down a gutter. "Please, Kate, you have to understand. I would never have done it unless I thought—" She stops abruptly as if finishing her sentence will break her.

"Thought what, Court?" I scoff. "Thought he was going to press his mouth over yours and give you the longest, most passionate French kiss of your life?"

"No," she says between sobs. "I mean, honestly, I felt something from him—there was a connection. At least I thought there was. God, I was so stupid. Obviously, I couldn't have been more wrong. And now I've ruined our friendship."

"Well, that was going to happen either way," I say definitively.

Her eyes register confusion, then acceptance, as she processes what I've said. "I know you probably won't believe me, but I didn't plan this. I never thought about Max that way until recently. I mean, I had just thought he was a nice guy and great for you."

"He is still a great guy for *me*. Just because you want him for yourself doesn't make him any less right for me. It just makes you a terrible friend."

She blinks several times as if I've just slapped her. "I know," she says quietly then blurts, "But . . ."

"But what?" I ask.

"But I need you to know that it was something that snuck up

on me—I never intended for this to happen. I never thought I'd feel that way about him."

Me either.

"And when I got the job with his company, I took it as a sign."

Her words hit me hard and I feel like a clamp is tightening around my chest—my own insecurities about the universe bringing them together swelling as I realized Courtney was beginning to realize it too.

Courtney quickly fills the silence. "And so I had to make this awful choice—the friend who had always been there for me, or the man I thought I was supposed to spend the rest of my life with."

"Decisions, decisions," I say sarcastically, looking down so I don't have to see the sincerity reflected in her eyes.

When I look up again, I see her lips part as if she's going to say something, but she doesn't.

"Sometimes I feel like I handed Max to you," I say. "I let you go to concerts with him while I stupidly buried my nose in some romance novel. While you guys were bonding over being adopted, I paid more attention to pictures of babies posing with dogs in my Instagram feed. I was so confident, so trusting. I was an idiot."

"No, don't say that."

"What should I say, then? I introduced Max to you before my own mother. I wanted you to meet him because I cared about your approval. I wanted you to like him. Not fall in love with him!" I slam my fist against the steering wheel, causing the horn to blare, and Courtney jumps in her seat. "And you know the worst part?"

"It gets worse?" she says under her breath.

"He's only fucking five feet eight and a half inches. Maybe

five nine. You always said you wouldn't be caught dead with a guy that *short*. With heels you are probably taller than him, no?"

"I don't wear . . ."

"That was a rhetorical question, Courtney! I don't give a fuck what shoes you had on when you were out trying to sink your claws into my fiancé," I say, seething now.

"I'm sorry," she says, her tears falling hard again.

"Me too," I whisper, taking in her porcelain skin and blood-shot eyes, hating that she still looks beautiful despite the fact she's been crying practically nonstop since she got into my car, remembering the night Max told me I had nothing to worry about. That his friendship with Courtney was just like mine with Liam.

"And now I've lost both of you," I hear Courtney saying, her voice shaking so much my instinct is to reach over and console her, so I slide toward my door just to put more distance between us. "I want you to know something, Kate. My friendship with you, every bit of it was real. Even if it doesn't feel like it right now." She wipes at her nose with the back of her hand and I reach for a package of tissues in my center console.

"Here." I jam the Kleenex into her hand.

"Thank you." She pulls a tissue out and blows her nose.

I stare at my steering wheel, letting my fingers trace the symbol in the center.

"Even if what you said is true, it doesn't matter now. What's done is done. You can't change the past," I lie, and wonder if Courtney had the chance to go back, what she would do differently.

"He won't talk to me, you know. At least you—you are giving me a chance to explain."

"That's not why I'm here. And I don't need your justification,"

186 liz fenton and lisa steinke

I say simply, but my voice sounds sharp and I notice Courtney flinch slightly. But she stays silent; even her tears have quieted.

"I just needed to tell you that you obviously can't come to the wedding or any other wedding-related event—" I stop when I see the expression in Courtney's eyes—she's feeling sorry for herself. And suddenly I remember I've seen that look before. It was when I'd found her and Max talking at my rehearsal dinner and naively asked her to take our photo. I hadn't been able to place it then—the emotion I was seeing reflected in them—but now I realize it was pity. She hadn't felt sad about what she and Max were about to do to me, she'd felt sorry for me. She had known that Max was going to leave me in just minutes *for her*, and she'd stiffly taken our picture then disappeared into the night so she didn't have to face her part in it. "But more than that, we—you and me, you and *Max*—*none of us* can continue being friends. This is not repairable."

Courtney's face turns ashen, but she simply nods. She knows what we all had is now broken. And without uttering a single word, she opens the door and steps out. I watch her walk away, wondering why I don't feel more victorious.

CHAPTER EIGHTEEN

....

Friendship is always a sweet responsibility, never an
opportunity. #truth

"I draw the line at sucking on peppermint pecker mints or penis
pops!" I laugh into the phone as Jules rambles on about the fa-
vors she's buying for my bachelorette party. I can hear her rum-
maging through the shelves of Sugar & Spice & Everything *Not
Nice* on Wilshire Boulevard, her high-pitched giggle breaking
into the conversation every few minutes as she discovers some
hilarious trinket shaped like a man's junk.

"Oh, honey, you better get on board—it's a *bachelorette party*!
You should see what I'm holding right now! Glow-in-the-dark
pecker ring toss! Oh my God, I didn't even know this existed—
they've come a long way since the penis straws we had at mine!"
We burst into laughter, us both remembering Jules dancing on
the bar as she sipped her *cock*tail—as she kept calling it—nearly
falling off the bar as she tried to mimic the scene from *Coyote
Ugly*, the night ending with us getting escorted out and hanging
our heads in mock shame on the curb until Ben came to get us.

For some reason, Jules had it in her head that she needed

to change my entire bachelorette party plan from what she'd done last time, even though the mellow night she'd organized before, when I'd simply worn a bride-to-be sash and subtle veil, had been perfect—me having no idea of the heartbreak that was waiting for me around the corner. "The only thing we need to change *this* time around"—I'd breathed heavily into the phone when I'd called Jules yesterday just minutes after my unsettling conversation with Courtney—"is *the guest list*."

Jules listened quietly as I told her about the talk Courtney and I had had in my car. As soon as I finished, she blurted, "You're a better woman than I would've been!"

"Why do you say that?"

"It would have been hard not to pop her in that gorgeous mouth of hers!"

"Don't get me wrong—it's not like I haven't thought about it. But it's weird. As angry as I am with what she did, part of me feels sorry for her too. I don't think she could feel any worse—not even if I gave her a black eye."

"If you say so."

"I do say so," I confirm. "I just want to try to move on from it all. To get on with my life with Max. To focus on our future."

"I agree. And first up on that agenda? A kick-ass bachelorette party! With penis necklaces!"

"Okay," I concede, too exhausted to argue. Besides, it seemed to make her happy—she'd been subdued lately, and planning this her way would hopefully snap her out of the funk she'd been in.

"Jules?" I try to get her attention over the beeping sounds suddenly ringing through the phone.

"Kate, you'll never believe what I just found!"

"I'm not sure I want to know," I say slowly.

"Electronic strip poker!" she squeals, and the beeps begin again.

"Jules," I say as I glance at the clock on my desk slowly ticking toward the time when I have to meet with Magda. "I've got to go. Have fun dildo shopping!"

After hanging up, I'm faced with an endless stream of emails that have appeared in my in-box during our short call. I start to click through them when a Facebook notification pops up on my screen—one of my college classmates has changed her status to married. I hit like and then scroll down my own feed, grimacing at the endless stream of celebratory announcements, staged photos, and carefully written statuses. In the past few days, I'd started to look at Facebook differently, wondering what the real story was behind the date-night photo or the pouty-lipped selfie. When I was in Big Bear, reconnecting with Max, doing things that provided endless photo ops, something had kept me from posting about it—I didn't even check in at the restaurant where we had dinner. Even though we were legitimately having a wonderful time, I held off. For reasons I didn't completely understand, I hadn't been compelled to share our private moments with other people the way I used to.

I click through my list of friends now to see if Courtney is still listed or if she's unfriended me. But as I'd expected, her name is still there, listed among those who claim they are ready and willing to receive my news every day. I wonder which of us will be the first to admit publicly that it's over.

• • •

I've always been convinced Magda has a sixth sense about what's on my mind. Whenever I'm about to do or say something, it's as if she already knows. Once, in a meeting, I parted my lips just the slightest bit and she whipped her head around and pointed at me, her long magenta fingernail hanging in the air. "Don't even think about suggesting we change the campaign slogan!" she'd warned, and I'd clamped my mouth shut, wondering how she knew exactly what I was about to say. So I've done my best to steer clear of her since I traveled back in time, keeping most of our conversations limited to the phone, worried that if I spend too much time in her presence she'll look at me and ask why I didn't use my power to wish her younger. So when I picked up the phone earlier to give her an update on how my search for a replacement for Courtney was going, I wasn't surprised that at the very same moment, my other line had blinked red and it was her telling me not to bother calling—she wanted to see me in her office this time.

I hover in her doorway at exactly 10:30 a.m. until she finally looks up from her work and curls her finger toward herself, indicating that I should enter.

I slide down into the seat across from her and wait, doing my best to keep my mind blank.

"You can stop avoiding me now," she says abruptly.

"Excuse me?" I say, using my most innocent-sounding voice.

"I know you haven't found someone to fill Courtney's shoes and—"

"I can explain."

Magda tilts her head to the side and purses her lips and I immediately stop talking.

"There's no need—in fact, you can stop looking."

"You've found someone?"

"No," Magda says simply, removing her blazer and smoothing the front of her black silk sleeveless blouse, her bony shoulders protruding from underneath it. "I've decided we don't need to hire someone. You're doing a great job picking up the slack."

I blink rapidly. There was no way I could keep up with the workload I'd been juggling. I'd been creating PowerPoint presentations rather than going to lunch and laboring after hours at home each night. I'd even had to write several emails and craft a pitch on the final day Max and I had spent in Big Bear. I knew I'd burn out if I kept this up for much longer. *Maybe I can just wish that Courtney never left in the first place?*

"But—" My pulse quickens, sending shivers of panic through my body as I start to argue why there is no way I can continue this pace—especially with the wedding coming up—but Magda cuts me off.

"My God, Kate, you look like you're about to pass out—I thought you were going to be relieved!" Magda says incredulously. "Weren't you and Courtney always in competition? Each of you trying to show me how great you were *individually*. Didn't you both desperately want my"—she waits for a moment, even though I can practically see the word she's about to say dangling from the end of her tongue like bait on a fish hook—"approval?" she finally says, dragging the word out one syllable at a time.

I sit silently, my palms wet with worry.

"And now she's gone. Don't you see, Kate? You've won."

I force myself to nod and quickly walk out, the look on Magda's face clear—there's nothing I can say that will change her mind.

I hurry back to my office feeling like I've just been punched in the gut, the to-do list in my mind so long it dizzies me. From the call I need to return to Stella to discuss a million wedding details to the three campaigns I am juggling—all with something due to the client at the end of the week—I'm overwhelmed. I duck into the bathroom to splash some water on my face, hoping the shock of cold against my cheeks will at least stop my knees from wobbling.

"Sorry, closed for cleaning," a woman's voice says from behind the stall.

I grip the sink, wondering when I'm going to feel like I'm in control again. I still can't shake the feeling that I'm riding in the passenger seat of my own life. As I stare at my sallow reflection in the mirror, a cart filled with mops is wheeled out of the stall. "Can I just splash some—" I start to say, then stop abruptly when I see Ruby's familiar curls.

Ruby pulls a yellow Caution sign out from the cart, sets it outside the bathroom door, then flips the latch and turns to me. "You don't look so good."

"Thanks." I roll my eyes at her.

"You've been a tough case, I must say."

"What do you mean by that?" I stare at her hard, willing her not to give me one of her cryptic answers.

"Well, just when I think you've chosen your path, you take a turn in the other direction."

"And that's a problem for you, why?" I demand. "Because you've never actually said why you've taken an interest in me. Is that the right word, Ruby, *interest*?" I say, unable to control the anger in my voice.

Ruby ignores my question, giving me a look I can't read.

"I'm sorry. I'm just frustrated."

"Because you have the chance to do your life over? To correct something that went wrong? That's frustrating?" Ruby puckers her lips.

"Well . . . yes and no. I mean, why won't you just tell me what I'm supposed to do? Isn't that why you keep showing up?"

Ruby shakes her head. "I'm just here to make sure you're all right."

"But not to offer me any actual help?"

Ruby ignores my dig. "As always, you can ask me *one* question," she says as she dips her mop in the bucket and starts gliding it back and forth across the linoleum floor.

I think for a moment, quickly weighing the questions sitting heavy on my mind like encyclopedias on a shelf. "Well, I'm sure you know this, but Max and I are back on the right path—" I stop, waiting for her to look up from her cleaning, but she keeps mopping. "So that means we're good, right, no more surprises? We're definitely getting married?"

Ruby finally looks up. "Yes, if that's what you want."

I feel a ball of fear slowly dislodge from my gut. "Thank you," I say, and start to leave. But something propels me to turn, and when I do, she's staring at me, mop in hand, a furrow in her brow, concern in her eyes.

• • •

The sun has set, the lampposts illuminating the street, when I finally leave the office. I'd worked through lunch and dinner, but still hadn't crossed as many things off my list as I'd hoped, my mind constantly wandering back to my interaction with Ruby, wondering if I'd imagined the look I'd seen or if it had been real.

I grip my steering wheel, but don't start the ignition, unsure of where I want to go. Finally, I pull out my phone and send a message to the only person I feel like talking to right now.

My cell dings a few moments later with a response from Liam and I smile. I'd felt so disconnected from him lately. He had always been the one person besides Jules I could absolutely count on, but lately it has felt like he is slipping away. I knew it was just because he had become so caught up in Nikki and her lifestyle, but it still made me uneasy. Everything and everyone seemed to be changing so much this time around, and I wasn't sure it was for the better. I fumble with the phone and quickly click on his name, hoping he'll say he has time to grab a beer with Elvis and me. But his message is curt.

Sorry, can't. At Nikki's.

Tears sting my eyes as I stare at her name and type several childish responses that I quickly delete, not sure why I feel so upset. Liam was just losing himself in someone in the way that people do when they are letting themselves fall. I had to get over the fear that his relationship with Nikki might mean he wouldn't be there for me anymore. That one of the few people who had always understood me might start spending that energy understanding someone else. I tap the phone against my forehead and tell myself to grow up. Liam was one of my best friends and I needed to let him be happy, even if it meant I might have to stand on my own without him.

Starting the car, I decide I'd been wrong about the place I needed to go. Taking a deep breath, I turn the wheel in the direction of my house, suddenly desperate to be wrapped in Max's strong arms, to let myself fall into him the same way Liam was falling into Nikki, to help him penetrate the silent wall that still stood between us.

CHAPTER NINETEEN

....

"I have a date," my mom announces when she appears on my doorstep the next morning, just minutes after sending me a cryptic text that she has something very important to tell me *in person*. Her lips are squished together, declaring this news as if she is telling me something impossible has happened, like she's just seen a potbellied pig flying across the sky.

That was fast. I had wished for my mom to meet someone just the night before. As I'd laid in Max's arms, I'd thought of her—no doubt sitting at home in her oversized mahogany leather chair, watching *Law & Order* reruns with her hands cupped around a mug of Earl Grey tea. It was like she'd given up on love the second my dad left—like a dancer who retires after an injury, too scared to get hurt again. So after Max fell asleep, I'd made the wish for my mom, hoping this one wouldn't backfire.

"Tell me everything—*immediately*," I say as I pull my mom by the wrist so she's standing inside my entryway.

We walk out onto my patio, my mom closing her eyes and exhaling as she sinks into one of the Adirondack chairs.

"So," I say, sitting across from her and kicking my bare feet up on an ottoman, the June sun already hot despite the fact that it's early in the morning. "Start at the beginning and don't leave anything out!"

When my mom had knocked on the door, I'd been about to put on my Nikes and go for a run before work, hoping Max would see it as a sign that I was taking a more active interest in something he loved. And who knows? Maybe once the endorphins kicked in, I'd be more ready for the long day ahead—one that included the Calvin Klein photo shoot for the neon underwear campaign. But as soon as I heard why she was there, I'd chucked my cross-trainers into the corner, deciding this conversation was going to take priority.

Since I was a little girl, I'd always been like a sponge, absorbing my mom's emotions. If she was having a bad day, I'd inevitably have one too, her testy tones and stinging observations easily rubbing off on me. If she was in a giddy mood, I'd catch that too, almost like it was a virus flying through the air. And when she was lonely, I could feel the ache in my gut so strongly it was as if I was also going through it—even last night while my head was resting on Max's chest, I'd felt that familiar twinge in my stomach that had prompted me to take action.

My mom pops her eyes open and starts talking. "Well, you know it's Thursday, and Thursday mornings are always busy, and I was on my driveway just about to get in my car to go to The Coffee Bean to get my—"

"Iced blended?" I interrupt, anxious to keep the story moving along.

"Right—and then Bill came walking up."

"Bill from next door?"

My mom blushes slightly.

"Bill who used to be married to Cheryl before she ran off with her personal trainer? That Bill?"

"That's the one," she says, the corner of her lips curving into a shy smile.

"And what did he say?" I ask, as I think of Bill, who has lived in the pale yellow house next to my mom's since back when my dad was still residing there. Bill, who used to grill out in his backyard, the smell of whatever steak he was cooking wafting into ours, always popping his head over the fence to ask if we wanted some. Bill, who once helped me change a flat tire in the pouring rain on a weekend I was home from college. Bill—of course. Why hadn't I thought of him before? As I watch my mom's face light up as she speaks, I realize that she had.

"He just, well, I thought he was going to make small talk like he always does and honestly, I was a little irritated he was holding me up because I needed to get to yoga right after I got my coffee." My mom giggles. "And then he just asked—asked me if he could take me on a date. That after all this time, why hadn't we?" My mom shakes her head. "Kate, honestly, it took me a full minute to even register what he said and—his face, you should've seen it. His cheeks were blotchy—red spots, you know—and sweat was trickling down his forehead."

"So? Don't leave me hanging here. What did you say?"

"I don't know what came over me, but I said, *sure, why not?* right there in my yoga pants with hardly any makeup on!"

I watch my mom's eyes dance with anticipation, her cheeks flush, and I realize I can't remember the last time I had seen her look happy. Sure, she'd smiled. Of course she'd laughed. But authentic happiness? I couldn't recall.

"So when are you guys going out?" I ask.

"Tonight!" my mom squeals.

198 liz fenton and lisa steinke

"Who *are* you right now?"

"I don't know." My mom pauses to stare at a hummingbird that's landed on the branch of my orange tree, its tiny wings fluttering frantically. "But whoever this person is," she says, tugging on her Lycra tank top, "she needs a new dress to wear to dinner!"

I reach over and impulsively hug her. *Thank you,* I think. *Thank you for making this wish come true.*

"What's up with your mom?" Max asks as he comes in the door from his run a few minutes later, having just passed her as she was leaving. His wet hair and the sweat dotting his face reminding me why we don't run together—we'd tried once, but his pace had been too intense and my lungs burned as I barely spit out the words *I need to stop now or I might die.*

I fill Max in on my mom's date as he makes his favorite power smoothie—beets, blueberries, ginger, apple juice, banana, coconut, and kale.

"Good for her," he says when I'm finished, pouring his concoction into a tall tumbler.

I frown slightly as I watch him take a long drink, remembering the one time he talked me into trying it. As he pulls out his iPad and starts reading the latest news, I debate whether to ask if Courtney had reached out to him after I talked to her yesterday. I knew if I walked out of the kitchen now, got ready for work, and left the house without bringing it up, he wouldn't either. It had been hard enough for him to tell me about Courtney's kiss, and he would probably do almost anything to avoid talking about it again. But there was a nagging feeling deep in my belly and I had to know if she'd respected the line I'd so clearly drawn in the sand.

When I'd returned home Monday night, I'd been too emotionally drained to bring up the conversation that I'd had with Courtney. All I wanted to do was curl up beside Max, to lose myself in the joy of having him there with me again—not wanting her to occupy any more space in our minds than she already had. But as I stare at him now, the elephant in the room palpable, I know we can't avoid it any longer.

"Max?"

"Yeah," he answers without looking up from his iPad.

"So I talked to Courtney."

He squeezes his eyes shut before quickly reopening them, the slight flexing of his forearms and straightening of his upper back telling me he was nervous about what I was going to say next.

"And I told her that our friendship was over."

"And how did that go?" He looks at me for a brief moment, then quickly turns back to whatever he was reading.

"She took it pretty hard. Which is interesting, considering what happened. Seriously, what did she think the outcome was going to be?"

"It's for the best," he says definitively, and gets up to make coffee, turning his back to me.

"I agree—I just hope she realizes that." I let it hang in the air. But he doesn't say anything as he dumps the grounds into the cone.

"Did you hear from her last night?" I ask casually as I pour myself a glass of orange juice. "After I spoke to her?"

I think I see him pause for a moment as he grabs the pot by its rubber black handle. "Nope. Not a peep."

"Okay. I just thought she might send one last text or something. You know, to say good-bye?"

I watch as he puts the carafe under the faucet and fills it with water, his face registering nothing. "I don't think I'll hear from her," he says with finality. "Except at work, of course."

My expression hardens slightly at the mention of them working together, and then, as if sensing my apprehension—that I'm not sure it's as simple as he's making it sound, especially when I think of Courtney's tears in the car yesterday—Max adds quickly, "I'm sorry about what happened, Kate. But you're just going to have to trust me. Okay? I promise that nothing like that will happen again." He leans in and kisses me softly. "Okay?"

I nod, deciding that I need to let go of the last of the uneasy feelings that are fighting so hard to break through to the surface. I think of Ruby and her observation that I keep switching my path. Was this what she was talking about?

• • •

"There you are!" Magda hisses at me as I walk across the soundstage at exactly eleven o'clock sharp, wondering why she's acting like I'm late when I'm actually thirty minutes early.

"You okay?" I ask.

She pulls me away from a gaggle of makeup artists who are huddled over the latest issue of *InStyle*. "The client isn't happy," she whispers, the smell of her perfume so heavy it makes me cough.

I can't use my gift of foresight to help me solve whatever the problem is because last time around, we didn't have this photo shoot on a soundstage. Last time, Courtney had still been the lead on the Bright Below the Belt campaign and had convinced the client to shoot on Figueroa Street in downtown LA despite the fact that it was way over their budget and included getting a ton of permits to close down the very busy street. The idea was to have the male model walking in his neon underwear in a sea of businessmen in three-piece suits. The caption would read: *The suit doesn't make the man. It's what's underneath it that defines him.* Which, of course, had a double entendre that was just the right amount of racy to capture a person's attention. And the ad had been a huge hit with the focus groups we'd shown it to. But after Courtney was taken off the account, then subsequently left the company, the executives at Calvin Klein got nervous, calling a meeting with Magda and me to "restrategize" the shoot, the doubt in their eyes strong as I'd tried to convince them why they should spend the thousands of extra dollars Courtney had so easily convinced them to do just weeks before.

And so here we were on a boring soundstage and shockingly, the client wasn't happy with any of the setups we'd pitched them. I sigh. Courtney would know how to fix this. But then again, we wouldn't be in this mess if Courtney were here. I think back again to her hollow eyes as she sat in the passenger seat of my car, realizing our friendship was over. That the man she cared about had stepped away from her. She had doubled down and lost this time, the advantage of my hindsight too much for her to overcome. But hindsight was a curious thing—yes, you could make tweaks to your life, but if you did that, if you used it to right the wrongs, was it still your real life?

By the time I finally leave the photo shoot, my legs feel like they are filled with lead. I haul myself to the car and slouch down in my seat. It had taken every creative fiber in my body to finally come up with the idea, still playing off Courtney's original plan but at a fraction of the cost. I could tell by the look in the executives' eyes that they'd be finding another ad agency if I hadn't. I'd pitched the idea that we set up a scene where our male model is having dinner with his beautiful date. She is fully clothed but he sits across from her in his underwear. The caption: *We all know it's not his clothes that make the lasting impression. It's what's below the belt that really matters.* I had seen Magda blush when I'd played around with different caption ideas, each rolling off my tongue with ease. I simply smiled when Magda arched her eyebrow and squinted at me, happy that I'd handled the situation without Courtney.

My phone rings, startling me and I answer it when I see it's an 808 area code. "Hey, Stella," I say, forcing my voice to sound upbeat despite how tired I am.

"Hi," she answers hesitantly. "You got a minute?"

"Of course," I say brightly, leaning back and closing my eyes.

"Well, I got an email from Max."

"Yeah? What did it say?" I try to imagine what he was adding to the list—a coconut stand or men dancing in loincloths?

"He said he wants to change everything back to the way it was originally planned," she says, her voice low, as if she's revealing a terrible secret to me.

"Really?" I ask, confused. Even though the thought of having my chocolate fountain and orchid centerpieces back on the wedding day made me smile, I also wondered, after all the effort I'd put into making the wedding more like what he wanted, why would he tell Stella to forget it?

"Change everything?"

"Everything," she repeats.

"The linen pants?"

"Gone."

"Pig?"

"Hasta la vista, baby."

"Wow," I say into the phone.

"You're telling me," Stella says, sighing loudly before adding,

"Kate, don't take this the wrong way, but you and Max really need to get on the same page here or I don't know what you're wedding day's going to look like."

Long after we've hung up, I think about Stella's words, realizing I'm now not sure what it's going to look like either.

CHAPTER TWENTY

. . . .

Life always seems simpler at dawn, the sun rising slowly outside my window, Max's gentle snores reminding me of the future we're working toward. Maybe it's because I wake up feeling light, like a feather dancing in the wind—something that seems to fade as the day wears on. Because I'll read too much into how Jules' smile never seems to reach her eyes the way it used to, why seeing Liam and Nikki's picture on the cover of *OK!* magazine makes my stomach lurch, and why Max's snores don't lure me back to sleep the way they once did—that I'm unable to match my breathing to his when I pull him close. It could be that even though I'm so happy to have him back, there's a small part of me that hates the fact that I needed a do-over to achieve the happiness that eluded us the first time.

"It doesn't matter how you did it. Life is complicated. If you and Max are happy here and now, then take it and run, Kate," Jules tells me later when I arrive at the restaurant where she works before we leave for my bachelorette party. "This is what you wanted. And now you'll even get the wedding you always hoped for as well. Why are you questioning it?" she says as she feverishly mixes fudge in a large stainless steel bowl. She barely even slows as a tall man sweeps in and dips a small spoon into the mix, the chocolate dangling precariously as he lifts it to his mouth, nodding his head in approval, Jules' only acknowledgment a quick sideways glance before he disappears into the dining room.

"Who's that?" I say with a smile. "Supercute coworker alert!"

Jules frowns at me. "He's one of the owners."

"How can that be? He looks about twenty-five."

"He's thirty."

I think back to the way his deep blue eyes crinkled at Jules. "He's adorable."

"I guess," she murmurs nonchalantly as she pours the fudge expertly into the waiting pan before placing it in one of the large refrigerators against the wall. "He's my boss."

"Really?" I ask. "Because boss or not, he looks as delicious as that fudge you're making."

"If you say so," she answers. "But stop trying to change the subject. I don't get it. You finally have Max back—you effing traveled *back in time* to make it happen, for goodness' sake. So please, tell me why you can't just go with the flow? Just accept that Max wants to make you happy and *that's* why he told Stella to change things back."

"Maybe," I ponder. "I guess I've come so far with him that I don't want to go backward again. The first wedding I planned wasn't at all what he wanted. And I want to make sure *he's* happy too."

"Sometimes you have to give up a little bit of your own happiness to make someone else's happen. That's what love is."

I watch Jules' face register a series of emotions as she says this. "What did you have to give up to make Ben happy?"

Jules' eyes narrow slightly. "Don't make this about me. Anyone who's been married and has kids would tell you the same thing."

"Would they? Because I'm only concerned about you."

"You've got precious little time to fix this thing with Max and I'm topping your list of worries?" She walks around and cups her hands over my shoulders. "You need to stop questioning *my* relationship and start talking to Max about *yours.*"

I didn't know why I hadn't mentioned Stella's call to Max the night before—it had certainly been on my mind as we ate dinner, as I poured him a glass of the Chianti Classico I had picked up on the way home. The words had sat on the edge of my lips as we opened the gifts that had arrived at our door earlier that day, both of us cringing as we realized the beautiful cherry-red KitchenAid mixer we tore open was from Courtney, who must have ordered it before everything happened.

"How did work go today?" I had asked Max as we sat on the floor together surrounded by light blue wrapping paper. "Did you see her?"

Max's eyes clouded over as if he was contemplating whether to tell me what he was thinking. "Okay—" he finally says. "I did see her once, in the elevator. She slid in right before the door closed."

"Oh? What did she say?"

Max's eyes met mine. "Just that she was sorry."

"And?"

"That was it. I told her I was sorry too."

The skin on the back of my neck pricked. "What are *you* sorry for?"

Max sighed and I could sense him formulating his answer. "I'm sorry things turned out the way they did. That two friendships ended. I feel bad about my part in all of it."

Trying not to read into Max's words, I'd turned the white and silver tissue paper over and over in my hands, until it dissolved into a small ball that I tossed in the direction of the trash can. "How did she seem?"

Max paused. "Miserable."

"Good," I had said under my breath and tried to mean it.

• • •

"I'll talk to Max about the wedding stuff," I promise Jules as she peels off her yellow and black apron. "If you pinky swear that you won't really make me wear that god-awful penis necklace tonight!"

"Not a chance." She laughs as she puts her arm around me and leads me out into the dining room and grabs her overnight bag from behind the bar. "You ready?"

• • •

"Vegas? Are you serious?" I ask as I lean my head against the leather passenger seat of Jules' SUV an hour later, after Jules finally revealed our destination.

"Yep." Jules nods, giving me a quick sideways glance as she merges onto the 15 freeway, the plastic penis that she stuck on the dashboard waving its approval as we speed past the tumbleweeds and shacks that sprinkle the side of the highway. "ETA two hours, thirty minutes!" she squeals, and high-fives Liam, who is sitting in the backseat sipping from his flask.

"Suite booked at the Aria? Check! Slutty outfit packed in your bag? Check! Bottle service at TAO? Check!" Jules says.

Liam chimes in, "But most importantly? Flask full of the smooth stuff to get this party started? Check!" He laughs and passes the liquor forward, me pursing my lips as I take a sip and

208 liz fenton and lisa steinke

feel the whiskey burn my throat, thinking I'm definitely getting used to the taste, and, dare I say, liking it a little.

"Do you go anywhere without that thing?" I tease.

"Not if I can help it," he retorts.

As I watch Jules gripping the steering wheel with a perma-grin on her face, I wonder why she is taking me to a place she'd always described as skanky. Anytime I had suggested a girls' trip to Las Vegas, she'd always rolled her eyes and exclaimed, *no way*.

Liam's phone buzzes and he smiles, texting back quickly with his thumbs. "Nikki says congrats and to have fun."

"That was nice of her," I say, and look over at Jules, wondering if she's having the same thought I am, that I'm surprised he was in the car at all. I'd half expected him to cancel at the last minute so he could attend some swanky Hollywood party with Nikki. "How are things going with you guys?" I ask, but am only met with silence.

"Liam?"

"Huh?" he mumbles, and I look over my shoulder to find him texting with the speed and intensity of a fourteen-year-old girl.

"I asked how things were going with Nikki."

"Amazing," he says, his eyes never leaving the screen of his phone as if he can't bear to let even a second go by without responding. He chuckles. "She wants to make sure we aren't being followed."

I glance back at the empty highway. "By whom?"

"The paparazzi."

"Really? Wow, how things have changed for you," I say, sounding more put off by this than I intend to. Liam had been getting a lot of media attention as Nikki's new boyfriend—having gone from my hipsterish best friend who was writing code for websites to the guy who was dating a huge TV star literally overnight. *Extra* had gobbled it up, wanting to know who this guy was Nikki had picked from obscurity. They'd even done a whole segment about him the other night: *"28 Days with Nikki?"* a tongue-in-cheek piece about how no guy had outlasted her stint in rehab.

"What's with the tone?" he asks, finally looking up at me. I wasn't sure I had a good answer for him, only that there was a small flutter in my chest whenever I thought about this life I'd wished for Liam. I couldn't shake the feeling that I was responsible for sending him careening down a path he wasn't meant to travel.

"Is your life *really* better now?" I question.

"Are you being serious?" he asks, his face contorted into a smirk that I wish I could wipe right off it.

"Yes, I really want to know."

"Of course it is!" he says, as emphatically as if I've just asked him if he'd be interested in winning the lottery.

"Okay," I say lightly.

"What do you mean, *okay*?" he challenges. "I can tell there's more swimming around in that head of yours. Just say it. You know you want to."

I look over at Jules again, but she only shakes her head as if she's warning me not to answer him. But there's something about the arrogance I swear I hear in his voice that makes me comment anyway.

"It's just that you've been kind of MIA since you started seeing her," I say, doing a mental calculation. I was sure we'd never gone more than a day without at least texting. Since he started dating Nikki, my texts would go unreturned for hours, if they were answered at all. And I hadn't talked to him on the phone in days. "And there's the car and the clothes. You just seem . . . different."

"Because I am!" He shakes his head. "I don't get it. I thought this is what you wanted. For me to finally find someone."

"Of course . . ." I trail off, not sure I want to continue, not even sure what I'd say if I did. They had just started dating and I knew he deserved his honeymoon period. He had a right to that giddy, fluttering-in-your-stomach feeling; that adrenaline rush when the other person's name pops up on your phone; that urgency to want to be in touch with them all the time, about *everything*. And as his best friend, I also knew I was supposed to want that for him.

When Max and I started dating, we spent all of our nights and weekends together. The only breaks we had from each other were when we were at work. Jules had once joked, "The sex must be amazing. I've barely heard from you in weeks! You haven't even posted on Facebook." But she hadn't been annoyed with me, and neither had Liam. Neither of them had called me to task over my absence or my behavior the way I was doing with Liam.

"I think what Kate is trying to say is you're moving really fast. We've never seen you like this. And we just want to make sure you're okay," Jules interjects.

"I'm better than I've ever been," Liam says, and leans back against the seat, staring out the sunroof, as if he's basking in happiness. "And what about you, Jules?" He meets her eyes in the rearview mirror. "Should we be concerned about you? The old you wouldn't be caught dead in Vegas, but now that you have a new look, we're on our way there. . . ."

"This trip is for Kate!" she says a little too quickly.

"Uh-huh."

"What's that supposed to mean?" Jules challenges, her cheeks turning red.

"Hey—" I interrupt. "I know I started this and I'm sorry. Can we just drop it? Pretend I never brought it up."

"Fine," they say in unison, and I lean my head against the window, letting the ensuing silence and the endless highway lure me into sleep, waking to the shiny casinos as we descend into the City of Sin.

"Are you sure there's no tiger in here or a baby in the safe?" I joke as we trail the bellman into the two-thousand-square-foot suite that Nikki's "people" had secured for us, passing three different TVs and two wet bars as I make my way to the window, gasping as I take in the incredible view of the strip, squinting my eyes to shield them from the late-afternoon sun. I turn to face Liam and Jules, who both seem lost in thought. "Hey, you two. I just want to say thanks. This is amazing." Pulling them in for a group hug, I squeeze them close to me. "I'm lucky to have you guys," I say, and am surprised when I feel tears burn my eyes, hoping the tension we'd felt earlier in the car will now melt away. "And I'm sorry if my wishes have hurt you in any way—I promise I was only trying to help . . ." I grip them both tighter, hoping Jules will take this opportunity to tell us both what's on her mind.

But she only breaks away and smiles at me. "No waterworks! At least until we get good and drunk!" She laughs, any signs she's struggling emotionally hidden behind her grin. She walks over to the bottle of champagne peeking out from an ice bucket that had been sent *compliments of the hotel* and uncorks it without fanfare. "To new beginnings," she says as she pours champagne for all of us and gives me a knowing look. "Just because you didn't get it right the first time doesn't mean it's not meant to be."

I take a deep sip, letting the bubbles tickle my throat as I ponder her words. She's right. It shouldn't matter that I needed to go back in time in order to make things right. This really wasn't any different than going to couples therapy to work through issues or going through a separation and then getting back together. The bottom line was we'd repaired our relationship.

"How about you, Jules?" I ask. "Is your life better the second time around?"

She pauses to refill her glass. "Hard to say," she says. "You're the only one who remembers living it the first time. You tell me."

My mind wanders back to the month leading up to the wedding. Jules had seemed a little distracted, but I had chalked it up to stress. Between Ben, her kids, and her job, and being my matron of honor, her life was so busy that there was little room for error. But now I'm sure I must have missed something more serious. "You did seem"—I search for the right word—"distracted."

A shadow passes over her face. "Interesting." She glances at her watch. "Hey, we've got reservations at Sushi Samba soon—I'm going to jump in the shower."

After the water is turned on, I glance over at Liam. "Do you think Jules has been acting weird lately? Is that why you asked her about why she *really* chose Vegas, because I agree with you, that's not like her at all. . . ."

"Define *weird*. Because you've time traveled, wished her a kickass makeover, and me a famous girlfriend. So it seems like a sliding scale."

"Touché." I laugh. "But in all seriousness, she's been different, right?"

"I don't know—like you said, I've been MIA," he says, and I can tell my comment bothers him.

"About that . . ."

"Forget it, let's just have a good time and not worry about how any of us is acting. I think we can agree that we're all doing the best we can under the circumstances."

"You're right, but what if this thing with Jules is more serious, like she might be having real problems, maybe even with Ben?" I start to tell him about what I overheard in Jules' foyer when the buzzing of his phone interrupts us. I grab it before he can. "Can Nikki handle not receiving a text from you for five seconds? I'm trying to talk to you about something important here."

I survey Liam as he searches for his answer. "Okay. She does seem slightly off. But if she has a problem, she'll talk to us about it—I'm not going to force her."

A dozen scenarios flare through my mind as I wonder what could be wrong between Jules and Ben—*if anything*. It was true that I could be reading too much into the fight I overheard. The reality was that couples argued, especially ones that had been together as long as they had. And it was possible I was being hypersensitive because of my own situation with Max. But the instinct in my gut told me something had happened to shift their dynamic dramatically. And I had wondered more than once, based on some of the cryptic comments Jules had made about her marriage, if Ben had cheated on her. It was possible—he traveled a lot and was a good-looking guy. But while there was a chance it had happened, I just couldn't believe he had it in him. He used to brag that he didn't need to look at other women after he met Jules—that she was the most beautiful person on the planet.

"I'm not saying we need to force her to tell us her secrets, I just want to make sure she knows she can confide in us. That we won't judge her *or* Ben." Max flashes through my mind, how I had ignored our problems until he'd been forced to look *other places* for the answers he needed. I didn't want Jules to make the same mistake. "After what happened to me, I just worry that if she's wearing blinders, it could make whatever she's going through worse."

Liam motions for me to give him his phone. "Well, you might have been given a special gift, but most of us have no other choice but to get it right the first time," he says, scrolling through his phone so his eyes don't meet mine.

CHAPTER TWENTY-ONE

....

"And you said we would *never* be able to finish it!" Liam raises his voice over the thumping sound of the music, pointing to the empty bottle of Ketel One vodka and mixers on the tray in front of us. He signals to the server who's been assigned to our plush couch in the VIP area of TAO. "Another one, please."

I try to shake my head, to tell Liam that I've already had too much, that I'm so buzzed I'm no longer embarrassed by the fluorescent penis beads I'm wearing around my neck. I had even let Jules talk me into participating in a ridiculous bachelorette scavenger hunt—I'd pinched some guy's ass on the dance floor and done a blow-job shot at the bar. But despite Jules' pleading, I had drawn the line at removing my bra and talking a man into wearing it.

But I was having a great time, the alcohol blunting any tension I'd felt among Liam, Jules, and me earlier.

"Having fun?" he yells into my ear, his breath hot.

"Of course!" I exclaim as that new will.i.am song starts playing, the one that Jules made us listen to on repeat so many times on the car ride here that Liam finally banned it.

"Oh my God—I *love* this song!" she screeches as she clumsily grabs for our hands, yanking us through the bodies smashed together like sardines on the dance floor. Once there, I lose myself in the moment, forgetting to be worried about Jules' marriage, about Liam's relationship with a young starlet who'd been in rehab just months before, about my own future with Max. Instead I close my eyes, raise my hands above my head, and shake my hips to the beat. And for a moment, I wish we were back in college—things had seemed so much simpler then. Just the three of us against the world. When I open my eyes, I catch Liam watching me with an odd look on his face.

"What?" I mouth to him.

He nods in the direction of Jules, who has her hands on the chest of a man I had caught staring at her earlier. He has his hands on her hips, and every few seconds, one of them leans in to yell something in the other's ear, but they never stop touching. When she finally glances over, I give her a questioning look, but she only throws her hands around his neck and grips him tighter. Concerned, I start to bob and weave my way over to her, but feel a strong hand on my shoulder. "Leave her be," says Liam.

"Are you sure?" I narrow my eyes. Jules has had a lot to drink.

"Come on." Liam tugs on my arm and leads me back to our table. "She's fine. We can keep an eye on her from here," he says as he mixes us each a vodka and Red Bull.

"I really don't need this—I'm already drunk," I say, taking a deep sip anyway.

"Reminds me of old times," Liam says wistfully. "When did we get old?"

I slap his shoulder. "We are not old! We've just grown up a bit. Or at least some of us have," I say as I wink at him.

"At least I'm still having fun."

"And I'm not?"

"I don't know. Are you?"

"I just said I was having a great time!"

Liam's eyes cut through mine, the speckles of brown in them disappearing as he squints, making his normal hazel hue appear dark green. "I'm not talking about tonight."

We sit for a moment, me not sure I want to ask him what he means and him not sure he wants to tell me. Finally, I break eye contact and search the dance floor for Jules, spying her at a table across the room with the man she'd been dirty dancing with, sipping her drink, her knees touching his. "Are you sure we shouldn't do something about that?" I set my drink down and nod in their direction. Something about the way he was looking at her didn't feel right to me.

"Yes," Liam says definitively.

"But don't you see what's going on over there?"

"I see it."

"And?"

"And what?" He shrugs.

"You're acting like they're just over there chatting about the weather or trading recipes!" I start to stand up so I can intervene, but Liam pulls me back and I fall awkwardly into his lap. "Liam! Come on. Let me go!"

I feel his arms tighten around me. "When will you learn that sometimes you need to let people live their lives the way *they* want? To let people make mistakes? To let yourself make them? If she decides to cross a line, that's her decision to make—not yours."

"So I just need to sit here and let her possibly make a mistake that could cost her everything?" I turn toward Liam, his face just inches from mine. The stubble on his chin is so close that I almost reach out to touch it.

"Don't you get it? This isn't about Jules and what she may or *may not* do with that guy over there. This is about *you!*"

"Me?" I say. "How does this have anything to do with me?"

"Because you are so damn scared." He rakes his hand through his hair, his face contorting as he strains for his next words. "Jesus, don't you get it? You are so petrified to make a mistake, to not seem . . ." He pauses to make air quotes. "Perfect . . . that you're putting that pressure on others too—that if you turn your back for a second Jules might willingly jump off the throne you've placed her on. It's too much, Kate. We're all fallible."

"You think I care more about being perfect than being happy?" I challenge, my cheeks burning with anger and embarrassment. Liam had never talked to me this way before.

"Think about it. You've wished your life exactly how you want it. You didn't like what happened with Max, so you're back here fixing it so you can have things *your way*. And you're still not happy—so maybe there's something to be said for life just working out as it should. Maybe we should just let Jules make whatever choices she needs to make—right *or wrong*."

Feeling as if the wind has been knocked out of me, I take a shallow breath, trying to decipher what Liam means. Is he saying I should have let Max leave me without trying to stop him? I stare at Jules, now flipping her hair over her shoulder and smiling the way she did back when she met Ben, and I try to remember the last time I have seen her flirt with her husband.

Liam's voice jars me out of my thoughts. "What I'm trying to say is people lie, people cheat, people *leave people*." His eyes lock with mine. "And sometimes you just have to accept that you can't edit life the way you do online. This isn't Facebook. It's the real world, for Christ's sake. Sometimes you just have to let your arm look fat in the picture."

I swallow hard, letting his words sink in, remembering all the pictures I'd scrutinized, retaken, filtered. "Well, you certainly didn't have a problem when I edited *your* life. When *I* made it possible for you to be with Nikki Day! Like she would have even looked at you twice in this *real world* we're living in," I shoot back, instantly wishing I could pull the words back after I see the hurt look on Liam's face, his grip on my waist slacking slightly.

I start to apologize when I hear a voice behind me. "Liam?"

Liam stands so quickly that I fall off his lap to the floor, Nikki Day standing above me, her hands glued to her hips. "What exactly is going on here?"

"Nothing," Liam and I say in unison.

"Didn't look like nothing to me—you looked pretty cozy together." Nikki pouts. "And here I thought I'd come out and surprise you guys. Looks like I'm the one getting the surprise. You were practically straddling my boyfriend!"

I clamber to my feet. "Nikki, it wasn't what it looked like," I say, still reeling from Liam's words and trying to figure out how Nikki could think crashing my bachelorette party would be a welcome surprise *for me*. But as I watch Liam's eyes light up, I decide that as uneasy as she made me, my desire for his happiness outweighs that, despite what I had just blurted out a moment ago. "I was going to go cock block Jules," I say, nodding across the room, where she's now sitting in the guy's lap. "But Liam physically stopped me—pulled me down so I couldn't walk away," I say, baiting Nikki to see what she'll say about it. Maybe she'll agree that I shouldn't sit here and let my best friend make a mistake just because it's apparently her fate to be unfaithful to Ben while she's drunk. What *were* the rules there?

A smile spreads across her face. "She's the boring married one, right?"

Ignoring Nikki, I shoot Liam a sharp look and he looks down. "Married, but never boring," he says quickly.

"Whatever," she says. "Marriage is overrated. I'm with Liam on this one. Leave her alone," she says, and she leans into Liam and kisses him, pushing him down on the couch hard as if I'm not even standing there. He pulls her in by her waist, his hand on the back of her sequined tank top, acting as if this isn't my party that she's inserted herself into. I pound the rest of my drink and slam the glass down. My deepest fear had come true—Liam's new girlfriend has finally infiltrated the inner sanctum of our friendship. I give them one last glance before striding away, Liam's words from earlier still ringing in my ears. My mind might be blurry with alcohol, but they had still stung sharply.

And another unsettling thought was also gnawing at me. Last time, Jules hadn't acted like this at my bachelorette party—causing me to think that even though she may have had the same problems with Ben last time, it was the makeover I'd wished for her that had set all this in motion.

I shuffle across the bar and order a glass of water, keeping a close eye on Jules the entire time and glancing occasionally at the crowd that has now gathered around Nikki and Liam. Finally, I make my way to where Jules is sitting, her face dangerously close to that of the man she's been flirting with, his hand now resting comfortably on her upper thigh, as he rubs it back and forth with the rhythm of the music. I cringe as I get up close—his eyes are glassy and squinting, his brow is covered with a sheen of perspiration, and there are sweat rings around the armpits of his T-shirt. Suddenly, I feel completely sober. "Hey," I say casually, forcing myself not to rip his hand off her leg and yank her away from him and into my arms.

"Hey!" she exclaims, and engulfs me in a tight hug, swaying

so hard that we both almost topple over. "This is my best friend!" she slurs to the man she introduces as Kevin. "She's getting married!"

I give a nod to Kevin, who holds up his drink while never letting his eyes leave Jules. "Yep, I'm getting married!" I say through the smile I've plastered on my face. "Now I'll be just like you, Jules. *Married!*"

Snapping her head up, she gives me a look I can't identify—a cross of anger, sadness, and something else. "Kate," she says, my name sounding garbled as it comes out of her mouth.

"Jules," I respond. "I think it's time to go."

She falls back onto the couch, Kevin's hand instantly draping around her shoulder possessively. "I don't want to go. Join us," she says, her glassy eyes pleading with me. Hoping I'll reserve judgment, that I'll pretend she doesn't have a husband and two children at home, that I'll say this is okay. But I can't. Even after what Liam said to me, I can't stand by idly and watch her make this mistake. Maybe it's because of the way Max left me for Courtney or because I've had to fight like hell to get him back. Or maybe it's just the simple fact that I really love Ben and Jules together and could never imagine them apart. No matter what my reason, I know I can't let her throw everything away on my watch—even if she thinks it's not a life worth coveting anymore. It's still a life she's spent years building.

"I'm sorry," I say as I perch on the edge of the table in front of them. "Kevin, right?" He nods. "Here's the thing: Jules is *married*. She has been for a long time. And as nice as you seem, I can't let her do this."

Kevin smiles. "I don't think that's your choice to make," he says, and tightens his grip, and I remember Liam's words from earlier.

"I couldn't disagree more," I say as I look at Jules watching our exchange with a faraway look in her eyes—she was even more wasted than I thought. "Listen, asshole," I say evenly. "I've just told you my friend is *married*. It's time for you to get lost. Because, honestly, the only reason she's even sitting here right now flirting with you is because of the half dozen drinks she's had tonight." I pause, daring him to challenge me, hoping I'm right. Praying that she wouldn't be acting this way if she were sober. But Kevin only winks at me. "I'm not leaving here without her," I demand, putting my hand on Jules'.

"Well, why don't *you* stay then?" he says, letting his eyes drop to my chest. "I've always wanted to have a threesome." He grabs my arm, digging his hand in as I attempt to pull away, the loud music pulsating in my brain as I try to wriggle from his grasp, his other arm still enveloping Jules' waist.

Kevin's grip loosens only when he's lifted off the couch a moment later, Liam's fist connecting with his nose swiftly, hurling him into a ball on the floor as he holds his face, screaming.

"Let's go," Liam orders, scooping Jules off the couch and leading us toward the exit as security quickly moves in. "Don't look back," he warns when I start to turn my head, Liam grabbing my hand as he holds Jules up like a puppet, placing her gently in the backseat of a waiting taxi as soon as we step out of the casino doors, the cab line miraculously empty. We crawl in behind her and sit in silence as the driver navigates the traffic, still heavy at 1 a.m., the honking and buzz from the streets drowning out the booming from the music in the club still pulsating in my ears. Jules passes out almost immediately, her breath heavy.

I finally break the silence. "Where's Nikki?"

He looks out the window, the Eiffel Tower in front of the

Paris casino lighting up the otherwise black desert sky. "She said she'd be waiting for me in her suite."

I glance at Liam's profile in the darkness of the cab. "I'm sure it makes ours look like a studio apartment." I laugh, hoping to break through the tension still lingering between us.

"There was mention of a basketball court and a lap pool."

"Because that's normal," I snicker, then sigh when Liam doesn't join me.

But then, a few seconds later, his chest starts to heave as he releases a hearty laugh, tears spilling from his eyes, and suddenly we're both howling so hard I wonder if we'll wake Jules. "How the hell did we get here?" he manages to say in between our roars.

Our laughter subsides as I stare up at the lights of the Aria as we pull into the circular driveway. "I was just thinking the same thing." I watch him rub his right hand. "Nice right hook, by the way. I thought you were a lover, not a fighter."

"Sometimes you have to be a little of both," he says as he throws the driver a twenty and delicately prods Jules awake. "Come on, sweetie. Let's get you to the room."

We lift Jules out of the cab, each of us holding on to an arm tightly as we make our way to the elevator. "Where's Kevin?" she slurs.

"Last time I saw him, he was in a pile on the floor," I say, smiling sideways at Liam as we step inside. "He was a jerk. Besides, you have Ben, remember? The love of your life?"

"Whatever," Jules says after a few minutes of silence, the only sound the soles of Liam's shoes scuffling against the carpet as we trudge down the hall. "He doesn't look at me that way anymore."

"What way?" Liam asks as he slides the key card into the

door, then watches Jules closely as she makes her way to the bed and falls into it.

"The way Kevin did. Like he wants to devour me," she says as she sprawls out. "The room is spinning."

I walk over to the bed and prop her up on the pillows. "Try to keep sitting up," I say as Liam hands me a Sprite from the minibar that I hold to her mouth. "Take a sip."

Liam sits on the edge of the bed. "Kevin looked at you like an object. He didn't give a shit that you were almost incoherent—he just wanted to fuck you."

"Exactly," she says. "At least someone wants to."

I think about how much Ben travels and wonder again if he is having an affair, if it is more than him just being exhausted. "Jules, did something happen? Did Ben—"

"You're not getting any other info out of her tonight, Detective," Liam interrupts, and wraps a blanket around Jules, her eyes sealed shut, her mouth hanging open.

"You still think we should have let her make the mistake?" I challenge as I follow him out of the room to the couch, my heart shattering a little over Jules' admission. If she and Ben couldn't make it, a part of me doubted if anyone could.

"Of course I don't!" Liam says, a flare of anger in his voice. "Not after that guy got rough with you." He shakes his head, as if remembering it all over again. "But I still believe what I said to you—this is Jules' life to live. We can't judge it. We can't control it. We have to let her make her own choices. Just maybe not when she's hammered!" He rolls his eyes and throws his feet on the table, stretching his arms out, the key to Nikki's suite resting on the table next to his cell phone. There was a part of me that didn't want him to leave—even after everything that has been said tonight, his presence was still warm and comforting, much like the soft blanket he had wrapped around Jules a few minutes earlier.

"Well, her life or not, it still makes me think. If she and Ben are in this much of a tailspin, then what does that mean for the rest of us?"

He pulls me in close against his chest and runs his hand through my hair. "When will you learn?"

"Learn what?" I whisper as I close my eyes, the pressure of his hand on my head making my eyelids heavy, all the alcohol and drama finally catching up to me.

"That nobody's perfect," he says softly, right before I drift off to sleep.

• • •

Memories from the night before come flooding back like high tide at sunset when I pull open my eyes, surprised to find myself next to Jules, who is facedown beside me in the king bed. I roll over, noticing my shoes sitting neatly on the floor. The last thing I remember is falling asleep on Liam's chest—had he carried me in here? I lean forward to see out the door of the bedroom, hoping to glimpse his long legs dangling off the couch, but it's empty. I feel a pang—he'd gone to spend the night with Nikki after all.

It still shocked me that he'd hit that guy last night—he'd always been the one to break up fights, not start them. What had gotten into him? The speed with which he was transforming made me uneasy. First it was cars and clothes. Now he was sucker-punching someone at a club. What would be next?

The room moves slightly as I stand and steady myself before moving forward, desperate to locate my overnight bag and the bottle of Advil tucked inside, my head almost exploding when I bend down to look for it. Finally, I grip the container in my hand and shake two pills out of it, gulping them down with a bottle of water Liam must have set next to the bed before he left. I palm the extra capsules I grabbed for Jules and lie back in bed, waiting for her to wake from the dead, worried that she's going to feel much worse than me, and not just because of the alcohol.

Instinctively I reach over and grab my cell phone, quickly sending Max a text to ask how his bachelor party went the night before, attaching a photo that we had taken at dinner, our heads tilted together as we raised our glasses in the air. I stare at Jules' face in the picture, the anticipation she was feeling now obvious. Last night, I had thought it had been because we were all together, but now I realize there may have been more to it. I had always viewed her as someone others were drawn to—she never had a shortage of women scrambling for her friendship at her kids' school, of clients wanting her to create a beautiful cake. She had even charmed the parking attendant at the Starbucks we frequented off La Cienega—him letting her park for free and saving her the best space in the lot. But clearly she was craving something more. Something she didn't feel like she was getting from Ben.

Max pings me back a picture of him with a line of full shot glasses, him shrugging his shoulders as if to say, "Well someone's got to do it!" He looked happy. I click over to my Facebook feed, cringing at Jules' incoherent status update from the night before about twerking at TAO. There are several typos, and no punctuation, so unlike her usual updates, which I know for a fact she double- and triple-checks, even sometimes asking my opinion before posting. I laugh despite myself when I see Ben's comment telling her to stop drinking and go to bed. *If he only knew what good advice that really was.*

I hear Jules moan before I feel her move beside me, rolling over as if she were filled with concrete. "Oh my God," she says as her hands shield her eyes from the daylight streaming through the slight opening in the curtain. I silently hand her the ibuprofen and bottle of water, alarmed by the green tone her skin has taken on.

"Thank you," she whispers, and lies in silence for a few minutes, eyes closed. I watch her closely—last night playing in a loop in my head.

"Jules," I finally say when her eyes open again.

"I don't want to talk about it."

"You—"

"Yes, I remember. At least most of it—parts of the night keep flashing through my mind like a slide show. I just can't remember how it ended," she whispers, her bloodshot eyes fearful, and I couldn't decide if her panic stemmed from not remembering if she had cheated on Ben, or if she was scared I'd be the one to tell him if she did.

"It ended with Liam smashing his fist into that guy's nose and shoving your drunk ass into a taxi."

"What?" Jules sits up quickly and then grabs her head in pain, leaning back slowly and taking a deep breath before continuing. "Liam? No way. I don't believe it."

"Believe it," I say as I fill in all the blanks of the night for her, including Nikki's appearance, her face darkening when I mention how the guy she was sitting with grabbed my arm.

"I'm sorry," she says, her voice small. "Did I ruin your night? I really wanted you to have a great night."

"Hey, stop. I had a great time. I'm okay. The question is, are you?"

"I don't know," she says, her sadness penetrating the air

between us, neither of us knowing the magic words to make it dissolve.

"What's going on with Ben? Or I should say, what's *not* going on with Ben?"

Jules squeezes her eyes shut as she tries to locate the right words. "I guess I just thought, when you gave me my makeover, that Ben would go nuts. That he was going to see me as hot again."

"You were hot before this!" I interject. "And Ben has always told you how beautiful you are. I've heard him."

"I know he still thinks I'm attractive. But we've been in such a rut. He's traveling more than ever, and when he is home, we're so busy with the kids that we can't even connect. I think I just want him to throw me up against a wall like he used to—when he was so into me that he couldn't control himself. And when you gave me a firmer stomach and killer haircut and he barely even glanced my way, I think something snapped inside of me," she says as the tears begin to fall down her face like a waterfall.

"What happened? Did he cheat on you?" I question, sitting up despite the pounding in my head, imagining what I'll say to him when I see him—how dare he hurt my best friend!

She shakes her head and I breathe a sigh of relief. They were still okay.

"I started to question things—to come apart on the inside." She takes a long pause before continuing. "But he isn't the one who's making the mistakes, Kate. It's me."

"But nothing happened last night, Jules. We stopped it before anything could—"

"You're right," she interrupts. "I didn't actually cross the line. But I wanted to. And not just last night." She shakes her head.

"I don't understand," I say gently, even though I think I'm

starting to, the pieces of the puzzle clicking together in my mind.

"Something happened with my boss recently. The guy you saw at the restaurant yesterday."

I remember how the energy shifted as he breezed through the kitchen, that I could feel a tension in the air as he'd sampled the fudge—an awkwardness between them I couldn't figure out. I swallow my breath and, as I wait for her to tell me the story, squeeze her hand to let her know that whatever she's about to reveal, I will understand. Slowly, she tells me that after a particularly stressful night at the restaurant, her boss, Tim, had grabbed a bottle of the restaurant's best single-malt scotch from behind the bar and offered her a deep pour. They were both distraught that the *L.A. Times* food critic had dined there earlier, and their server had tripped and spilled an entire glass of wine all over his crisp white shirt and Burberry tie, causing him to leave abruptly. Three glasses of scotch later, they had gone from being incredibly depressed and wondering if the restaurant could survive a bad review, to laughing about the look on his face as the waiter frantically attempted to wipe the reviewer's crotch with his napkin. Another half glass later, he'd tucked a strand of hair behind her ear, whispering how much he liked her new look as he'd leaned in so closely that she could see a light speckle of tan freckles dotting his skin that she'd never noticed before. Just as their lips began to come together, the executive chef had banged on the back door, in search of the cell phone he'd left behind. They had broken away from each other quickly, Jules grabbing her bag off the counter and rushing out the door into the cold wind without saying good-bye, shaking at what might have happened if they hadn't been interrupted—perplexed that she had felt both excited and sickened at the same time.

"I threw up when I got home. All those years of marriage and that's all it takes for me to want to throw it all away? Four glasses of scotch?" She cries harder.

I let her catch her breath before responding. "I get that you came close to making a big mistake—you're human. But you chose to leave the situation. You could have stayed and picked things back up the second you were alone again, yet you didn't. That counts for something."

"Maybe," she says as she wipes her nose with the back of her hand. "I felt terrible."

"Okay. But then why almost do it again last night?" I ask gently, afraid that if I push too hard she'll shatter into a million pieces.

She sits quietly for a moment before answering, her chest heaving up and down. "As much as I felt disgusted with myself for almost cheating on Ben, for how much I had *wanted* to kiss my boss, there was a part of me that loved the rush of it all—the way it felt to not be Evan's or Ellie's mom, to not be Ben's college sweetheart. To be desired like that again—I can't explain the feeling, but it's overpowering. It's almost like the whole world slips away for those moments. I don't expect you to get it. I'm not sure I even understand it myself. All I know is last night, I wanted to feel that way again—no matter the consequences."

I put my hand over hers but say nothing. It was true, I didn't understand. I'd give anything to have what she and Ben have, problems and all. But what I did know was that whatever she was feeling, it was real. "So what happens now?" I ask slowly, still trying to sift through my own conflicted feelings—that Jules was on the brink of throwing everything away and I wasn't sure how to stop her. Even though she was like a sister to me, I had no clue about the one thing that was eating her up inside. Was it because she knew I didn't want to see that her relationship could be flawed—that I couldn't accept that people's lives were far more complicated than they let on, even my closest friend's?

"I don't know," she says as she takes a small sip of water. "I need to think."

"Where do things stand with your boss?"

"He pulled me into the freezer the next day and we both agreed that it was the scotch talking. But to be honest, there's still something there, an undercurrent that keeps drawing me to him. And I'm pretty sure he feels it too."

"So what are you saying? That it's going to happen again? Is that what you want?"

"I don't know what I want anymore," she spits out.

"You dodged a major bullet, Jules. I say to stop while you're ahead." I walk over to the bay window and lean my head against it, the sidewalks below not yet cluttered by the tourists—the people, many of them just like Jules, who are hoping to fill a void in their own lives in this City of Sin. Where the allure of the slot machines and the lights and the alcohol help people escape their own realities. "Both times, there's been something that's stopped you right before—maybe the universe is trying to tell you something?" I add, trying not to think about the messages the universe had been sending me about my own life.

"Maybe." Jules materializes beside me, the blanket from the night before still wrapped tightly around her. "I know what the right answer is here. And I really *want* to assure you that I'll never put myself in that position again. But you're the one person I can be honest with—and the truth is I can't make that promise. Not right now."

"Okay," I murmur without meeting her gaze.

"I'm sorry. All you want is to get married to the man you love, while I'm throwing my own marriage away. You must hate me," she says, apprehension dancing in the backs of her eyes when I finally look up to meet them.

There was a part of me that wanted to shake her—to convince her that sex is just sex. To make her realize how rare it is to have a man like Ben, who not only loves her, but is also completely devoted to their children, even if his job was pulling him away from them at the moment. But I knew I was watching her marriage from the cheap seats, and despite what I *thought* I knew, she was the one living it every day. And by the way she viscerally described her pain, I knew it was slowly ripping her apart—that I needed to be there for her the way she'd been for me. She'd literally kept me standing after Max left; she'd believed me when I told her my incredible story about traveling through time; and she'd never once judged me for my own mistakes or treated my problems as trivial, even when we both knew they were.

"I could never hate you," I say as I grab her hand, the heat from the early morning Las Vegas sun already beginning to scorch the window. "It's all going to be okay," I promise, gripping her palm tighter, hoping I'm right.

CHAPTER TWENTY-TWO
....

"What happens in Vegas stays in Vegas!" I joke as Max smirks at me over his UCLA mug, the light blue script of the word *Bruins* so faded you wouldn't know what it said unless you knew he'd gone to school there, that it was his favorite mug to drink coffee from. It's always been the subtle things like this, the little nuances that make him who he is, many of which only I know, that have made me feel connected to him. Like how he can only read a magazine from the first page to the last page, never skipping around like I do; or the fact that he talks in his sleep after he's had a cocktail; or the way he runs his hand through his hair when he's nervous.

"Come on! Tell me *something* about your night." He reaches in and kisses me softly. "I can make it worth your while," he says seductively.

As I drove us away from Las Vegas this morning, watching the city disappear into the hills through the rearview mirror, Jules sleeping soundly in the passenger seat, Liam high above us in the air, having texted he was flying back with Nikki on the Gulfstream jet she'd chartered, I had prepared myself for how I would answer Max's question, for the way I could describe my

234 liz fenton and lisa steinke

night without having to lie. Jules had sworn me to secrecy about how she was feeling, and of course I would never betray her confidence. Besides the fact that she was also Max's friend, she had told me she didn't want to put her problems on anyone else's shoulders. In fact, she'd repeatedly asked me if *I* was okay—if knowing the betraying thoughts that lingered inside her head had changed something inside of me, had altered the way I saw her or viewed marriage in general. The truth was, of course it had changed things, but I told her, if anything, it had pushed me closer to Max. It had reinforced why I didn't ever want to lose him again.

"It was like old times!" I say brightly, because in so many ways, it was. Before Kevin and Nikki infiltrated my night, it had been just the three of us laughing and dancing the way we used to. I immediately launch into a recap of the evening, leaving out Jules' incident, but including Nikki, a part of me wanting Max's opinion on what her arrival meant for my friendship with Liam.

"Don't take it personally. He's a guy, which means he's only thinking about *one* thing right now." Max laughs and raises his eyebrows.

Maybe that's the problem.

I smile at Max's joke, but his words rest heavy on my mind. Did we put too much importance on our sex lives? Did we overlook other, possibly more meaningful things because our partners weren't throwing us up against a wall? Did we let our animal instincts take over when instead we should be focusing on our emotional ones? Jules had contemplated having an affair because her husband wasn't paying enough attention to her, but what if it was just a phase—if he really was just busy and distracted? If she'd tried talking to him about how lonely she was feeling, would things be different? And Liam. He was head over heels for a twenty-four-year-old woman who'd struggled with alcohol and drug addiction and, according to the latest gossip, had barely graduated from high school—because the sex was good? He was changing who he was and even letting his friendships fall by the wayside because he only had one thing on his mind?

"What?" Max asks when he sees me shake my head.

"Nothing," I say, deciding I'm overthinking it. I need to take Liam's advice and let my friends live their lives the way they want to. And I need to focus on my own life—the one right in front of me, the one I plan to live with Max.

Stella had called while Jules and I were on the way back from Las Vegas to let me know about yet another obstacle she'd run into. Apparently, all of the DJs and bands on the island of Maui were now booked on our wedding date and the only way to play music would now entail a more DIY approach. She'd wanted my approval to set up speakers and an iPod. "It's what anyone who's anyone is doing now anyway," she'd squeaked, her voice sounding as tight as a drum, and I'd known better than to argue.

Not surprisingly, it turns out, when you plan a wedding, then replan it, then change everything back to the way it originally was, the only way to pull it off, or as Stella lectured, *even have one at all*, is to prioritize.

Having Max as my husband is priority number one, I'd thought as I'd tried to block the image of my bright pink iPod propped up next to the shrimp cocktail. *That's what's important.*

I heard myself suggesting we go back to the luau theme, and after a long pause during which I could almost hear the words Stella wasn't saying rolling around in her mind, she'd finally spoken.

"We can't," she'd said slowly, exasperation creeping into her voice. "As soon as I let the dancers go, they were immediately booked by another couple. And they were the last troupe available. Same thing with Louie's Luau, the company that was going to roast the pig, the whole nine yards. They'd done me a favor saying yes at all—" She didn't finish her sentence, as if she knew she'd just be adding salt to the wound.

"I'm sorry, Stella."

"It's fine—just promise me one thing," she'd responded, her tone suddenly lighter, and I'd found myself assuming that was a skill she'd obviously honed through her job—to be able to dance through a conversation without losing total control, no matter how frustrated she might be.

"You name it."

"Just don't change anything else."

"Cross my heart," I'd said, imagining Max in the crisp dark suit we'd originally selected for the ceremony, remembering how he'd tugged at the collar and dusted imaginary lint off the lapel as he'd examined himself in the mirror. I drew in a long breath as I drove past the world's largest thermometer in the tiny town of Baker, the dial ticking up to 105 degrees, hoping that was the explanation for why I'd felt a bead of sweat forming on my brow.

• • •

"Did you see the *Enquirer*?" Jules asks the next morning when we meet for coffee before work, both of us still bleary-eyed from our weekend.

"Do people still read that?" I ask.

"If by 'people' you mean me, then yes!"

I shake my head, and she slides her hand into her bag resting at her feet and pulls it out.

"You shouldn't have your purse on the floor!" I scold her.

"Why not?" she says as she flips through the magazine.

"Bad feng shui! The idea is that money spills out of the bottom of your purse when you leave it on the ground," I say, remembering the look I'd given my consultant when she'd first told me. But now I was always careful to set my tote on a chair. "And, girlfriend, you don't need any more problems!"

"Tell me about it." She continues to turn the pages until she finds what she's looking for. "Here it is, look." She holds the magazine out to me.

"Do you want to talk about things?" I ask, hoping her comment was an opening that she's ready.

"Nope," she says, and her lips form a tight line, one I've seen when she tells one of her children that their time on the iPad is over. It's not negotiable.

"You sure?" I push anyway.

"I've already said too much. I shouldn't have laid all of that on you. I'll figure it out, I promise."

"But . . ."

"Kate, please. I'm not ready. But when I am, I will tell you, okay?"

"All right." I acquiesce, still concerned and wanting another chance to convince her not to stray. To stop her from doing something that can't be undone. I exhale deeply and grab the magazine from her, reading the headline: "New Direction for Nikki Day?" Under it is a picture of Nikki in the passenger seat of a car being driven by one of the members of a boy band currently topping the charts—their latest single ironically titled "I Got Your Girl, Yo." "Is this true?"

"Hell if I know." Jules rolls her eyes. "Liam says it's not."

I raise my eyebrows at her. "What?" she says in response. "Of course I asked him about it! And he swore it was bullshit."

"But she is in the car with this guy and her head is resting on his shoulder!"

"I know, I know, but he says it's Photoshopped or something. Then he reminded me about her party this weekend."

"He's still going? After this article basically tells the whole world she's probably cheating—" I say, and then catch myself, but it's too late, the words are already out there. "You know what I mean, Jules. It—it's different than your situation," I stammer.

"You really believe that?" Jules says.

"Yes, of course. I'm just not a fan of Nikki. I don't think she's right for him. That's all I meant, I promise. And he can go to that party, but there's no way in hell I'm going to attend. I don't care what she told him, these pictures don't lie."

"Okay, but if you're secretly judging me for how I'm feeling, now is the time to tell me. It's better to get it out on the table." She slaps her hand on the wood tabletop for emphasis. "Because I would think *you* of all people would understand . . ."

"What's that supposed to mean?" I ask, feeling my chest tighten.

"Because of what Max did to you with Courtney."

"He didn't actually *do* anything."

"He fell in love with someone else!" She bristles and my eyes fill with tears.

"In another life, not this one," I start to argue before Jules interjects.

"True. I'm sorry if that came out a little harsh."

"A little?" I say, my voice catching in my throat.

"Okay, a lot. Maybe I just got overly defensive because of my own stuff. But what I'm trying to say is, you forgave Max. You understood that there was more to the story." When I don't respond, her face softens. "I'm sorry, I didn't mean to be such a bitch."

"I know," I say. "It's okay."

"I was just trying to make the point that you should give others the same consideration you've given Max."

"Like Nikki Day? I'm sorry, Jules. I love you, but comparing her to Max is a stretch. Why would I give a shit about her?"

"Because Liam does," she says simply.

I pause for a moment. "You're right," I reluctantly agree, her reminder about accepting Liam's choices bringing back the talk he and I had at the club.

"Great," she says, clapping her hands together. "So that means you'll go to this party no matter what your feelings about Nikki are? Because even though Liam acts like he doesn't need us, he still does. We should be there for him. In good times," she says as she points to the article about Nikki, "and bad."

"I'll go," I say, and swallow the lump in my throat, trying to ignore how quickly things seemed to be spinning out of control—like a merry-go-round that I can't escape without flying untethered through the air and falling to the ground.

CHAPTER TWENTY-THREE

....

Going through old photo albums—OMG, who gave me that god-awful bowl cut when I was a toddler? #momIknowitwasyou #dontdenyit

As a little girl, I remember feeling like time always went slowly when I wanted it to speed up, like the first day back to school after winter break when I was still dreaming of the presents I'd opened on Christmas morning. And time seemed to fly by at lightning speed when I wanted it to decelerate, like summer vacation when I spent my days with my bare feet kicked up over the handlebars of my bike, the wind ripping through my long hair. But now, over twenty-five years later, as I stare at the date on the calendar, I wonder why the opposite is happening. My wedding is fast approaching, yet I find myself wanting the hands of the clock to move just a little slower. There is a pressing feeling in my gut, one that tells me to take my life one day at a time, to not be in such a rush, that Max will be my husband soon enough.

I pull out my cell phone and listen as it rings, wondering if my dad will answer or if I'll get his voicemail, where Leslie hums in the background as he chants his greeting, trying to sound like he's rapping, but the result sounding more like he's preaching. It's so ridiculous that I can't help but laugh every time I hear it. They'd moved to Northern California last year so I didn't see them as often as I liked, but it was always good to hear his—*and her*— voice. And I realized my dad was the one person who needed to answer a question that had been sitting heavy on my chest.

"Daughter!" my dad says cheerily.

"Father!" I answer, smiling at the memory of trading this greeting for years.

"So you're almost a married woman—how are you spending your *final* days before you become an old ball and chain?" My dad releases a hefty laugh and I imagine him sitting in his leather recliner, his feet perched on the matching ottoman, CSPAN on mute on the TV.

"Dad?" I start, ignoring his question, my voice suddenly sounding like it did when I was a little girl. "Can we talk about Mom?"

He exhales deeply, and for several moments there is only silence between us. Finally, he answers. "I know she's upset about Leslie wanting to be in the family picture at the wedding—"

"I don't want to talk about that. That's not what I mean."

"Oh? Then what is it?" My dad's voice lightens.

I think back to what my mom had said to me—that my dad had been her everything, and I wonder, if that was the case, why hadn't that been enough for them to make it? "What happened between you and Mom? Why didn't you stay?"

"Whoa, I'm going to need something stronger than this coffee I'm drinking to have this conversation." My dad laughs again, but this time it's stilted. "Hey, Les, can you bring me a beer?"

"If you don't want to talk about it, I understand—" I start to let him off the hook, deciding as I curl my knees under me, the photo albums from my childhood strewn across my dining room table, the little girl with the strawberry-blond pigtails staring up at me, that maybe I don't need to dredge up the past after all. Maybe figuring out where my parents went wrong won't unlock the answers inside like I hoped they would. As I listen to my dad and stepmom's muffled voices, I wonder if it's better to preserve the memories I have, not taint them. My dad had left, that was true. But he hadn't left me.

"Sorry about that. I'm in my office now. Don't want Leslie to overhear this."

"Dad, on second thought, we don't have to talk about this. It's probably none of my business—" I flip through one of the albums, fixating on a school picture of me in the first grade, my front tooth missing, the freckles on my nose pronounced from the summer sun.

"Actually I think we should discuss it. I know your mom has always had ideas in her head about why I left." I hear him take a drink of his beer. "I know she's always felt I left her for Leslie— that I was having an affair with her."

The word *affair* hangs between us, like a chime dangling in the air, silent until a gust of wind blows it and causes it to release a musical sound. I chew my lower lip, removing a photo of my mom and dad from behind the plastic in the album, one taken on their wedding day, the picture sticking slightly to the backing as I pull it out. My mom's dress is ivory, with an antique lace overlay, her hair swept up in a bun with loose curls falling around her face. She has her arms wrapped around my dad's neck, kicking her leg up behind her. My dad's tie is loose and he is leaning his head toward her, his eyes closed.

"Kate? You still there?" my dad asks, his usually sturdy voice sounding weak.

"Yes," I answer as I turn the picture over in my hand. My mom had written: *The end of a perfect day but the beginning of a perfect life.*

I think of Jules. I thought she'd been in a perfect marriage too. And I was engaged to be married to a guy I had always thought was perfect for me. How do we know the difference between what's real and what we tell ourselves is real? Did perfection even exist? Or maybe it was just a very dangerous notion, one that we can only see in others' lives, but never in our own.

"Kate . . . I didn't have an affair."

"Then what happened?"

"Sweetheart, there is no *one* answer to that question," my dad says, and I hear ice cubes hitting a glass. I imagine him now mixing a drink in the bar in his office. "We just grew apart."

"Then why doesn't Mom see it that way? Why is she still so . . ." I pause, choosing my next word carefully. ". . . stuck?" I finally say.

"I'm probably to blame for that."

"Why?"

"Because I didn't give her a whole lot of warning, Kate. I said *we* grew apart, but maybe what I should've said is *I* changed." He takes a breath. "By the time I came to her and talked to her about how I was feeling, it was already too late—something inside of me had shifted. I wasn't the twenty-four-year-old man she married anymore and I needed to figure out who I was, and I didn't feel like I could do that with her. That's the thing people don't realize about the forever part of marriage—you're going to change, and if the other person doesn't adapt, things can go sideways pretty quickly."

"So then why did you get married again right away?" I ask,

knowing that's the sticking point, the thing my mom can't accept. That my dad pulled away in that U-Haul intending to go find himself, but instead he found the woman of his dreams.

"I know your mom has always thought I had an affair because of the timing, but like I told her back then, I didn't know Leslie before I moved out. I met her after. Believe me, another relationship was the *last* thing I was looking for—but it just happened. Life is short, and when you meet someone who makes you as happy as Leslie makes me, well, let's just say everything else seems to fade away," he says.

Was my love for Max so strong that the rest of the world stopped when we were together? Yes, I had come back in time for him. But maybe it wasn't because nothing else mattered to me but my love for him—maybe I just couldn't bear being left alone.

"If you could do it all over again, would you still have married Mom?" I ask.

"Of course—because we had you. But, Kate, even if I had the opportunity, I wouldn't want to rewrite the history of my life."

"Not even if you were given the chance to go back in time and change anything? You wouldn't?"

"Nope. Sometimes your mistakes turn out to be your biggest blessings—so you can't live your life second-guessing every choice you make."

"Why not?"

"Because then you're really not living it at all."

I consider my dad's words as I place the wedding photo back in the album.

"Kate? What is this all about? I know it was hard on you when I left. But I really thought it was the right thing to do. I didn't want you to grow up in an unhappy household. I hope you know that." I can hear the panic in my dad's voice. That maybe I don't. That maybe I've been bottling up a secret anger toward him for leaving my mom.

"Yes, I'm okay, Dad," I say, and can picture his jaw softening as he hears my words. "I mean, of course I was sad—no kid wants her parents to get divorced. But you were always there for me," I say, thinking about how my dad never missed a soccer game or a spelling bee, never tried to shove Leslie on me, instead letting me come to accept her on my own terms, which I did eventually. "Plus, you know I love Leslie," I say, feeling a pinch of betrayal of my mom for saying it out loud.

• • •

The conversation with my dad sits with me long after we've hung up. As I'm getting ready for Nikki Day's party, I'm still replaying my dad's words—that he wouldn't rewrite his history, even if given the chance. Was he just saying that to spare my feelings, because if he hadn't married my mom, I wouldn't have been born? Would Jules have to give the same response about her marriage to Ben because of her children? Or was my dad right—does life work out just as it should, even if it doesn't feel like it at the time? And if that was the case, why couldn't my mom accept that? Even though she had already been on three dates with Bill, she was still bringing my dad's name up in every conversation, the thought of seeing him and Leslie at the wedding consuming her. I had hoped that dating another man would ignite a spark in her, one that would let her leave the past behind once and for all—but for whatever reason, she still seemed to be clinging to it.

"What should I wear to this thing?" Max says, startling me as he enters our walk-in closet.

"Shit, sorry, didn't mean to scare you!" He grabs for a pale blue button-down. "You okay?"

"I was just thinking about a conversation I had with my dad today. I was asking about why he left my mom."

"That's a heavy topic for a Saturday." He searches my eyes. "Why were you asking? Is your mom giving you shit about Leslie again?"

"Yes, always." I release a hollow laugh, pulling a blue wrap dress down from the hanger and holding it up against my body. "Can I ask you something?" I meet Max's eyes in the full-length mirror on the wall and he nods.

"Yes, definitely wear that. It brings out the blue in your eyes." He smiles.

"Thank you. But that's not my question." I pause, looking around, thinking how much my life has changed since I was in this closet when this all began—when I was giddy over a pair of sandals that had magically appeared.

"Oh?" He runs his hand through his hair, sticking up slightly in the back from the baseball cap he'd been wearing earlier.

"Do you think life works out just as it should? That you can't mess with destiny?"

Max's lips curl upward and I think I see his chest contract slightly, as if he's just released the breath he was holding. Had he been worried I was going to ask him something else? "Have you been reading *The Power of Now* or something?" He laughs.

"No!" I swat him with my dress. "I'm being serious, Max. What's your opinion?"

"Well, if I *must* weigh in on this . . . I would say that we control our lives, not the other way around. I don't believe there's some predestined plan for me."

"Good answer," I say, kissing him deeply.

"Oh, yes. Definitely wear that," he says, running a finger down my arm as I grip the dress. "And if you do, I can't be held responsible for what I might do to you later."

"Oh, really?"

"Yep," he says, kissing me again.

"Why wait until later?" I start to pull his T-shirt over his head.

"Don't have to ask me twice," he says, pulling me down to the closet floor. I let myself get lost in his kisses, in his touch, detaching myself from the conflicting thoughts about fate and destiny that are wrestling inside of me, and decide the only moment that matters is the one I'm living in right now.

CHAPTER TWENTY-FOUR

. . . .

Once, Magda had given me some valuable advice. It was right before my first client pitch, a proposal I had been working on for weeks, barely sleeping or eating, my hair falling out at the slightest touch from the stress. As we sat in the reception area of the cosmetic company we were courting, the fire-engine-red walls making my temples pound, Magda had uncharacteristically put a hand on my trembling knee and smiled. "Kate, you've put together a fantastic presentation. I wouldn't let you pitch this if I didn't think you were ready."

I had nearly jumped at her touch. "But what if I'm not . . ." I'd paused before finishing my thought, not sure how vulnerable I wanted to appear.

"Not what?" Magda squinted her eyes.

"Ready?" I'd finally said.

"I'm going to tell you a little secret," she said as she leaned in. "No one's ever *really* ready for anything. You just fake it till it feels right—and eventually it will."

I had nodded silently, trying to reconcile this kinder, gentler Magda with the one who had fired questions at me like bullets the entire way there.

"Okay? So pull it together. I don't want to have to fire you," she said, and laughed quietly to herself, leaving me to wonder whether or not she was joking. I never did find out—I had held my shaking hands steady as I'd impressed the executives, signing them as my first client. I have given countless pitches since, but I have never forgotten that moment—or the tip that had gone along with it. Advice that would come in handy tonight.

As we all sit silently in the valet line that wraps around the block for Nikki's party, Max's Jeep Cherokee trapped between Escalades and SUV limos, I wish I could read everyone's mind. Max stares straight ahead with a blank expression. Ben and Jules sit in the backseat, their hands brushing lightly, almost as if by accident.

"Liam's already in there," I say, my voice almost echoing in the quiet car as I glance back at Jules, who looks up from her phone, her emerald eyes slightly vacant despite how stunning she looks in her cap-sleeved charcoal-gray sequined dress, her legs crossed tightly to combat its short length.

Max had whistled as she walked out her front door, shooting me a guilty look immediately afterward. "It's okay," I had said, laughing. "She looks smokin' hot." And when Ben had material- ized through the same doorway a few beats later—the entrance to the two-story house they'd owned for nearly a decade, the home they'd been so proud to be able to purchase, me helping them move in and paint because they'd used all of their savings for the down payment—there was something that felt discon- nected between them, like an unplugged power cord straining for the outlet. I watched Max as they slid into the backseat, curious if he had noticed. He hadn't seemed to, launching into a debate with Ben over whether Los Angeles would ever get an- other professional football team, both of them laughing as if they didn't have a care in the world, and I decided I was just being sensitive because I knew that Jules' fidelity to Ben was hanging on by a tiny thread.

I quickly reapply my lipstick as we inch toward the valet stand, while all of us attempt to guess which celebrity is going to emerge next from the sanctuary of their limousine. Jules and I let out a squeal when we spot her favorite celebrity couple stepping out of the car ahead of us, him grabbing for her hand as they expertly maneuver the microphones and cameras assaulting them as they meander down the red carpet.

"They're going to be pretty damn disappointed to see us." Max chuckles as he puts the car into park, the valet, a young model type with a shaggy haircut, opening our doors with a flourish. We hurry self-consciously down the carpet, the flashing of the cameras stopping briefly as we shuffle past, me looping my arm through Jules' and pulling her back slightly from Max and Ben.

"You doing okay?" I ask, glancing over my shoulder at Ben and Max.

"Yes!" she snaps. "Don't be like that, Kate."

"Like what?"

"Reading into every single thing, each look or moment of silence. It's not that simple," she whispers. "Please don't make me regret confiding in you."

"Sorry," I say, slightly hurt by her tone.

As if reading my mind, she squeezes my arm. "I know you're just trying to be a good friend. But, I promise, it's all going to be okay. I'll figure it all out."

"With you and Ben?"

"With everything. Stop worrying so much." She touches the thin skin under my eyes. "It's going to give you wrinkles!" She laughs and I join her, deciding she's probably right. Here I am, at this incredible party, surrounded by the rich and famous, with Max and all of my closest friends—I need to take a deep breath and enjoy it.

• • •

"Have you tried the ceviche?" Jules calls over her shoulder later as she walks in the direction of the bar to get us our third round of champagne, tripping slightly as she looks past me to a good-looking man—one I think I recognize from an action flick Max and I saw a while back. The movie star catches her elbow as she starts to fall and soaks in the broad smile Jules gives him as a thank-you. They have a brief discussion before walking slowly to the bar together, continuing their conversation as they stand in line, Jules' leg propped out, her hand sitting on her hip flirtatiously. I take a bite of my crab cake and glance over at Ben, who's talking to Max while keeping a close eye on his wife. He catches me staring at him. "She's just drunk," he says confidently, but I hear some defensiveness hiding behind his words. "I'm just making sure she makes it back without falling over again," he adds quickly, as if he needs a reason to be watching her.

"Totally! She's just blowing off steam," I add a little too eagerly and wonder why we're trying so hard to convince each other that what we're witnessing is harmless. But then I remember Jules' warning—to stop reading into every little thing. If I'd bumped into a hot actor who had headlined the last blockbuster I'd seen, I'd probably be flirting too.

Ben finally peels his eyes away. "You know how it is—a night away from the kids, and you go crazy." He laughs. "She deserves to let loose. I've been traveling a ton lately. We've barely seen each other."

"You should whisk her off on a weekend away after the wedding," I say, fighting the urge to shake him, to tell Ben that he is on the verge of losing the woman he's loved for more than a decade, that she is slipping through his grasp like hot sand on a summer day.

"Maybe. It's so hard to find a sitter," he says, and takes another sip of his Jack and Coke.

"We'll watch them," I say firmly as Max whips his head up and starts to say something. I give him a look that immediately silences him.

"We'll see," he says noncommittally as Jules walks carefully in our direction, clasping two flutes so full of champagne that the liquid is spilling over the tops.

"Did you see who I was talking to?" she says, her cheeks flushed as she sips the bubbles off the top of her glass and hands the other to me. "That was the guy who was in *First Night*! You know, he was the one who got the girl in the end?"

"He sure did," Ben says under his breath and drains his glass. Max throws me a *What the fuck is going on with them* look and I shrug my shoulders in response, Jules either not hearing him or not caring as she sways to the beat of the band that begins to play.

"Let's go find Liam," I suggest as I glance behind me, surprised I haven't seen him yet—we had spied Nikki earlier giving an interview, but Liam was nowhere to be found.

"Looking for me?" I hear Liam's deep voice and spin around, his normally rumpled hair expertly slicked back, giving his usually slack features a hard edge that I can't decide if I like.

Liam greets Max and Ben with a firm handshake before pulling Jules and me in for a hug. "You girls look stunning."

"Thanks," I say, resisting the impulse to reach up and touch his hair, convinced it will feel like a Ken doll's head. "Where's Nikki?"

"Around," he replies vaguely, and my mind immediately wanders to the picture of her and the guy in the *Enquirer*, wondering if he'd also be making an appearance here tonight. Hoping, for Liam's sake, that he won't. "You know how these thing are," he adds, all of us bobbing our heads in agreement, even though we have no clue about *these things*.

Liam grabs a drink from a passing waiter and settles in, telling us funny stories about walking the red carpet with Nikki, confiding that it felt weird to stand by her side and hold her sequined clutch while she regaled each reporter with sound bites she'd rehearsed in the limo on the way here.

"Must have felt amazing being someone's purse handler," I say sarcastically.

"It beats sitting at home obsessively binge watching some TV show on Netflix, which you could've been doing tonight," he says pointedly, and I stick out my tongue.

Several glasses of Moët & Chandon and turns on the dance floor later, we're all having a great time. Max and I jump up and down to the beat and Liam joins us in the brief windows when he isn't being pulled away by Nikki's "people" for a photo op. Ben is even swinging Jules, instantly taking me back to their wedding day when they'd surprised the guests with a synchronized dance.

When the band begins to play a song I don't recognize, I pull Max toward the dessert table, which is overflowing with gorgeous delicacies I had been looking forward to tasting all night. But his hand goes slack as we reach the edge of the dance floor and I twist my head to see why, my stomach doing a somersault when I see what he does—Courtney dancing closely with a tall man with salt-and-pepper hair. He raises his hands in the air and she slides herself toward his toned body as if she doesn't have a care in the world. Gone is the girl who had cried in my car, her red-rimmed eyes now sparkling, her hair sleek, her body tucked into a mini that leaves little to the imagination. I put my hands on my own dress, suddenly feeling like an old maid—Courtney's beauty had a way of making your own luster dim.

"Max?" I say softly, the noise from the band swallowing my words. I shake his shoulder slightly and say his name again before he finally turns his head, the anguish in his eyes hitting me like a sucker punch to the stomach, the alcohol he'd consumed earlier ripping away the veneer that I realize now must mask his true feelings.

"Courtney," is all he says.

"I know, I see her too," I say, and grab for his hand. "Come with me," I plead, not wanting to sound desperate, even though I am. Desperate to pretend that I don't see Max's love for Courtney written all over his face; desperate to still believe I can outrun our fate. I think about Jules' messed-up life and Liam being turned into a Hollywood cliché. It's as if by coming back here, I have taken a sledgehammer to everyone else's story in order to write my own happy ending.

Max gives Courtney one last look before turning back to me and grabbing my hand. "I'm sorry, Kate," he says, and I'm not sure what for and I don't want to ask.

"It's okay," is all I say because I don't trust myself to say anything else. "I'll be right back," I say, pointing in the direction of the restroom, just wanting to put as much distance as possible between me and what's happened in the last five minutes.

Walking in a haze through the crowd, I almost collide with a server wearing a crisp white shirt and black pants. "Excuse me," I say automatically without looking up.

"You better watch where you're going," a familiar voice says, and I do a double take when I find Ruby holding an empty tray, smirking at me.

"Why am I even surprised?" I say, more to myself than to her. "Of course you would show up now. Is this your *I told you so* moment?"

Ruby's smirk evaporates. "Is that what you think? That I'm here to teach you some sort of lesson?" she says as a drunken starlet walks by and hands her an empty glass with a cigarette butt in it. Ruby tosses the glass into the trash before grabbing my arm and pulling me away from the crowd. "Whether you believe it or not, I'm here to help, *not hurt,* you."

"Could've fooled me," I say, my anger at Max spilling out of me onto Ruby. "I did everything, *everything* right this time. And he still loves her. She still wins," I say, my voice cracking.

"Maybe that's the problem, Kate. You keep treating this as if it's a game."

"Isn't it, though? Aren't we all trying to triumph at life?" I think about Callie from college, who just this morning had posted a picture of a letter her eight-year-old had written telling her what a wonderful mommy she was. He even had incredible handwriting that seemed unlikely for a child who had only just graduated kindergarten. But the fact remained the same—if life was a game, Callie was in the lead by a mile. And even given a second chance, I had still lost.

Ruby presses her lips together and looks me over with wonder as if I'm a rare animal at the zoo. "After everything you've been through, that's what comes to mind?" She steps into an alcove as a real catering waiter walks by briskly. "And to think I believed you were *finally* getting it." She untucks her shirt. "I'm done here," she says, her eyes glistening as she turns to leave.

"Wait," I say. "This is it? You're walking away from me, now?" I ask, feeling panicked. "How do I fix this? Do I have any more wishes?" Maybe there was still a chance I could make this all right—if we hadn't come to this party, if he'd never seen Courtney dancing with that man. If I could erase it all, Max and I could still be happy together.

Ruby sighs heavily, looking tired. "You do have one final wish. My advice to you is to use it wisely." She pats my shoulder lightly. "Just remember, some things just aren't meant to be fixed," she says before disappearing into the darkness.

CHAPTER TWENTY-FIVE

....

The cold water tingles my skin as it splashes up onto my face, wiping away in an instant the careful work I'd done applying my makeup earlier tonight, when I stood barefoot on my tiled bathroom floor, my heart still beating quickly after making love to Max, a nervous excitement coursing through me as I anticipated coming to this Hollywood party with him on my arm. Blotting my face dry with a stark white monogrammed napkin that reads *Nikki's Night*, I sneer at my reflection in the mirror, wanting the answers I am seeking to be reflected in my eyes. Was Ruby right? At least I have one more wish. I could use it to go back in time again. Third time's a charm, right?

I pull a tube of gloss out of my black sequined clutch and glide it over my lips, thinking about what I could have done differently with the wishes I'd been granted. Obviously it had been a mistake to use them to try to help Jules and Liam, my efforts to make their lives better completely backfiring. If I did decide to do this all over again, I wouldn't have any more wishes, which means I would have to rely on my own power of persuasion to convince my best friends I had traveled through time. And Liam was so skeptical, I wasn't confident I could make him believe me on my own. Or that I'd even want to try. It might be better not to tell them at all—not to involve anyone else in my inability to get my own life right.

Yes, I decide as I push open the bathroom door, the bass from the band's speakers vibrating in the hallway. Traveling back again will be worth it because it will solve two major problems: Jules will hopefully be satisfied with her marriage and Liam won't be at the center of a celebrity cheating scandal. Those two reasons alone are enough to convince me to do it. Even though I know I'll be back to square one with Max and Courtney—but I'll just have to figure out what I can do differently so my actions don't keep pushing them together instead of pulling them apart.

I'd definitely need to go back further in time. Maybe two months? Six? When had their friendship shifted to something more? Was it when I sent Max to pick her up after her car broke down on Sepulveda Boulevard? Or had it been when Courtney scored backstage passes to meet the members of Toad the Wet Sprocket, Courtney sweet-talking her way onto their tour bus where she and Max partied with the band? What had been the exact moment that had changed the course of all of our lives? If I could pinpoint that, I might have a chance.

I make my way through the crowded ballroom, trying to keep my composure as I pass the entire cast of my favorite sitcom, finally spotting Max sitting with Ben and Jules in a lounge area in the corner, Jules cocking her head in the direction of the dance floor where Courtney is still gyrating with her date. I throw my hands up and shake my head, refusing to look in her direction again. As I start to make my way toward them I spy Liam's lanky body sitting at the edge of the party where the dimming lights and darkness meet.

"Hey," I say gently, and sit beside him as he raises a bottle of tequila to his lips, his hair now rumpled, his bow tie loose around his neck, looking so much like the old Liam that my heart jumps—I hadn't realized how much I had missed this version of him.

"Hey," he echoes, and passes the bottle of Patrón to me.

I hesitate before taking a large swig, coughing slightly and wiping my mouth with the back of my hand as it burns my throat. "Damn, Liam. How much of this have you had?"

He shrugs his shoulders. "It was full when I snagged it from the bar."

I look at the bottle, a little over a quarter of the liquor gone. "You okay?"

"This night has not turned out at all like I thought it would."

"Tell me about it—check out who ended up on the guest list." I point the bottle to where Courtney is on the dance floor.

"What are the odds of that?" Liam says, shaking his head.

A *gazillion to one.*

"You should have seen Max's face when he noticed her." My stomach curls as I remember the look, one I wish I could erase from my mind. "It was like he'd seen a ghost," I say, a single tear escaping from my eye, and I reach up to brush it away, but Liam beats me to it, his fingertip dissolving it.

"Come here," he says, and pulls my chair closer to him, wrapping his warm arm around my shoulders.

"I found out I have one more wish. I'm thinking of using it to go back in time again. But I'm planning to go further back—maybe as far as six months."

Liam takes another long drink from the bottle. "What if you don't? What if you stay here? If you saw him look at her that way, after everything, maybe it means it's time to let him go."

The tears begin to fall more rapidly and I turn my face into his chest and wipe them away with his shirt. "I'm worried that I don't know who I am without him."

"That's funny."

"What?"

"I don't know who you are *with* him."

I pull back, startled by his reaction. "What do you mean?"

"Nothing." He shakes his head. "Forget it."

"No, tell me."

"I don't even recognize this version of you—you've had tunnel vision this entire time, so closed off from everything that you can't see what it's done to you. You've changed, Kate."

Stunned by Liam's words, I try to formulate my response. I knew I was different, but I wasn't sure that was a bad thing. My eyes were wide open this time. I wasn't letting my relationship slip through the cracks while I paid attention to all the wrong things.

"And what about love?" he asks before I can respond.

"Love?"

"I tell you to let him go and the first thing you say is you don't know who you are without him. Why didn't you say it was because you loved him?"

"I don't want to live my life without him. That *is* love."

Liam shakes his head. "Not in my book. I say that's fear."

With each hurtful word Liam throws at me, anger begins to build up inside me like logs being stacked to make a fire—I'm worried I might erupt into flames if he struck a match against me. "Since when did *you* become a relationship expert? Aren't you the guy whose buddies take over/under bets on how long before you find a flaw and dump the girl you're dating? The man who's Nikki's puppet?" He flinches slightly when I say the last part.

"Not anymore."

"Which one?"

"Either. Both. Whatever. Nikki and I are done. Tonight was all for show. Even though there was a part of me that still thought she'd change her mind."

"The boy bander?"

"True. All of it."

"But you told Jules the press got it wrong."

"I wanted to believe they had. But then she admitted it to me this morning and begged me to still come as her date." He closes his eyes for a moment, as if remembering their conversation. "I don't know why I agreed—guess I'm just a sucker."

"Or a nice guy." I rub his back, suddenly ashamed of the things I said. "You're too good for her anyway, Liam."

"That's what Nikki said too." He smiles sadly. "Right before she dumped my ass for a guy who has a swagger coach in his entourage."

"I'm sorry," I say, and mean it. I might have not liked Nikki, or the way she changed Liam, but I never wanted to see him hurt.

"No, it's okay, really," he says. "Honestly, I got caught up in it. I think I liked the lifestyle more than I liked her."

"Still, it never feels good to be dumped." *Especially not for someone else*, I think, remembering the rehearsal dinner as if it were yesterday.

Liam looks at me. "I know Max really hurt you." He points to where Courtney and her date are still wrapped around each other. "That he's still hurting you."

I start to defend him, but Liam puts his hand up. "Don't make excuses for him. *Please*. I know he's not a bad guy, but it's not him I care about." He gives me a long look, his eyes fixated on me, the things he wants to say swirling in them.

I stay silent, staring at my engagement ring, remembering the night Max asked me. Had it been a proposal like something out of the movies? No. But it had been special and I had said yes without a second thought. But now it was like Liam was shining a spotlight on Max, forcing me to look at him in a way I hadn't wanted to before. The night Max asked me to be his wife, I knew he was as excited about our future as I was, but it was possible the not-so-subtle hints about my age I had dropped pushed him down a road he hadn't truly been ready for.

Liam leans his head down toward mine. "Remember, right after college, when I was up for the lead in that sitcom? I went through, like, thirty auditions. It was down to me and one other guy and they called my agent to tell me the part was mine? And then, when we were expecting the contract to be sent over, we got a phone call that they chose him?"

I nod, cringing inside at how devastated Liam had been, how humiliated he was when he had to call his friends and family and tell them they'd retracted their offer.

"Do you recall what you said to me after I told you I was going to quit acting? When I said it wasn't fucking worth it anymore?"

I shake my head, my eyes filling with tears.

"You said the only way to get through something is to go straight through it. Not hide from it. Just feel it, learn from it, and then pick up the pieces and move on with your life."

"I said that?" I smile weakly as Liam nods, touched that he's held that advice with him all this time, but my chest feeling hollow at the thought of following it myself. "It's solid advice, Liam. But I can't."

"Why not?" He frowns.

"Because I'm not like you."

"What's that supposed to mean?" Liam's shoulders tense.

"I can't compartmentalize my feelings like you do."

"Is that what you think I do?"

I sit up straighter so I can meet his eyes. "You give everyone these small scraps of yourself, always careful not to get too involved, too attached. You never let anyone hold your heart long enough to hurt you. But you think I should just dig in and feel the pain?" Liam's eyes glisten but I can't stop, thinking again how he'd judged me for not wanting to let Max go. That he inferred that I didn't love him enough. "What do you even know about love anyway?"

"I know more than you think," he says cryptically before whispering, "I know what it's like to have the person you love be in love with someone else."

"What?" I say, confused. "You mean Nikki?" I whisper back, our faces so close that the tip of his nose grazes mine.

Liam laughs. "God, you're so dense sometimes," he says before tentatively placing his lips on mine, almost like his kiss is a question he's looking for an answer to. My eyes widen in shock and I instinctively try to pull away, but he holds me close.

"Liam," I murmur.

"Shhh," he says, holding my chin gently in his hand. "Stop thinking so much. Just follow your damn heart for once in your life." He kisses me again, his lips so soft and welcoming that I have to force myself to pull back a second time.

"I can't. Max—"

"Your fiancé who is clearly in love with someone else? Does he really get a say in this?"

I pull even farther out of his embrace at the mention of Courtney. "That's not fair. If I do this with you, then I'm no better than he is." I stand abruptly, my purse falling to the ground. Liam picks it up and our hands brush.

"I'm not going to apologize for kissing you. I'm not going to spend one more day pretending I don't care—even if it means I get *hurt*." He stands and grabs my shoulders, but his eyes soften quickly when he looks into mine. "Don't go back in time again. Don't marry Max. Stay here and be with me."

My mind spinning, I watch him as he chews his lower lip, his eyes squinting at me so hard it's as if he's trying to see inside of me. Liam is in love with me? The question materializes in my mind like skywriting as we continue to lock gazes, neither of us ready to break eye contact or the palpable silence. I loved him too, of course, and would do anything for him, but I couldn't give him this—not when I had fought so hard to make things work with Max. "I can't do this right now," I say, and his shoulders sag. "I'm sorry." I reach for him, but he moves away from me.

"I'm sorry too . . ." He finally averts his gaze, staring out at the crowd of partygoers oblivious to the drama unfolding between us. "But I had to tell you. I needed you to know there's a life here, with me. If you're brave enough to take the leap."

"I'm sorry." I shake my head, thankful that the darkness is helping to conceal my watery eyes, the disappointed expression I imagine in his eyes, suddenly remembering his words before the rehearsal dinner—that I didn't have to go through with the wedding. He had quickly laughed it off, but I wonder now if he had been harboring a sliver of hope that I really would call it off. I hear Nikki's voice echo from the main stage as she thanks everyone for coming tonight—wondering suddenly, as the sound of thunderous applause fills the air, if the *real* reason I had fought against Liam's relationship with her had nothing to do with her celebrity and everything to do with my own feelings for him. I think back to how unsettled I was when he began to choose Nikki over me, how my heart had felt vacant as I'd stared at yet another unanswered text message on my phone, and wonder if the idea of losing him had sparked something inside of me that I hadn't let myself realize was there, or more likely, was too afraid to acknowledge.

"I have to go back," I say more to myself than to him, deciding that I still owed it to myself to see things through with Max.

"Then I have just one request," he says, his voice low and scratchy. "Don't tell me when you get there."

"What do you mean?"

"Don't tell me about coming back here, about what Max did to you the first time. About what I just confessed to you."

"Why?"

"Because I don't want to know—I *won't* want to know." He stands up and starts to walk away, then stops himself and turns back abruptly. "Have you ever thought about why I haven't gotten serious with anyone?"

I think of his last string of girlfriends: Daphne, Erica, Janie, or was it Jamie? Many of whom I'd never even met, but had, of course, heard about. After a month or two, he'd inevitably announce their departure, then tell me why it would've never worked. I'd listen as he explained why he'd broken things off with her—always wondering about the real reason he wasn't settling down, guessing it was a commitment issue because of his absent father. But I never pried. I figured he'd eventually find the one who would rise above the rest and weed through the bullshit and ultimately get to his heart despite his greatest efforts to tuck it away. And all along that person was . . . . "Me," I hear myself say. "It was because of me? " I ask, the words sounding strange as I say them out loud.

He rubs the stubble that's lightly dotting his chin and nods slowly. "I compare them all to you," he says quietly. And suddenly, I flash back to that night in college Liam kissed me and I blew it off. Has he loved me since then?

"You really shouldn't," I say. "Clearly, I've got issues!"

"That's just the way I like you," he says, and we both laugh awkwardly. "Here's the thing—the man you marry should find your *issues* endearing. The guy you spend your life with needs to understand you—needs to know you don't come with a manual, but you're pretty damn easy to figure out if he knows how to get inside your mind." He raises his eyebrows. "He needs to accept that you can *and will* piss him off like there's no tomorrow—especially when you are trying to make everything around you so damn perfect. But ironically, he should also realize that you have an incredible ability to make him feel like his imperfections are the best part of him." He looks away for a moment and I don't speak. I can't speak—my throat is thick with tears as I absorb his words. He grabs my hands and pulls my face close to his. "Does Max get you? Does he know not to try to stop you when you are obsessing over taking the perfect photo or that you always think the book is better than the movie? Even *The Godfather?*" Liam shakes his head. "Does he know that short of your boss or your mother hiring a plane to pull one of those banners that says KATE IS FUCKING AWESOME, you will never be satisfied with what their opinion of you is? Does he know you might cry like a blubbering baby over something seemingly innocuous—like the series finale of *How I Met Your Mother*—and he should just let you? Does he know you hate running and only do it to impress him? Does he know how insanely smart you are? How beautiful? Does he even know the *real* you?"

I suck in a deep breath and release it slowly, processing his words, realizing they represent so much more than friendship. He really loves me. In a way I never realized was possible.

"I don't know—I thought so, I think so . . ." I stammer.

"Because if he doesn't, then that's not true love. And you will both be settling."

"And you are the expert because?" I ask, but I already know what he's going to say.

"Because that's how I feel about you—how you make me feel."

I cross my arms over my chest, trying to warm myself from the chill running through me as I try to make sense of his confession. It was true, he knew me in a way that Max never had, but I wasn't convinced that was reason enough to throw everything with Max away, not after all I'd done to repair our relationship. "I've come this far with Max. I need to see what happens with him," I say, rubbing my hand along his arm to take the sting off my words.

He flinches slightly, but finally nods. "Can't knock a man for trying, right?" He half laughs. "I guess you've dragged me to so many of those rom-coms that I got caught up. Who was I to think I could give you some big speech and you'd fall into my arms and say you felt the same way?"

"Liam." I hold my hand out to him, but he doesn't take it.

"It's okay. You don't have to feel sorry for me. I love you, but I want you to be happy."

I squeeze my eyes shut, afraid the tears that are brimming behind them will spill over if I don't, not wanting to think about what might or might not make me happy.

"But I meant what I said earlier—please don't tell me any of this if you go back, especially not this conversation." He looks down. "Kicked to the curb twice in the same night," he says under his breath. "I just want to live my life like there's no opportunity for second chances."

"Okay," I say, reaching for him again. This time he accepts me into his arms. I hug him tightly, not wanting to let go. He grips me hard, like he might not see me again, and I resist the urge to stay, knowing I need to get back to Max. "I have to go."

"Okay," he says, and sinks back down in his seat, picking up the bottle of tequila again.

"I'm sorry," I say again, not sure if I'm apologizing for leaving or for not loving him back the way he wants me to.

"It's okay—it's all going to disappear soon anyway, right? None of it will matter."

"It's for the best. For everyone."

"Keep telling yourself that, Kate," I hear him say to my back as I walk away, into the lights of the party, gripping Max's hand firmly when I find him, hoping our bond is just as strong.

• • •

"You want to talk about what happened tonight?" Max says as I crawl into bed later, and for a second I think he means Liam, but then I realize he's talking about Courtney. I'd been quiet on the way home, my mind spinning like a tornado with the memory of Liam's words and the visual of Max's face when he saw Courtney, whipping around and around. I lay my head on the pillow, not wanting to talk, especially because it was all going to be pointless once I had made my wish.

"We just can't seem to escape her," Max says, and curves his body around mine, laying his arm over my waist and pulling me closer.

"No, we sure can't," I say softly.

"I'm here for the long haul," he whispers into my ear.

His words comfort me—I can tell how much he wants to mean them. But is he staying because it's the right thing to do, or because he wants to spend the rest of his life with me? Last time, I'd been so caught up in the wedding planning that I'd made it easy for him to convince himself that my love had faded too, that he had been doing us both a favor by ending things before we were legally bound. But the difference this time is that I have fought like hell for it—but is the sentiment still the same? Should it be this hard?

"Me too," I whisper, all at once terrified to go back in time and start over again, but even more scared to stay and try to make something out of the mess I've made here.

CHAPTER TWENTY-SIX

....

The first time I saw my wedding dress, it didn't look like much on the hanger. But I'd been drawn to it anyway—I'd loved the gray sash wrapped around the waist that tied into a bow in the back and the way the organza felt between my fingertips. I'd handed it to the sales associate and figured it would most likely be one of the dozens I'd end up rejecting, because, as Jules and I agreed on our way into the boutique, who finds *the dress* on the first day she starts looking? Between the anxiety of finding the gown and the fact that my pear-shaped body didn't cooperate with a lot of styles, I knew the odds were stacked against me. But when I'd stepped onto the platform in front of the three-way mirror, Jules walked up behind me and nodded her head, and we'd both started to cry before falling into a fit of giggles, because we were officially *those people* we'd made fun of so many times on those bridal reality shows.

As my mom and I walk into the boutique for my final fitting, my breath catches at the memory of being here for my final fitting last time, when I'd still been wearing my engagement like it was a neon sign above my head. I catch my reflection in one of the large mirrors as I pass through the showroom and hardly recognize the look in my eyes this time.

I'm still not sure why I decided to come here, why I didn't post the status that would send me back further in time after I got home last night. I had sat on the toilet in the bathroom, clutching my phone, unable to press my finger down, determining that I needed more time to figure out why, despite all of my efforts, Courtney and Max remained intertwined in each other's lives. Maybe the only way to prevent them from falling in love would be for them to never meet—for me to go back in time to before I first introduced them. A twinge of concern tickles the back of my mind—would the universe have them meet another way if I didn't facilitate it?

I had also thought that seeing myself in my wedding gown one more time, feeling the way the fabric swayed as I walked, memorizing the way it made me feel to pull it up around me, would help bring me clarity. But as I stood here now, I was unwilling to believe that my decisions didn't hold any weight. What about free will? I imagined there were going to be some pretty pissed-off philosophers when they heard about this development—that some things may be predetermined, no matter how much we try to change them.

"I can't wait to see you in your dress," my mom says, her eyes brimming with tears as she watches a young redhead walk into the back room to retrieve my gown.

"Are you going to cry?" I ask, pulling her down beside me on a pale pink velvet-covered bench.

"Maybe just a little." She smiles, blinking back the moistness in her eyes and hugging me tightly. "I'm just so happy for you. They say the day your little girl gets married is one of the best of your life."

You didn't get to enjoy it last time, I think, recalling the look etched on her face as Max told everyone there wouldn't be a wedding—the disappointment coupled with sadness had only added to the pain I was feeling.

"Here it is," the redhead says cheerily, presenting it to me as if it's one of those giant checks you receive when you've won the lottery. "You can try it on in there," she says, and points to a white beveled door in the corner. "Champagne?" she asks, and my mom and I say yes in unison.

I grip the padded hanger tightly, holding the dress up so the bottom of it doesn't brush the floor. I close the dressing room door and hang it on a hook on the wall, the emotions of the morning after the rehearsal dinner rushing through me in a violent wave. As I pull the zipper down to remove the dress, the sound takes me back to the moment Jules sealed my gown inside its garment bag and called the concierge, agreeing to pay God only knows what to have it shipped to her house so I'd never have to lay eyes on it again.

I push the memory aside and step into the dress, calling for the salesgirl to help close it in the back before walking backward, away from the mirror. "It's still amazing," I say more to myself than to her, but she nods excitedly in agreement as she helps me slip my feet into the heels I bought.

"Oh my God," my mom says as she's drinking her champagne, nearly spitting it out as she chokes a little on her words. "You look beautiful."

"Thanks, Mom," I say as I step onto the platform and twirl around, admiring the dress from the back, then catching my mom's reflection in the mirror, the tears she promised now spilling down her cheeks. As I watch her watching me, mine glisten too, imagining my future daughter one day doing the same, saying a silent prayer that her heart will be sure as she spins on her platform, that she'll choose a man worthy of her. That she'll get it right the first time.

"Mom?"

"Yeah?"

"You seem really happy."

"Of course I'm happy for you, honey."

"No, I mean there's something about you that's different. Lately, you seem—"

"—lighter?" my mom offers.

"Exactly." I smile, thinking of the man she's been dating. "Is it Bill?"

"Oh, no, I told him we can't see each other anymore."

"What?" I knot my forehead. "Why? I thought things were going so well."

"They were, but we, well *I*, quickly realized that we didn't have a damn thing in common other than living next door to each other," she says with a laugh. "You know about the only things he likes to do are grill out in the backyard and tinker with that old Chevy in his garage? I'd die from boredom!"

I study her face for a moment. "So then why are you so happy?"

"Because dating him was the best thing that's happened to me in a long time."

"But it didn't work out," I say, taking a careful sip of my champagne as I hold the flute away from my body, curious for her answer.

"I don't know how to explain it exactly," my mom says, holding out her glass so the associate can fill it again. "I feel like a huge weight has been lifted, because even though he wasn't the one, I had a great time figuring out he wasn't. It gave me hope that the right guy for me might be out there."

She walks over and stands next to me in front of the mirror, putting her arm around my waist. "I think I'm ready to finally move on."

"Really?" I ask.

My mom nods before answering. "I was devastated when your dad left. And I worried for a long time how it would affect you."

"Me?"

"I guess I didn't want you to fear marriage because ours had failed."

"I don't, I mean I never did. Sometimes people just outgrow each other," I say, wondering about my own relationship with Max, wondering if we'd outgrown each other and not even noticed.

"Anyway, it took me a long time to figure out who I was without your dad. Even longer to actually *like* the person I was without him." She laughs awkwardly.

I shiver, goose bumps covering my bare shoulders and arms. I'd said similar words to Liam last night.

"Maybe my only daughter getting married has made me really think about my own life, but I'm starting to lament spending so much of my time focusing on my regrets," my mom adds as she takes another sip of her champagne.

"I'm really happy for you," I say, still shocked that I'm finally hearing the words I've been waiting for her to say.

She puts her arm around me and we stare at each other in the mirrored wall in front of us. "Now this doesn't mean that I'm going to be Facebook friends with your dad and—"

"—the wife?"

"Leslie," my mom says slowly, and I give her a short smile. "It's time for me to finally let go of what could have been."

"What could have been?"

"I think I was so stuck on what life could have been like if your dad hadn't left—all the things we would've done together, so bitter that he was doing those things with someone else—that I really wasn't living."

"Wow," is all I say, happy for my mom's breakthrough, but sad thinking about all the years she lost.

"I know, right?" she says as she points at herself. "I've been putting all this time and effort into keeping this body fabulous and then not even using it!" She laughs as I cringe, the thought of her being sexual with someone making me want to gag. "The point is," she continues, "even I know when it's time to give up and move on to something better."

I walk back to the dressing room, replaying my mom's words. Of course she picks today to finally decide to start living her life again. I debate whether it would be selfish for me to go back now, knowing she might not have the same realizations next time. As I step out of my dress, it feels heavier this time, like a weight bearing down on me—the understanding that there were more lives than my own hanging in the balance.

• • •

"Welcome to Starbucks," a peppy, fresh-faced girl greets my mom and me. We've decided to stop for a coffee before I drive her home, our heads still buzzing slightly from the champagne.

After we order, we're making our way to a table in the corner when I think I see a familiar face. Before I can get the words out of my mouth, my mom cuts me off, "Isn't that Callie, your old college roommate?" She scrunches up her nose as if trying to decide.

"I think." I study her as she stands in line, rubbing her protruding belly as her two children demand cake pops and Cotton

Candy Frappuccinos. Through gritted teeth, she barks, "For the fiftieth time, the answer is *no*," the lines around her eyes deepening as she says it. But her kids' begging is relentless, and when they reach the cash register, Callie finally gives in, mumbling something about how they should just take all the money in her wallet and buy whatever they want because they always do anyway.

She leans on the counter as her children feast on their treats, her younger one dropping the cake pop on the floor before picking it up and shoving it furiously into her mouth, Callie just shaking her head in defeat as she attempts to wipe the face of her son, who pulls away dramatically. Callie finally looks up and catches me watching her, her pale cheeks reddening as she recognizes me, me hoping my thoughts aren't written across my face. These kids look nothing like the little angels I'd seen on Facebook last week, running down the beach holding hands.

"Callie?" I say hesitantly as I advance toward her. She gives me a weak smile as she nods and pulls me in for a hug, holding it for a beat too long.

But when she steps back, she's recovered, grinning widely and making jokes about her kids being obsessed with sugar because she *never* gives it to them *normally*. I am amazed how quickly she has transformed from a normal tired mom with unruly kids into her Facebook persona. That even here, in real life, she feels like she can't show me, an old friend, her true self.

It had been so long since we'd shared a dorm room, so many years since we'd even had a live conversation, that it didn't feel right for me to tell her that it was okay, that she could bitch at her kids and I wasn't going to judge her. I knew she'd never understand how, after everything I'd been through, seeing her act like a human being made me like her so much more. So instead I tell her what I hope she needs to hear, that she looks beautiful and her kids are adorable, as she politely shuffles her brood out the door, mentioning something about a birthday party at the trampoline place down the street.

"Whew!" my mom sighs after Callie is gone. "She really has her hands full with those two. The exact reason why I only had one." She laughs.

"It was really good to see her," I say as we sit down.

"I'm not sure she'd say the same about seeing you—she seemed pretty embarrassed. Almost like she wanted to crawl under the table when she saw you watching her."

"I know," I say, taking a sip of my coffee, thinking about how I would've felt if I had run into her in Starbucks the morning after I got back from Maui, when I felt like a shell of myself. I probably would have reacted the same way she did, assuming she was going to judge that I had come so undone, that I had fallen so far from where I thought I'd be. Not unlike Callie, I had often spent a fair amount of time manipulating the way others saw me on Facebook. Now I wondered if we'd both be a lot happier if we spent more time cultivating relationships with the people right in front of us.

• • •

The smell of garlic envelops me when I walk in the front door. I slip off my shoes and follow it into the kitchen, where I find Max opening a bottle of red wine. "What's all this?" I ask as I look around, the table set, a pot of something that smells delicious simmering on the stovetop, chopped tomatoes, basil, and garlic on the cutting board for his signature bruschetta.

"Do I need a reason?" He smiles and kisses me.

"No, I just wasn't expecting—"

"Exactly why I did it. I knew you probably didn't eat today because you were with your mom . . ." He pauses and I nod my head to let him know he's right. "And I thought I'd surprise you with your favorite—eggplant Parmesan and bruschetta."

"Thank you," I say, happily accepting a piece of bread from him. I take a bite and close my eyes as it melts in my mouth.

"It's been too long since I cooked for you," he says as he mixes the garlic, basil, and tomatoes, sprinkling salt and pepper before spreading the mixture on the toast he just pulled from the oven. "Too long since I've done a lot of things," he adds, and I know last night is still on his mind—that the bruschetta is a peace offering.

"Well, I'm glad you're cooking for me tonight. This is delicious," I say, spooning some of the mixture out of the bowl. I debate commenting on the last part of what he said, knowing that after I make my last wish he won't remember the conversation anyway.

But I will—I'll take every single memory with me. The way Max and Courtney seemed to come together no matter how hard I tried to tear them apart, the way Jules and Ben's marriage began to unravel, and the look in Liam's eyes when I told him I didn't think I could live a life without Max, that I couldn't give Liam the chance he wanted. I'll never forget the way my heart broke a little bit when I realized that I was crushing his.

I watch Max as he scurries through the kitchen, pouring the wine, finishing the last touches on our meal, trying to memorize every detail of his face, the way he tilts his head when he's concentrating, the way his brow furrows as he tosses the salad. I swirl the red wine in my glass and bring myself to ask the question that needs to be answered.

"Max?"

"Yeah?" he responds, still concentrating on the wooden mixing bowl.

"Why do you love me?"

His hands are still clenching the salad tongs and he slowly looks up at me. "Why are you asking me that? Is this about last night? Because—"

"No," I interrupt, and the forcefulness of my answer makes him flinch a little. "I just want to know."

He grabs a towel and wipes his hands. "I love the life we've built together. We're a great team, Kate." He walks over and kisses me. "I love you. I want to make you happy."

"I know," I say, unable to meet his eyes. I knew he meant his words. I had witnessed his determination in putting Courtney aside for me, all in the name of our happiness. I grab him and pull him in tight, burying my face in his neck, drinking in his spicy smell, trying to freeze this moment in my head.

Finally, I pull back and Max stares at me, waiting for me to say more. "I want you to be happy too," I say as I kiss him, forcing the corners of my lips into a smile as I turn toward the stairs.

"Where are you going? Dinner's ready!" he calls after me.

I give him one last look. "There's something I need to take care of," I say. "I'll be right back," I lie as I head up the stairs and grab my phone off the dresser before I can change my mind.

CHAPTER TWENTY-SEVEN

....

Back where it all began. #wouldnthaveitanyotherway

I sense the change in scenery even before pulling open my swollen eyes, remembering the way the fluffy white down comforter had wrapped around me like a cocoon that morning, no doubt Jules' handiwork after I had finally passed out the night before. I sit up slowly, inhaling the salt in the air through the slightly ajar sliding glass door and look over to my right, where I already know I'll find Jules slumped in a stiff wingback chair in the corner, watching me intently.

"Oh, honey," she says, her tear-stained face softening when she sees I'm awake.

I swallow, my throat dry and scratchy, and I reach up and rub it.

It worked. I'm right back where it all started.

I hold my body still, waiting for the crippling emotion to cascade through me as Jules perches on the edge of the bed, her bloodshot eyes regarding me. I force my eyes away from her, to the area of the room where I'll locate the one thing that will signify this is actually happening.

"Kate?" Jules' voice sounds raw.

Feeling as if I'm watching a movie of my life, I look toward the closet, my chest seizing for a moment when I fixate on my wedding dress hanging there, steamed and waiting to be worn. I stare at it for several seconds, bracing myself for the fear to set in, waiting for the panic to be unleashed, the doubt to ensue. But the only emotion I feel is relief.

"Say something, *please*," Jules tries again, and I cover her hand with mine and smile. "You're smiling?" She half laughs.

I nod. "Everything's going to be okay," I say.

"Isn't that what I'm supposed to be telling you?" Jules frowns and places the back of her hand against my forehead like she had when Evan had strep throat last month. "What were in those pills your mom gave you last night? Because this is not *at all* how I thought you'd react when you woke up this morning."

"Me either," I say, thinking how, when I decided to bring myself back to this day, I had been sure the feeling of losing Max all over again would hit me hard and fast like the snow from an avalanche. I never imagined the opposite would happen, that I would feel as if my lungs had expanded so I could finally breathe.

When I'd lumbered up the stairs last night, I'd known what I had to do—that I had to finally let Max go. I'd debated changing my mind as my fingers hovered over the keyboard, but his words to me in the kitchen hung in the air like red flags. All this time, I'd been fixated on Courtney, as if she were the real problem. But when I'd finally mustered the courage to ask Max why he loved me, my temple pulsed as I heard my own doubts echoed in his answer—knowing in that moment, I had to stop hiding from the truth.

Yes, Max would have married me this time, I was sure of it. His eyes would have been moist when he watched me stride down the

282 liz fenton and lisa steinke

aisle toward him. I could imagine him twirling me on the dance floor and carrying me through the doorway of our suite at the end of the night, throwing me down onto the bed as we laughed. He would have done a great job of convincing himself he'd chosen the right girl, and I'd have done an even better one of pretending I'd made the right decision too. But deep down, I knew he would never love me the way I deserved to be loved. And for me, he'd always be a prize I'd fought for, but never really earned.

"Is he gone?" I fling back the comforter, startling Jules.

"Yes—Ben just texted me that he saw him at the desk checking out," she says slowly, as if she's trying to take the sting off the words.

I fling my legs over the side of the bed and rummage through my suitcase.

"Are you going to try to stop him?" Jules asks, and even though my back is to her, I know she's looking at me like I'm batshit crazy. "Kate."

"No," I say as I pull on a pair of jeans and a tank top and quickly run a toothbrush over my teeth.

"Then why—"

"I'll explain later," I yell as the door to the hotel suite clicks closed behind me. I rush down the carpeted hallway in my bare feet, hoping to stop him before he leaves, needing to say things to him that can't wait another minute, that have waited too long already.

When I get to the reception desk he's not there and I stop running, bracing myself for the fact that I might have missed him. But then I see him stepping into a cab out front. "Max!" I call.

He turns when he hears my voice, his face ashen, probably expecting me to yell at him, or worse, beg for him to stay. I think of the last time when Jules told me he was gone. I hadn't asked any more questions about Max. Instead, I'd started questioning her about the guests and the wedding details, worried about what people were going to think, what I would say in my own defense of how I let a relationship I had portrayed as perfect detonate like a land mine. That day felt like a lifetime ago.

"Can I talk to you for a minute?" I ask when I reach him, now standing stiffly outside of his taxi, running his hand through his hair, and I want to pull it away from his head and tell him he doesn't need to be nervous. "Don't worry, I'm not going to try to change your mind again."

Max gives me a long look, then asks his cabdriver if he can wait for a few minutes. As he walks tentatively beside me toward a bench at the edge of the circular driveway, I notice the dark shadows under his eyes. He hadn't slept last night.

"Kate, I don't know how many more times I can say I'm sorry," he starts, but I put a finger to his lips.

"I know. That's not what this is about. I just want to clear the air before you leave."

"What changed? Because last night you were so"—he starts, then stops, remembering my reaction—"upset, so angry." I raise my eyebrows and he quickly adds, "Not that I didn't deserve it. I guess I'm trying to reconcile that Kate with the one sitting here."

I wish I could tell him the truth. How thankful I am that he tried so hard to make it work the second time. That he might have done me the greatest favor of my life. "I had some time to think about things," I finally say, looking down at my bare finger, my engagement ring resting in a velvet box in the safe in my hotel room, knowing I'll return it to him as soon as I get back home.

"Okay," Max says, giving me the same skeptical look Jules did in the hotel room. Wondering how, in just twelve hours, I could have swung so fiercely in the opposite direction.

"I just want you to know that we're okay and *I'm* okay. I still wish you hadn't waited until we were *here* to tell me." I sweep my hand toward the hibiscus bushes lining the property, the rolling green hills of the golf course, the koi pond next to us. "But I agree with you—we aren't meant to be married."

"Really?" he says, his face so full of relief that I have to swallow back an involuntary tear. "Because, Kate, I really do believe that. And I'm so sorry I waited so long," he says as he wrings his hands, and I imagine he's thinking about Courtney, sure I won't be quite as forgiving once I discover he's leaving me for her—that she's the reason he can't see our future together anymore. "I was so confused. I want you to know, it was such a hard decision for me. I never wanted to hurt you. Please remember that."

I grab his hand, which is soaked with sweat. "I know. Sometimes the truth has to hit us over the head before we can see it," I say, thinking about Ruby, realizing now that going back had never been about fighting to stay with Max, it had been about learning to push beyond my fear to find clarity, even if it meant I might get hurt.

We both digest my words, our hands still locked together as we watch the palm trees swing hard with each wind gust stretching toward the sky but their trunks solid and secure. Exactly how I felt at this moment. "Max, I know about Courtney."

The color drains from his face as he opens his mouth to respond. "How—"

"Does it even matter how?" I ask.

He shakes his head. "Nothing happened—I swear to you . . ." He looks down at his hands, wringing them like a wet dishrag.

Finally he meets my eyes again. "I don't know how to explain it, but there's something between us and I need to find out what it is."

"I know that too," I say, and sigh as Max releases his explanation fast and furiously, like each syllable makes him feel less guilty, telling me how hard he tried to fight it and how conflicted he's been. I finally put my hand up to silence him. I'd already witnessed firsthand why Courtney and Max were meant to be together, I didn't need to hear it from him again.

"Here's the thing," I begin, searching for the words to explain to him why I was so seemingly calm, despite the fact he was leaving me for someone I had considered a friend. Because the truth was, their betrayal still hurt—the searing pain had morphed into a dull ache that would reside in my chest for a long time to come. But it had become clear that they were the puzzle pieces that fit, not us. And as crazy as it might sound, there was a part of me that admired them for not letting life lead them around like it had them on a leash—the way I had let life lead me for so long.

I turn toward Max, letting myself look into his eyes. I may not be his soul mate, but there's no doubt in my mind that we still have love for each other. "I think I'm finally learning that I can't force something that isn't meant to be." I think about the battle I'd waged for Max, the energy I'd exerted to change the course of my life, thinking I could conjure my own happiness along with it. I squeeze Max's hand tighter. "I just want you to be happy. And if she's the person who can do that, then you have to follow your heart toward her."

"Thank you. I want you to be happy too," he says softly.

"I know you do," I say. "And that's why I'm letting you go."

Max's eyes search mine for the rest of the answers I can't give him—he'd never believe me if I told him anyway. "And you can tell Courtney she can have custody of Magda. I'm sending my resignation later today," I say, having decided before I made my wish that the best thing would be for me to leave the advertising agency. I knew Courtney was better at the job than I was anyway—I just didn't have the same passion for it. And I was done fighting for Magda's acceptance.

"Are you sure? Maybe you should think about it for a few days. Don't make any rash decisions, especially after what happened last night. I don't want you to regret anything."

"I won't," I say definitively, but quickly adding, "It's time for me to move on. And even though I meant it when I said I'm okay with everything, that doesn't mean I want to see Courtney every day. My friendship with her is over," I say, gently reminding him that even though I wasn't unraveling at the seams, there were still consequences to the choices they had made.

"What are you going to do?"

"I don't know," I reply honestly. "But that's okay too," I say in the same breath. I wasn't sure what my next career move was, but I had money saved and I knew I would take the time to figure out what I really wanted.

The cabdriver gives a short honk and leans out the window, gesturing that it's time to go. "So, I guess this is good-bye?" Max says.

"It is," I say, hugging him tightly and watching as he climbs into the taxi, looking back one last time as it pulls away from the curb.

• • •

"Un-fucking-believable!" Jules exclaims when I finish telling her about my exchange with Max. I had sat on the bench long after he left, with my legs curled up beneath me, breathing deeply, letting the fresh air penetrate my lungs until Jules had come rushing out, frantically looking for me. I had patted the seat beside me and filled her in, her mouth flying open as I revealed Max was in love with Courtney, it growing wider when I told her that I'd already made peace with it.

"Hey, so there's something I need you to do for me," I say.

"Anything."

"When I cancel our honeymoon," I say, thinking of the suite I had booked us on the remote island of Lanai, the way the lush green land reached the ocean, "I'm going to rebook it for next month. For you and Ben."

"What? Why?"

"It's already paid for. And I thought it might be a nice getaway for you guys. You know, to reconnect?"

"What about the kids?" she asks.

"I'll watch them."

"What about your job?"

"I'll be able to get the time off," I say, not ready to tell her I was quitting just yet—she was still trying to digest that I wasn't falling apart over Max.

"We couldn't possibly—"

"Shush," I interrupt. "You're going. End of story."

"Why are you doing this?"

"A very wise person once told me that marriage is hard—that you have to keep fighting for it every day," I say, thinking of Jules' own words to me. "Maybe this will make it a little easier to do that."

Jules' chest compresses as she exhales. "How did you know this is just what we need?"

"I had a feeling," I say cryptically.

• • •

I nearly spit out my coffee as it burns my tongue.

"I told you to be careful, I had them make it extra hot," my mom says, looking concerned.

"It's fine," I say. "I think I'm just desperate for caffeine."

My mom had tracked me down in my hotel room with two lattes in hand and a worried look on her face. And like Jules, she'd eyed me warily as I'd weaved the same story—that I had woken up with a new outlook on life. But then she'd hugged me tightly when I'd finished, her shoulders caving with relief.

"That's interesting," my mom says, brushing a strand of hair away from my face. "I had my own little wake-up call this morning," she says as she adds a packet of raw sugar to her coffee. "I woke up feeling so emotional. I think Max leaving you reminded me of how your dad left me. But then I ran into this woman— she had the most beautiful curly hair and dark brown eyes!"

I perk up as my mom begins to describe Ruby, how she met her as she was getting coffee, and for reasons my mom couldn't explain, she'd felt compelled to spill her entire life story to her as Ruby nodded her head and sipped on her mocha. When my mom had finished rambling, Ruby gave her a serious look before asking if she was finally ready. My mom, confused, had asked, "Ready for what?" To which Ruby had replied, "To begin living your damn life again, woman!"

"For a minute, I was shocked. I mean, who did this woman think she was?" my mom says with a laugh. "But then I realized she was right. And I wanted to find you immediately and warn you not to make the same mistakes I did. To not let what Max did define the rest of your life." She pauses, staring out the window at the ocean. "And then I get up here, and you're not crumpled in a ball on the floor like I would have been. I had no idea you were so strong. It makes me realize how weak I've been. I'm so sorry." She puts her arm around my shoulder and I lean into her.

"Don't be," I say, her silky hair pressing against my cheek. "Maybe we can work on moving on together. Okay?"

An hour later, I've convinced both my mom and Jules, who'd also showed up at my door saying she was still *very worried about me*, that they could leave me in the hotel room by myself. After they've gone—I ordered Jules to pack for the red-eye home that night and my mom to go lie by the pool—I make a quick call to the front desk, then pick up my cell phone. Last time, I'd been terrified to show any weakness on Facebook, to let people know that life wasn't turning out the way I'd hoped it would. This time, I pull up my profile, smiling as I read all the congratulatory messages on my timeline and decide that everyone deserved to hear the truth from me. I type the words without hesitation, that Max and I decided not to get married today, but that I truly appreciated everyone's kind thoughts. I hit post and throw my phone into the drawer before collapsing onto the bed, relieved to have the truth out there, closing my eyes and letting the sound of the waves lull me to sleep.

A knock at the door wakes me and I jolt upright. "Room service!" a familiar voice calls out.

Ruby's curvy silhouette takes up the threshold as I swing the door open and see a plate of fresh fruit in her hands. "Hungry?"

I wave her in and we walk out to the lanai, the hues of the golden sunset filling the sky. As I place a piece of mango into my mouth, letting the sweetness slide down my throat, I remember standing out here on the night of my rehearsal dinner, my chest tight with anxiety. And now, the calmness that fills my body is so foreign it feels almost like a drug. "Thank you," I say to Ruby.

"I figured you were probably starving."

I laugh. "I'm not talking about the food. For what you did for my mom."

Ruby grins. "Consider it a parting gift."

"But how did you know that was exactly what she needed to hear?"

"I can't believe that you're still questioning how I know things!" she says as she firmly places her hands on her hips.

"Sorry!" I say. "I guess I still don't understand all of your powers."

"Clearly," she deadpans, and I swat her arm. "So tell me," she says, her smile fading slightly. "Where do you go from here?"

"You know, I always thought that somehow my life wasn't perfect unless other people thought so too." The image of Callie Trenton materializes in my mind, her hand wrapped around her swollen belly as the sun casts a glow across her face. The same picture I'd seen on so many Facebook feeds. "But I would still constantly wrestle with that idea, often wondering, when I still didn't feel authentically happy inside, if I needed to mimic what other people were doing to achieve that."

"And now?"

"Now I don't give a fuck," I say, and smile. "I just want to live a happy life, no matter what that life looks like."

Ruby puts her arm around my shoulder. "I have a feeling you're going to find that happiness you're looking for. Just don't make me come back here again, okay!" she mock scolds me, her laughter vibrating her chest. "You take care, Kate," she adds, before disappearing through the door almost as quickly as she came.

"Bye, Ruby," I call after her.

"Who's Ruby?" Liam's head peeks through the sheer curtain.

"The woman who just left? Isn't that how you got in here?"

Liam shakes his head. "How long were you in the sun today? There's no one here. Jules gave me her key—she wanted me to check in on you. You haven't been answering your texts."

"Sorry, I threw my phone in the drawer and fell asleep for a few hours."

"And you were dreaming about a woman named Ruby who was in your hotel room? Tell me more!" He laughs and deflects the swat I give him.

"Come. Sit with me," I say as he plops down onto the chaise and wraps his arm around my shoulder, the same way he had at Nikki's party right before he told me he loved me. But did that mean that those feelings would translate here, to the life I came back to?

"Are you really okay?" he asks, his tone turning serious. "Jules told me you said you were, but I need to hear it from you."

"I am," I say. "Things have a way of turning out exactly the way they're supposed to." I grab a grape off the plate, popping it into my mouth. "Where's What's-her-name? Your date?"

Liam glances at his watch. "Probably about halfway over the Pacific Ocean by now."

"She left without you?"

"She wasn't happy that I spent most of last night here with you and Jules. She said she didn't want to compete with something like that."

"I'm sorry," I say. "I feel like it's my fault."

"Don't be. It wasn't going to work out anyway."

"Why? Does she have a bunion or something?" I tease.

"Worse—she has a hamster. Named Mr. Magoo. What adult woman has a hamster as a pet?"

"What a travesty!" I smile and grab another grape, this time tossing it at Liam's mouth, and he cranes his neck to catch it.

"So what now?" he asks. "You heading home?"

"No. I'm going to stay another week," I say. I had called down earlier and extended my reservation, deciding that it would give Max plenty of time to move out of the condo and me enough time to absorb the new direction my life was going in. I look over at Liam. "Want to join me?"

Liam's eyes shoot up and our eyes meet. "Are you sure?"

I nod my head. "Absolutely."

"Then of course I'll stay," he says softly.

I reach over and wrap my hand around his, not knowing if it's the right thing to ask Liam to stay, not sure if we might ruin our friendship if we try to make it something more. But as his fingers meet mine, I decide that I'm ready to take the journey, no matter where it might lead us.

Acknowledgments

So many people to thank. So little time. (Actually, that's not true. We have all the time in the world. We've just always wanted to say that.)

To Greer Hendricks: How can we ever properly thank you for making our publishing dreams come true? Because we know the DryBar gift certificates are definitely not enough! We are so lucky to have you as our dream editor, championing us every day. Big kisses to you! (And, btw, it doesn't hurt that you write the *nicest* editorial letters!) And Sarah Cantin, we love you, even though we kind of want to hate on you, because you just might be the cutest, sweetest, best-dressed woman *ever*. Not to mention, you give amazing restaurant recommendations. We're also so appreciative of our publisher, Judith Curr. We are simply in awe to be working with you. You're the best of the best. And a big thanks to the entire team at Atria. We feel like the luckiest girls in the world to work with y'all.

We adore you, Elisabeth Weed. You are the best agent we could ever ask for. (And a blast to share a bottle of wine with too!) And we so appreciate that we can always count on the wonderful Dana Murphy.

Ariele Fredman, we feel lucky to have you as our publicist. Thank you!

Huge love to all of the authors and bloggers and readers who have supported our journey. We appreciate every post, every picture, every review, every seat filled at a book signing, everything. Thank you.

To our faithful early readers—Mike, Matt, Cristine, and Heather—know that your feedback was invaluable in shaping this story. We could never thank you enough.

Mike and Matt, we love the hell out of you for stifling your eye rolls as we chat endlessly, for laughing at our jokes even when they aren't that funny, and for reminding us it's okay not to be perfect. Simply: Thank you for loving us just the way we are.

And to our Facebook friends: Thank you for sharing your lives with us each day and allowing us to crowd your news feeds with our endless selfies. (We just can't help ourselves!) We hope you read this story and realize that no one's life is as picture-perfect as it may seem, even if the photos and status updates they post might make you feel otherwise. And let's be honest, an ideal life would be pretty damn boring anyway, wouldn't it? Embrace your imperfections—and we guarantee everyone else will too.

XOXO, L&L